ALMOST
a
BRIDE

Books by Jody Hedlund

The Preacher's Bride
The Doctor's Lady
Unending Devotion
A Noble Groom
Rebellious Heart
Captured by Love

BEACONS OF HOPE
Out of the Storm: A BEACONS OF HOPE Novella
Love Unexpected
Hearts Made Whole
Undaunted Hope
Forever Safe
Never Forget

ORPHAN TRAIN
An Awakened Heart: An ORPHAN TRAIN Novella
With You Always
Together Forever
Searching for You

THE BRIDE SHIPS
A Reluctant Bride
The Runaway Bride
A Bride of Convenience
Almost a Bride

THE BRIDE SHIPS ⚓ BOOK FOUR

ALMOST

a

BRIDE

JODY HEDLUND

 NORTHERN LIGHTS PRESS

Almost a Bride

Published by Northern Lights Press
© 2020 by Jody Hedlund

www.jodyhedlund.com

ISBN: 9781733753449

Scripture quotations are from the King James Version of the Bible in the Public Domain.

This is a work of fiction. Names, characters, incidents, and dialogues are products of the author's imagination and are not to be construed as real. Any resemblance to actual events or persons, living or dead, is entirely coincidental.

Cover design by Roseanna White Designs

That the trial of your faith,
being much more precious than
of gold that perisheth, though it
be tried with fire, might be found
unto praise and honour and glory
at the appearing of Jesus Christ.
1 Peter 1:7

one

CARIBOO, BRITISH COLUMBIA
AUGUST 1863

"*H*ello, beautiful. Will you marry me?"

Kate Millington stumbled on the boardwalk in an attempt to avoid plowing into the man who'd maneuvered directly into her path.

"Whoa, now!" He grasped her upper arm and steadied her.

At the evening hour, the raised sidewalks of the mountain town of Williamsville were teeming with all manner of men. Having just arrived with a pack train, Kate was eager to explore, in spite of the busyness, and had convinced Becca to accompany her down the narrow main thoroughfare.

The tightly confined buildings constructed from hewn logs were squat, unpainted, and nearly identical except for simple signs protruding above doorways announcing the establishments: Bibby's Tin Shop, McPherson Brewery, Kelly Saloon, Lee Chung Laundry, and more.

Tucked at the foot of the Cariboo Range, the town was hemmed by a hill of ponderosa and Douglas pine on the eastern side and bordered by Williams Creek on the west. Framed by the sky's ever-changing shades of blue and violet, the mountain peaks towered above everything, and Kate's fingers itched for her paintbrushes and watercolors.

But along with all her other worldly goods, her art supplies were packed in her bags still secured on the back of a mule. Nevertheless, she'd been giving herself over to her imagination, cataloging every detail of the town and recording every nuance of the surroundings so she could recreate the scene later.

The proposition of marriage jarred her back to reality . . .

With the grip tightening around her arm, she forced her attention to the man blocking her way, noting he was as burly and shaggy as the moose she'd spotted when their caravan had camped last evening.

"You'd make me a very happy man if you'd agree to marry me." His expression was hopeful—at least what she could see of it beneath his facial hair.

Of course she had to reject his offer. Yet at the same time, she searched for kind words that wouldn't cause him undue pain. "Your offer is very sweet . . ."

Becca slapped the man's arm, apparently feeling no need for any kindness whatsoever. "Get your hands off the woman!" As if the slap wasn't scary enough, Becca's furrowed brow, flattened lips, and flaring nostrils had the power to intimidate the stoutest of hearts.

Eyes widening at the sight of Becca, the moose released Kate and took a step back. Though Becca's hazel skin was as warm as a summer woodland, her girth was broad and big-boned, and her expression as inviting as that of a mother bear protecting her cub.

"Miss Kate already got herself a man," Becca stated in a tone loud enough to stop those who hadn't already halted to stare at Kate.

Once upon a time, Kate would have been mortified by all the attention. But after living for over six months in Victoria, where the male population outnumbered females ten to one, she'd grown accustomed to men staring at her with unabashed admiration.

Even so, she self-consciously tucked a flyaway strand of her blond hair behind her ear and brushed at her dusty skirt, the once-blue calico now almost gray.

"Go on with you." Becca took hold of Kate's arm and propelled her around the moose, coming to Kate's rescue, as she had since the start of their journey out of Victoria weeks ago. "We got to find your Mr. Frank before nightfall."

"Mr. Frank, as in Herbert Frank?" the moose asked.

"Mm-hmm." Becca leveled a stern look at the man. "You know where he at?"

The moose glanced in the direction of Kelly Saloon. "Is she the bride Herb's been yapping about nonstop?"

"She the one." Becca picked up her pace, dragging Kate along.

"Heyday for Herb." The moose whistled under his breath. "Lucky dog."

Kate tripped after her friend, unable to make her feet cooperate. And her heartbeat turned sluggish, as if protesting the forward momentum.

"Wait, Becca." Kate found her voice. "Perhaps I ought to change my attire first. Or, at the very least, wash up."

"You pretty enough just the way you is."

Their footsteps against the planks made a sharp *thunking*, drawing even more attention. At a foot or more above the street, the sidewalks were like a stage, raising her and highlighting her for all the men to see. For Herbert Frank to see. Herbert Frank who was waiting and planning for her arrival. Herbert Frank who would likely marry her this night—if a reverend could be found.

Raw panic burst through Kate, and she glanced frantically for a place to hide.

The sign above the nearest place of business read *Hart General Store.* Jerking away from Becca, she veered toward the open doorway and the overflowing shelves inside.

"Where you going now?" The exasperation in Becca's voice trailed after Kate.

She didn't know how to answer the dear woman. How could she explain this strange moment of dread to Becca when she didn't know how to explain it to herself? "My, um, tooth powder. Aye, my tooth powder canister is near to empty, and I need to purchase more—"

"Miss Millington?" came a call from the direction of the saloon.

With one foot inside the store, Kate froze. The deep baritone with a Cornish accent belonged to none other than Herbert Frank.

Another wave of panic crashed through her. She closed her eyes and fought against it, drawing in first one deep breath, then another.

"Katherine Millington?" Herbert called again. "Is that you?"

As much as she wanted to disappear behind the wares stacked floor to ceiling, Kate forced her feet to remain where they were. She silently counted to five. She could do this. After all, this was why she'd left Manchester last fall and sailed halfway across the world on the *Robert Lowe* bride ship. She'd come to find a husband and get married.

She'd lived in the Marine Barracks in Victoria at the government complex for the first couple of months after arriving and had agreed to marry James McCrea, a local hotel owner. When her plans with Mr. McCrea had fallen through, she'd gone to work as a domestic. During that time, she'd continued to entertain suitors through the spring until she met Herbert Frank.

Over the several weeks they'd courted, she liked that he was handsome and church-going and kind. He made her smile and had promised they'd be happy together in Williamsville. With his claim pulling out a decent profit in gold, he'd needed to return there by the time the spring thaw opened the way through the Fraser Canyon for travel. Before he left, he'd wrested a promise of marriage and arranged for her to travel to the small mining town where he said he'd be waiting for her.

"Miss Millington." His tone turned urgent. "It's me. Herbert Frank."

Even if she wasn't ready to face him, she couldn't simply walk away and ignore him. He was a decent fellow—a good listener, fun-loving, and doting. He'd even paid every shilling of her travel arrangements, so she'd be safe and well fed during the arduous trek up into the mining district.

Why, then, was she having the misgivings?

With another deep breath, she slowly pivoted.

Becca stood less than a foot away, her hands fisted on her ample hips, her keen eyes rounded beneath raised brows. "What you doing, Miss Kate? I thought you ready to marry your man."

"And I am. I'm just a little nervous. That's all."

"You said he a good man. You ain't been lying to me now, have you?"

"No, of course not."

"Then quit your dallying and go greet him proper-like."

Kate squared her shoulders. "You're right, Becca. I'll go greet him this very moment." Then before she could find another excuse, Kate skirted her friend and made her feet march directly toward Herbert. When she reached the edge of the plank walkway, Herbert was there, peering up at her.

"Miss Millington, I'm delighted to see you." An enormous smile lit his face—a face that wasn't quite as handsome as she remembered. Had it been so narrow in Victoria? Had his ears been so big? And what about his nose? Had it been that long?

She was just being flighty. He was the same. Same brown hair, same trim mustache, same thin brows.

"Mr. Frank." She wasn't delighted to see him in return. But she couldn't very well say so and instead scrambled to find a polite response. "I'm delighted to finally arrive in Williamsville. The town is—" She surveyed the main street again, this time seeing the mud, the shanties at the far end, the canvas tents beyond, a hillside of stumps, and the piles of crumbled rocks. "It's quite interesting."

Interesting? The moment the word was out, she wanted to palm her forehead. She'd always been better at expressing herself in sketches and paintings than in words.

Herbert studied her as though she were a famous masterpiece on display. "You're as lovely as always."

"Thank you, Mr. Frank." Herbert's examination felt too bold, and she moved to descend.

"Allow me." Herbert held out a hand to assist her from the boardwalk.

She hesitated before accepting his proffer. Once she was on the ground, his grip tightened, and she realized he had no intention of letting go.

"How was your trip here?" he asked. "I hope it wasn't too difficult?"

"Oh no. I liked it." Liked? That wasn't exactly the right word. Traveling through the canyon on narrow paths had been harrowing. Hiking over the rocky terrain had been tiring. The dirt and dust had been endless. She was gritty, sore, and weary. Even so, the sights she'd seen, the creatures she drew, the vistas she viewed—everything had been more beautiful and glorious than she could explain.

"Then you had no troubles?"

"Nothing to speak of." Their camp had flooded one night. They never had enough food. A mule slipped and fell down a ravine. Natives threatened when they'd drawn too close. And several travelers had become ill. How could she explain all that here, now?

Every man on the street was still staring at her. Those within businesses were peering out windows and doorways. Nevertheless, the attention from everyone else felt less daunting, less uncomfortable, less threatening than Herbert's. His presence in front of her was overpowering.

With a wiggle, she attempted to extricate her hand, but his grasp remained unyielding.

The same panic from a moment ago surged through her, and she quickly fought it away by distracting herself. "I did meet a wonderful friend during my traveling."

"A friend?" His voice was skeptical.

"Aye. Her name is Becca." Waving toward her friend, Kate tried to nonchalantly break free from Herbert.

His hold didn't slacken.

From her position on the sidewalk, Becca was watching the interaction, more creases appearing in her forehead with each passing moment.

"Rebecca St. Germaine," Kate continued. "She was living in Victoria with her brother and his family. Now she's moving here to do washing"—Kate located the sign down the street—"at Lee Chung Laundry."

Herbert nodded at Becca. "Ma'am."

Becca's response was to lift her nose and peer down it haughtily.

"She was heaven-sent." Kate smiled at her friend. Even though Becca had been the only other female in the group and was slightly older than Kate's eighteen years, they'd easily bonded. "I don't think I could have made this trip without her."

Again, Herbert nodded at Becca. "Thanks for taking care of Miss Millington."

Becca sniffed. "I ain't nobody's servant. I sure enough didn't leave bondage behind only to end up enslaved again."

"Of course not," Kate said. "You're free here. We're all free here." She'd had plenty of conversations with Becca during the trip, enough to know she had run away from slavery, traveled to California, and from there made her way to Vancouver Island with the hope she'd be safe from anyone intending to make a gain in returning her to her master.

Kate's smile faltered. Why, with each passing moment, did she feel as though she was about to lose *her* freedom?

"I bet you're hungry." Herbert tugged her closer.

The tug was innocent enough. He was only excited about being with her again after the months of separation. Yet the pressure only seemed to open the gate for the emotions that had been gaining momentum, and now they spilled out in a flood she didn't understand.

All she knew was that she didn't want to go with Herbert.

"I'm sorry, Mr. Frank." This time she yanked hard enough to free her hand and take several steps backward. "I'm really sorry."

Confusion rippled across his features.

As he opened his mouth to question her, she blurted her answer. "I'm sorry. But I cannot marry you."

two

eke Hart couldn't tear his attention from the unfolding drama happening outside the store between Herb Frank and his newly arrived bride-to-be, one of the brideship women who'd come over on the *Robert Lowe* from Manchester, England. Herbert Frank had been lucky enough to be in Victoria when the ship arrived, and he'd also been lucky enough to win the hand of one of the brides.

Stop staring and get a grip, Hart. He hadn't been able to focus on the mining board meeting since the second he noticed the young woman walking through town. At least, Putnam and Blake hadn't been able to focus either. They'd been gawking, just as speechless as he was, their cigars and whiskey forgotten, their scrawled meeting notes abandoned. Middle-aged and with families they'd left behind to chase after gold, the two fellow mining bosses were each old enough to be his father, but certainly not immune to the charms of a new pretty face in town.

"I cannot marry you." The young woman's words carried

inside as if she'd been standing next to them. When she spun and stalked toward the store entry, Zeke pushed away from the table, just as he had the first time she'd almost entered.

His chair scraped against the rough-hewn planks, but he held himself in his seat, not wanting to appear too eager. After all, the meeting wasn't over, and his assistant could handle the woman.

Zeke glanced at the counter where Wendell was bent over a ledger. With spectacles perched on the end of his nose, the young man's lips moved rapidly as he silently calculated the column of numbers, oblivious to the scene unfolding just outside the store.

Truth be told, Wendell was almost always oblivious to his surroundings, especially when he had a page of numbers in front of him. And not for the first time, Zeke decided he needed to hire someone else to run the store and free Wendell to focus on the accounting.

The woman's hurried footsteps drew nearer, and Zeke's muscles tensed. Would she enter this time?

"Miss Millington, wait!" Herb hopped up onto the boardwalk, his face rigid with anxiety.

Millington. The name was familiar. In fact, the woman herself looked familiar. Zeke dredged the far reaches of his mind. Where had he seen her? Why did he have the feeling he ought to know who she was? No doubt she was someone he'd met back home in Manchester before he ran away. Perhaps he had a dalliance with her during his last days there, when he'd been at his worst with his carousing, when he hadn't thought twice about charming a woman into his arms, only to leave her brokenhearted.

It would be just his luck if she happened to recognize him.

He picked up his shot glass, tipped in the last mouthful, and let the liquid burn down his throat.

As the woman stepped into the open doorway again, Zeke zeroed in on her lovely features even though his gut warned that he was heading toward danger. Her face was gently rounded with a flush highlighting her cheeks. Her eyes were wide, revealing a dark brown richer than the deepest layers of earth. And her lips were slightly parted, her fingers pressed against them, as if to stifle any words that might try to escape.

In spite of the dust of travel, she radiated beauty and sweetness. Like a lone mountain flower that somehow had managed to flourish amidst the waste-rock debris. Though worry etched her face, something in her expression reflected an innocence that tugged at his protective instincts.

Before she could make it inside the shop, Herb appeared behind her, grabbed her arm, and spun her around so swiftly that she let out a startled cry.

Zeke leaped to his feet. His chair bumped against a shelf and knocked several tins to the floor. He started across the store. "Let her go, Herb."

Herb took hold of the woman's shoulders. "Miss Millington, please don't walk away. I love you."

Behind Herb, a stout black woman swatted Herb on the back. "Let go of Miss Kate or you gonna be in real trouble."

Herb was oblivious to everyone except for the young woman. He leaned in as though he planned to kiss her.

She tried to wrench free, releasing another cry, this one louder.

In three long strides, Zeke reached the doorway and pinched Herb's wrists, giving the miner no choice but to let go of his captive. Once the woman was loose, Zeke shoved Herb, causing him to stumble backward out the door, trip across the boardwalk, and fall into the street on his backside.

Zeke dodged past the woman and went after Herb.

"What do you think you're doing, Hart?" Herb yelled up at him, red-faced, his hat knocked off and rolling down the street.

"Coming to the lady's defense. I can't abide any man using force on a woman."

"She's my woman—"

"Not anymore."

"She agreed to marry me, and I aim to hold her to it."

"You can't force her. Not when she's changed her mind."

"That right!" The black woman now stood next to Zeke on the boardwalk, fists on her hips, glaring down at Herb.

"Zeke?" the woman said from behind them. "Zeke Hart?"

Zeke froze. A colorful word slipped out. The woman *was* one of the broken hearts he'd left behind in Manchester. And now he was caught. His backbone stiffened in preparation for the coming wrath and the tongue-lashing he deserved.

"Zoe's been looking for you. In fact, you're one of the reasons she came to the colonies." The woman's tone rose with a tinge of excitement. "Does your sister know you're here?"

For a long moment, Zeke refused to turn, refused to meet the woman, refused to come face-to-face with one more of his many past mistakes. But now that every eye in Williamsville was trained upon him, he had no choice but to acknowledge her presence.

He shifted in a slow turn until he faced her. The anxiety in her pretty face was gone and replaced with wonder and— awe? Her lips rose into a smile, one he ought to remember but couldn't.

He studied her features more closely, taking in the softness of her skin, the lushness of her lashes, the fullness of her lips. How had he forgotten a face like hers?

She seemed to be taking him in every bit as much as he was her. The openness of her expression, the interest, the warmth—everything about her invited him into her life and her world.

No wonder Herb had fallen for this woman and couldn't let her go.

She clasped her hands together as if she was genuinely happy to see him. "Even though I haven't seen Zoe since she got married and moved up the Fraser River to Yale, I know for certain she'll be thrilled to find you."

Zeke cleared his throat. "Zoe and I met back up already."

"You have?"

"Aye, I saw her last month when she opened the home for foundlings." Because this woman had come over on the bride ship, she'd obviously become a friend of Zoe's and was well aware of his rift with his twin sister. Maybe that's all she knew about him. Maybe she wasn't one of his past conquests after all.

A playful glimmer brightened her eyes. "You don't remember who I am, do you?"

"You look familiar. But I admit my memories of my last years in Manchester are blurry." Especially since he'd been working hard to forget them.

"Remember your friend, Jeremiah?"

After first arriving in the colony, *Jeremiah* was the name he'd taken as an alias, the name of his best friend from Manchester. But once he'd learned from Zoe that he was free of the accusations against him, he started using his real name again. Most people referred to him by Hart, so the adjustment hadn't been too difficult. "I remember Jeremiah. How do you know him?"

Her smile quirked higher on one side than the other, which only made her look younger and more innocent. "He's my older brother."

Zeke's mind rushed back years to his boyhood, to the ragged school, to his companion and best friend, Jeremiah Millington. They'd done everything together in those early years—played, learned, and even found their faith together. Until they started working at the mill. Until the long days of operating the spinning machines zapped them of energy. Until the factory had begun to take away the people they loved. Until they'd had so little left to live for . . .

"I'm Katherine. But everyone calls me Kate." She paused, giving him time to place her name and face.

She didn't have to remind him they'd been neighbors

most of their lives, that they practically grew up together, and that if he'd been a decent human being and less selfish, he might have taken more time to concern himself with the well-being of others.

But she said none of that and instead nodded at him encouragingly.

"Kate." He tried to conjure up a picture of Jeremiah's many siblings. Mostly brothers. Aye, there had been one sister. A sweet little girl. She tried to keep up with them, especially when they'd been younger. With her blond hair and brown eyes, he could see the resemblance to Jeremiah now. "You've sure grown up."

"You still don't remember me, do you?" Her smile was forgiving.

"'Course I do. You tagged along with Jeremiah sometimes."

"I suppose you thought I was a pest?" Her voice contained a note of teasing, almost flirtation. The tilt of her head seemed to beckon him.

"If I ever did, I regret it." He'd show her he could flirt just as easily in return.

She heaved a breath, the rigidness of her posture easing and only bringing attention to her lovely form.

Lovely wasn't the right word to describe the generous curves in the right places, along with a trim waist and the long legs outlined in the folds of her skirt. Somehow, against his better judgment, his gaze lingered over her, which only sent a spear of heat into his gut.

Zeke jerked his sights away and scrubbed a hand over his

mouth and jaw, surprised at the immediacy and strength of his desire. What was he thinking? Kate Millington was Jeremiah's little sister.

His friend had always been fiercely protective of his family, especially when he'd stepped into the role of caretaker and provider after his father had run off. He'd only been thirteen at the time, too young to shoulder such responsibility. But Jeremiah had done it without complaint. If he'd been able to read Zeke's wayward thoughts just now about Kate, his friend would have pounded him in the face.

The trouble was that Jeremiah would have had to pound every man in Williamsville. Zeke wasn't the only one with wayward thoughts about Kate. And Herb wouldn't be the only man who'd want to marry her. Once word spread that she was no longer engaged, every unattached man would be lining up at her door to propose marriage.

Zeke's muscles tightened at the remembrance of Herb's manhandling. What was to stop Herb from going after her again?

Herb was in the process of dusting off his trousers after picking himself up. The Cornish miner might be pushy at times and have trouble holding his liquor, but overall he was a good man. There were worse—much worse—who'd think nothing of preying upon Kate.

Zeke eyed the black woman who'd moved to Kate's side, angling her glare to include him now. Even with this guardian angel standing next to her, Kate still wouldn't be safe. "Williamsville is no place for a single young woman like yourself."

"I'll be fine, Zeke." His name rolled off her tongue as

soft as velvet. And for a second, all he could imagine was the stroke of her fingers and how her touch would surely be just as soft.

"You'll need a safe place to stay," he insisted even as he fought to push away his strange reactions to her. Like every other man in the Cariboo, he'd gone too long without the pleasure of female company. And the deprivation was going to his head.

"I'm sure I'll find accommodations," she responded, but with less certainty and a sideways glance toward her guardian angel.

"I've got a fine log house ready for you, Miss Millington." Herb situated his hat back on his head. "It's just down the street, and I'm sure you'll like it once you see it."

Kate edged closer to her protective angel. "You've been very kind to me, Mr. Frank. And I do thank you for the offer. But I've realized we're just not suited to each other."

"You can stay with me." The words were out before Zeke had time to process what he was saying.

Kate's brows flew up. "Stay with you?"

"Aye." Now that he'd made the offer, he couldn't take it back. "I have the room."

"Oh, I see what this is about!" Herb shouted. "You're trying to steal Miss Millington away from me by tempting her with your big house."

"I'm not stealing or tempting her away," Zeke said. "How can I, when she's already walked away?"

Herb jerked on his vest to straighten it. "You think that

just because you've got a bigger claim you can start putting on airs and doing whatever you want."

"You know as well as everyone else around here that I'm doing what I can to make this town and the surrounding mines safe." Zeke braced himself for the onslaught of accusations that had become all too common from his competition. He'd once assumed he'd find peace and contentment if he had wealth and prosperity and power. But the past year had been anything but peaceful. And his life had been anything but content.

"You're not taking my bride away, Hart." Herb's deep voice echoed in the silence. "I won't let you."

"I'm not planning to marry her. She's just a childhood friend. A playmate's little sister. Nothing more."

three

Kate's singing heartbeat faded into silence. She was just a childhood friend to Zeke and nothing more?

She studied his handsome face, hoping she'd see the spark of interest in his eyes again, the one that had flamed to life only moments ago when he'd been looking her over and seeing her as a grown woman instead of a girl.

At least she thought she'd seen desire. And at least she thought he'd been viewing her as a woman. Had she been wrong?

Disappointment rushed in to replace the melody that had started playing the instant she'd recognized Zeke Hart. She'd always fancied Zeke, even when he'd been but a boy. With his dark hair, long lashes, and stunning green eyes, he made her heart patter faster and her skin flush every time she'd seen him.

It hadn't mattered that he hardly looked at her in return. She'd admired him and allowed her daydreams of him to take life in her sketch pad. After he'd run away from Manchester to escape a crime he hadn't committed, she'd pined over the drawings of him and prayed one day he'd be able to come back home.

Fortunately, she hadn't wallowed long before other young men took notice and distracted her from the girlhood infatuation with Zeke. She'd had several serious relationships and had even considered marrying one of the men. But in the end, none had been right for her.

Perhaps if life in Manchester hadn't been so hard, she would have been willing to settle down. As it was, when Miss Rye of the Female Immigration Committee had come looking for women to sail to Vancouver Island and British Columbia, Kate had been all too ready to go, especially to ease Jeremiah's burden by having one less sibling to care for.

Of course, she'd thought of Zeke from time to time over the past couple of years, especially because Zoe had been eager to find her twin brother and make amends with him. But Kate hadn't expected to encounter him, certainly not here in Williamsville just moments after arriving.

He looped his thumbs into his belt and stared into the interior of the store as though he'd tired of the conversation and was ready to get back to work. Obviously, it was his store. The sign above the door shared his name.

Zeke had clearly done well for himself here in the colony, much better than he could have if he'd stayed in Manchester like Jeremiah. And Zeke had also grown more handsome. He was all man now, and her fingers twitched with the need to sketch him. His shoulders and arms had filled out proportionately, and his chest formed a beautiful upside-down trapezoid.

The planes of his face had always been easy to draw. The lines, shadows, and symmetry had been so perfect, classical, like an ancient Greek god, with a straight nose, high cheekbones, and strong chin.

And the dimples in his cheeks, she'd added them to almost every sketch she'd ever drawn. She'd only gotten the tiniest glimpse of them when he briefly smiled a moment ago, not enough to satisfy her.

As if sensing the mental drawing she was making of him, he glanced at her, lifting one of his dark brows. Was he expecting an answer to his invitation to stay in his home?

"Thank you for the offer, Zeke—"

"No," Herbert interrupted as he approached the edge of the boardwalk and looked up at her with pleading eyes. "I paid your traveling expenses here. You owe me now and can't just walk away from our arrangement."

Kate opened her mouth to respond but couldn't find an answer. Herbert was right. She hadn't thought about the consequences of breaking off her engagement and repaying him. What could she do now?

As her mind scrambled to find a solution, Zeke crossed his arms, his shirtsleeves stretching tight against his biceps. "I'll cover Kate's expenses."

"I don't want your money, Hart." Herbert hopped up onto the sidewalk.

"I don't want Zeke's charity either," Kate interjected. "I'll find a way to earn my own money so I can repay you."

Herbert turned his back on her and faced off with Zeke. "The entire town can see as plainly as me that you're stealing my bride."

"Now hold on, Herb." Zeke's voice was loaded with exasperation. "I already told you I'm not aiming to marry her. I'm not in the market for a wife. And if I was, I wouldn't have to steal from you to get one."

A few guffaws arose from the men watching the interaction.

Becca took hold of Kate's arm, her worried eyes upon Zeke and Herb.

Kate patted the woman's hand. "Maybe I can work in Lee Chung Laundry with you, Becca. Surely Lee Chung could use an extra hand."

Becca pursed her lips and tugged Kate back a step.

"I'm the one who found Miss Millington first." Herbert advanced upon Zeke. "And I plan to keep her."

"Just accept the fact that she's changed her mind and doesn't want you anymore."

"She won't get you either." Herbert bent and slipped his fingers into his boot. An instant later, he rose with a knife in his hand. Kate barely had time to suck in a surprised breath before Herbert thrust the blade into Zeke.

Kate screamed and darted toward Zeke, but Becca's strong grip wrenched her back. In the same moment, Zeke swung a fist into Herbert's stomach, doubling him over. Before Herbert could gather his wits, Zeke had a hold of the man's arm and was twisting it, causing him to cry out and drop to his knees.

Thankfully, other bystanders had jumped into action and rushed to Zeke's aid. Several took custody of Herbert while another man propelled Zeke toward the open doorway of the general store, shouting instructions for someone to fetch the doctor.

As Zeke passed by, Kate glimpsed the handle of the knife protruding from his upper arm, his shirtsleeve stained crimson.

Kate's airways cinched, cutting off her breath. If Herbert had been aiming for Zeke's heart, he'd come close.

Zeke stumbled into the store, brushing off the assistance. "I'm gonna be fine. Just a little knife wound is all."

Kate moved to follow him, but once again Becca's hold kept her in place. "I can help." She wiggled to free herself. "I have a little practice doctoring wounds." As the only girl in a family of all boys, she'd seen enough brawls and blood to have a basic knowledge of how to treat injuries.

"I don't know, Miss Kate." In spite of the doubt grooved into her forehead, Becca released her.

Kate rushed into the store, a handful of onlookers parting to make room for her.

"Best let the doctor treat that man." Becca's words trailed after her. But as Zeke lowered himself into the nearest chair, Kate was already bending over him and examining the way the blade had entered his flesh. It wasn't deep and hopefully hadn't hit a major artery.

Zeke closed his eyes and leaned his head against the shelf behind him. The pallor in his face and the throbbing vein in his neck attested to the pain he was beginning to feel.

The first thing she needed to do was cut away his shirt and try to determine the angle of entry.

"I need a pair of scissors," she said to a short man hovering nearby and peering at Zeke through spectacles on the end of his nose. "I'll also need a couple of clean strips of cloth."

The man didn't question her but moved to obey her orders. Zeke, on the other hand, was less obliging. "Don't trouble yourself." His eyes flew open. "I can wait for Doc."

"Fiddlesticks." She didn't know much about Williamsville, but if it was anything like Victoria, the doctor would already be busy and might not be able to visit Zeke at a moment's notice. "I had to remove a stake from Elijah's foot once. This isn't much different."

"I remember Elijah," Zeke said almost fondly, even as his breath came out in a puff.

"How comforting," she teased, hoping to distract him from his pain. "At least now I know I'm the forgettable one in my family."

"I didn't forget you. Besides, Elijah could keep up with Jeremiah and me."

"I guess you liked him better," she teased again as she probed around his wound.

At the touch, Zeke flinched. "I can't see how I would have."

"Don't worry. I understand. I always got in the way whenever I tried to join your adventures."

"We did have plenty of adventures, didn't we?"

"Aye." Her designated assistant returned with the items she'd requested. As he held out the scissors with trembling hands, his spectacles slipped off and hung by one ear. His young face was pale and perspiring, and his pupils were dilated as if he were about to pass out.

Zeke took notice of the man's condition. "I'll be alright, Wendell."

He attempted to hang his glasses, only hooking them behind his ear after the third attempt. "You sure, boss?"

"I'm sure."

The young man swallowed hard, his Adam's apple rising and falling.

"I'll take good care of him," Kate added.

"At the very least, she promises not to kill me," Zeke said in an apparent attempt to lighten the mood.

The young man blanched and swayed, Zeke's words not comforting him.

"Oh dear." Kate grabbed the man's arms in time to keep him from buckling. Gently, she guided him to the chair next to Zeke's. Once he was sitting, she maneuvered his head down. "Put your head between your legs and take some deep breaths."

"How many?" He bent his head until it almost touched the floor.

"How many what?"

"Breaths."

Kate paused in pressing against his back. "I don't think it really matters."

"Six, twelve, eighteen, or twenty-four?" the young man persisted in a muffled voice.

"At least thirty-six," Zeke interjected dryly. "Maybe even forty-eight."

"I'll do forty-eight to be safe," came another muffled reply.

Kate glanced between the two, and at the sight of Zeke's lips lifting into a half-smile that revealed a dimple, she allowed herself to breathe and smile in return. "So, tell me about your favorite adventure with Jeremiah."

As she worked cutting away Zeke's shirt, she forced herself to ignore Zeke's intense gaze following her every move, his muscular arms and chest, and the nearness of his mouth. Even if his smile and dimple hadn't lasted long, she was entirely too conscious of the way his lips formed words and sentences, and the evenness of his breathing in spite of his pain.

Becca had pushed her way through the men who'd swarmed into the store and were crowding around Zeke. Becca shooed them back, so Kate had enough workspace and then issued additional orders in her no-nonsense way.

As Kate inspected and attempted to discover the unseen damage the blade had done in Zeke's arm, she had to work harder to keep Zeke talking, especially as the pain intensified. From what she could tell, the blade had severed layers of skin and flesh but not much more.

Finally, after catching Becca's attention and silently communicating the need for her assistance, Kate clutched the knife and jerked it out.

Zeke's long lashes fell, and he pinched his lips closed.

Becca took the knife from Kate and handed her the rags. Immediately, Kate pressed the cloths against the wound to staunch the blood. She didn't want to squeeze too hard and cause Zeke more pain, but she had to be sure he didn't lose an excess of blood.

Without the knife acting as a cork, wet warmth seeped beneath her fingers as the blood flowed.

"I need to hold his artery here at the joint below," Kate said to Becca as she slipped her hand above his elbow. "You tie a strip above the injury to slow down the blood loss from above."

Becca used her teeth to tear a long strip from the bolt of material Zeke's employee had brought them. Soon enough, she had the tourniquet tied tightly in place.

As Kate waited long minutes pinching the artery as well as the wound, she became aware of the store interior for the first time. It was a one-room log structure, each wall filled with shelves piled with every conceivable item the men in town might need—trousers and hats, axes and knives, cups and skillets, blankets and tarps, and numerous items Kate guessed had to do with mining.

The spicy smoke of cigars lingered in the air along with the metallic and musty scents of new goods mixing with the old. With a dusty front window letting in some natural light and a gas lantern hanging from a rafter, Kate tried to imagine Zeke working within the confines of the store day after day.

Was he happy here with the new life he'd built for himself?

As if hearing her unasked question, he opened his eyes and met her gaze. The green had turned dark and murky with his pain. Even so, something glittered in that green, something she'd thought she noticed there before. Desire.

Did Zeke Hart desire *her*?

The very idea sent warmth spiraling through her chest. After all the years of admiring him, was it possible he was finally admiring her in return?

She couldn't tear her eyes away—didn't want to break the connection for fear she'd never get it back. But even as his dark gaze held her captive, she remembered Zoe's concerns, concerns that Zeke had turned his back on not only his family and friends but also on God. Kate had been the one to comfort Zoe on the day Zeke had walked out of the house and away from his faith.

Every day on the voyage from England, Kate had joined Zoe in praying for Zeke, that he'd make his peace with God and return to following Him. Had Zeke done so?

She held his gaze a moment longer, wishing she could see down to his soul, but then dropped her attention to his wound. She had no business letting herself become interested in a man who didn't share her faith, particularly one who'd spurned God.

Whatever the case, after her broken engagement to Herbert, she couldn't start another relationship without learning more about the man first. Perhaps that's the mistake she'd made with Herbert. She'd moved too quickly after ending her engagement to James McCrea.

For her next suitor, she needed to be more careful, get to know him better, and be wiser in her choice. Maybe then she'd finally find the right man.

four

"Please, Kate." Zeke ambled next to her on the boardwalk. "I want you to stay at my house where you'll be comfortable and safe."

Darkness had fallen hours ago, bringing with it cooler air that provided relief from the high-altitude sunshine. The streets were alive with revelers, all the men who'd come down from the hills and nearby mines to sate their hunger and quench their thirst. Once again, in spite of the cover of nightfall, Kate was the center of attention, garnering whistles and calls.

He'd managed to keep her to himself at the store after everyone else had taken their leave. Becca had stayed, and Wendell had been there off and on, nearly passing out every time he glanced at the wound.

All the while Kate had tended Zeke, she'd distracted him by relaying news from home, as well as telling him about her voyage to British Columbia on the *Robert Lowe*. He'd also asked about her months living in Victoria and had found himself growing distressed as she talked about her engagements, first with a hotel proprietor and then with Herb.

Doc had arrived at the store not long after sunset. By then, Kate and Becca had not only cleaned his wound but had also bandaged it. When Doc had looked at everything, he gave Kate a lecture about the dangers of removing puncturing objects and the chance of bleeding to death as a result.

Becca quickly rose to Kate's defense and listed all the precautions they'd taken. Even so, Doc grumbled for the length of his visit, until he left after giving further instructions he knew Zeke would ignore.

Now Becca walked a short distance ahead of them, casting Zeke distrustful glances every few seconds as if she expected him to pick Kate up and run away with her. He guessed he'd been lousy at concealing his attraction.

Kate was too pretty for her own good. And his. Once again, he blamed the flaring interest on the fact that he'd gone too long without any women in his life—not since he'd left Manchester. Even then, his last months there had been filled with unemployment, hunger, and bitterness.

Regardless of what he was feeling, he owed it to Jeremiah to look after Kate. "My home is one of the newest in town and one of the few made of mill-cut boards rather than logs."

"You know I appreciate your thoughtfulness," Kate replied as she had the other times he'd asked her to stay at his house. "But I need to get a job and find my own way."

"'Course you can still get a job." Zeke tried to ignore the

throbbing in his shoulder. "You'll just have a safe place to stay is all."

Would she be safe at his house with him? Even though he'd hired Mr. Peabody to manage his home and had given the older man the second floor as his living quarters, having Kate so close was only asking for trouble. And the last thing he wanted to do was dishonor her.

"I'll be safe enough staying with Becca in the cabin behind the laundry."

With the trouble he was having persuading Kate to live in his house, he'd sent Wendell out earlier to secure backup living arrangements for Becca and Kate. Lee Chung was stubborn, but he was also a shrewd businessman and hadn't been able to turn down Zeke's generous payment if he'd move out of his place and let the women live there instead. Wendell had also taken measures to have the women's belongings transported to the cabin.

Even though living behind the laundry was better than renting a room at one of the taverns or boarding houses, Zeke didn't have a good feeling about letting Kate go.

Several men stumbled out of a tavern onto the boardwalk, and Zeke placed a steadying hand on Kate's arm to keep her from colliding with the group. As soon as they saw Kate, they ogled her. Zeke directed her around the men, glaring at each one. They'd better catch the hint not to bother Kate, or they'd have to answer to him.

"Lee's place is a shack." Zeke spat the words as they started across the street, dodging horse droppings and a moving wagon. He didn't want Kate living in a shack. And he didn't want her doing the hard labor of washing the dirty clothing that miners and other townspeople brought to the laundry. She deserved better.

Kate gave a pleasant, lilting laugh, one that reminded him of her sweet spirit and innocence. "I won't mind living in a shack. You know what my home was like in Manchester. We never had much. But we had each other, and that's what counted."

"Amen," Becca said over her shoulder.

Kate's slum apartment had looked nearly identical to his family's, only a building away. Their lives had also been nearly identical, both of them dealing with loss and poverty and hardship and lousy fathers. He was relieved she'd found a way to escape, like Zoe had. And he was relieved she was in a new place where she could have a better life.

He simply wanted to make sure her life was better. He had the means to help. In fact, he had more wealth and resources than he could use in his lifetime. And since he could ease her discomfort and provide for her, that's what he wanted to do. If only he could convince her to let him.

"If you won't live in my house, then let me build you your own place."

She peered up at him, the moonlight highlighting her eyes filled with both surprise and amusement.

Did she think he was as pathetic and desperate for a woman as Herb? Maybe he was, but he didn't want her to know it. "Just as a brother. That's all. I'm only doing what Jeremiah would have done for Zoe if we'd switched places."

"Jeremiah would have married Zoe if she'd given him the chance." Though her tone was light, something serious edged her words.

"Are you saying I should marry you?" He tried to keep his tone as light as hers, but his muscles tightened in anticipation of her answer. He couldn't possibly want to marry Kate, could he? She wasn't exactly a stranger. But he didn't know her anymore—if he ever really had. What was wrong with him to consider the possibility? Hadn't he said earlier he wasn't in the market for a wife?

Thankfully, she laughed at his question, sparing him the embarrassment of speaking—and perhaps proposing right on the spot. "I guess I should wait on getting married. After what happened with Mr. Frank, I need to stop rushing into relationships and take more time, so I can be sure I'm marrying the right man."

"Good answer. But none of the men here will care one whit if you're rushing." He glared again at more miners passing by who were eyeing Kate with too much interest.

"Well, I care, especially after you got injured on account of my *rushing*." Her expression was earnest, making her pretty face even more irresistible.

With the laundry only a dozen paces away, he halted. The motion sent fire racing from his wound down his arm, and he turned his face away from her to hide his grimace.

"Zeke?" She touched his uninjured arm lightly. "You should be home abed. I told you the pain would be unbearable even with the laudanum."

Ahead, Becca paused underneath the *Lee Chung Laundry*

sign. The windows of the laundry reflected the lantern light from inside, showing Lee still busy at work in front of one of his large tin tubs, scrubbing vigorously on a piece of linen. Lee often worked eighteen hours straight. Some nights his lantern burned until one or two in the morning.

The hardworking man could use the extra help. Just not from Kate.

Zeke forced down the pain and took a breath. "I'll go home to bed if you promise to let me help you."

"I've been managing on my own these past months just fine." Her voice contained a gentle rebuke.

"I've got the means—"

"I can see that your general store has done well. But I can't accept charity."

His general store was a good investment. Wendell had been wise to direct him to open it. Providing supplies to miners was lucrative and brought in more income than his other businesses—the livery, the men's boardinghouse, and the sawmill. Wendell had assured him that eventually the sawmill would generate even more income than his other businesses combined. But for now, nothing could compare to the success of his gold mine.

At the mining board meeting today with two other bosses, Putnam and Blake, he'd discussed the possibility of opening a hospital. Wendell, with his accounting smarts, didn't consider a hospital a financially sound investment since they'd likely lose more money than they'd earn. But, as Zeke had said to the other men, since they'd been the lucky ones to strike it rich, didn't they have the responsibility to take care of their community?

After despising the wealthy mill owners in Manchester for the calloused attitude toward him and their many other employees, Zeke wanted to be different, to take care of his workers, and to help Williamsville prosper. Unfortunately, Putnam and Blake didn't share his vision, and half the time Zeke felt like he was striding upstream against the current.

"But I do thank you," Kate continued. "You have a kind heart that you're so willing to give from the little you have."

Little? He opened his mouth to correct her, to explain that he was one of the wealthiest men in the colony. His mine was producing thousands of pounds of gold every week, even a year after he'd struck pay dirt.

But then he stopped. He didn't want to impress Kate with his newfound riches. Didn't want to win her by his wealth. Not that he wanted to impress or to win Kate at all. But if he did, he wanted her to like him because of who he was and not for what he owned.

"Why'd you change your mind about marrying Herb?" His question tumbled out into the night air. Once there, he wished he could swat it away like he would the pesky mosquitoes that plagued them during the summer, especially when she focused her attention on the plank walkway beneath their feet and bit her lower lip. "I'm sorry. I shouldn't have asked. It's none of my business—"

"No, it's alright." She toed a tobacco juice stain. "I don't mind telling you."

He waited, conscious that Becca was also listening, her expression interested, as though she, too, wanted to understand Kate's decision today.

"I—" Kate started but paused. Then she raised her hands in an attitude of defeat. "Honestly, I don't know why I changed my mind."

Her confusion made him want to comfort her. He could only imagine the pressure she was under after having come over on one of the bride ships and being expected to pick a husband and get married.

"All I know is that I set off on this trip to Williamsville fully expecting to marry Herbert. But now that I'm here, I can't go through with it."

"Listen, if you're uncertain, then you're better off waiting than rushing into a marriage and living with regrets."

She looked up and met his gaze. "Thank you."

Warmth pooled inside him.

"I'm glad you're here, Zeke." She reached for his hand and squeezed it.

The touch of her fingers only stirred the warmth. He gave a gentle squeeze back, fighting the urge to hold on to her, and forcing himself instead to let go.

With a word of good night, she followed Becca inside the laundry.

Once the door closed, a blanket of darkness descended upon him. He frowned and stared for long moments at the laundry. His mind filled with images of his childhood, of Jeremiah's easy smile and laughter, so much like Kate's.

Jeremiah had been the best of friends, even when everyone else had deserted him, because they believed he started the fire at the mill. Jeremiah had been the one to lower him down into the sewers when the constables had come to arrest him. And his friend had been the one to hide him in a dung cart and drive him out of town so he could leave Manchester undetected.

He owed Jeremiah his life. The very least he could do was watch over Kate like he would a sister. Jeremiah would have wanted it, especially here in this lawless town when men could get away with almost anything, including attempted murder.

'Course, Herb was adamantly denying he'd tried to murder Zeke, saying he'd only meant to scare him off. Without the proper authorities and justice system in place, Herb would spend the night in the makeshift lockup behind the livery before going free.

Kate didn't belong in such a town. And yet, hadn't Zeke just recently complained at one of the mining board meetings that they needed more wives and families for Williamsville to prosper and grow more civilized?

If Kate stayed, not only would he make sure she had everything she needed, but he'd oversee the men who came calling on her, discouraging away the unfit and only allowing the best to have access to her.

With the pain in his arm making him nauseous, he returned to his shop. Wendell once again stood behind the counter, poring over the ledgers.

"The day's done, Wendell." Zeke dropped wearily into a chair. "Take a break."

Wendell finished writing down several numbers before raising his head and peering at Zeke through his spectacles, which doubled the size of his eyes along with the concern there. "You should take a break too."

"Can't. I'm too worried about Kate."

With his forefinger, Wendell delicately slid his glasses up his nose and then cleared his throat. "If I recollect the incident correctly, you're the one with the injury, not her."

Zeke leaned back in his chair, propped his boots on the table, then closed his eyes, wishing he could as easily block out the throbbing in his arm. "I've decided I'm gonna personally take charge of her courtship process."

Wendell didn't say a word, which usually meant he didn't like Zeke's suggestion and didn't know how to respond.

Zeke lifted his lids. The young man still watched him, his glasses having slid back down his nose. "Spread the word that nobody's to seek out Kate's attention or court her unless they get permission from me first."

"That's rather dictator-like, don't you think, boss?"

Zeke had once told himself he wouldn't use his money or position of power in the town to lord himself over others. But this case was different. "Tell them I'm the closest thing she has to family—that I'm like a brother. And that I have her best interest in mind."

"And you don't think they'll see through your threat to the fact that you want her for yourself?"

"No. I mean, yes." Zeke dropped his feet and let the legs of his chair hit the floor. The jarring reverberated up his torso to his arm and down into his wound.

Wendell's pale eyebrows rose.

Zeke drew in a deep breath to stave off the pain. "You know what I'm trying to say. Nobody's gonna see anything, because I don't want Kate for myself."

"Ninety-five percent of the eligible men in town will see exactly what I have, that you like her and think she's beautiful."

"Ninety-five percent?" Zeke couldn't keep from teasing his assistant. "Are you sure it's not more like ninety-six?"

Wendell gazed off into space and silently mouthed several calculations, as though mentally tabulating, before shaking his head. "No, I'm quite certain the total is ninety-five percent."

Zeke pushed back from the table and stood. "Even if one hundred percent object, I don't care. I've made up my mind, and I'm not allowing anyone to call on Kate unless I give permission."

Zeke crossed to the door, exhaustion and pain making each step feel like a dozen.

Wendell sighed. "Very well, boss. I'll make sure the ninety-five percent knows."

"Good answer." Zeke opened the door.

"There's just one problem."

Zeke paused halfway out. "What's that?"

"Miss Millington. She doesn't strike me as the kind of

woman who will take kindly to having a man meddling in her business."

"Then we won't give her any reason to suspect we've meddled, will we?"

Wendell pushed his glasses up on his nose and swallowed hard. "No, boss."

Zeke continued on his way. "Night, Wendell."

"Good night, boss."

five

Perspiration trickled between Kate's shoulder blades, down her spine to her hips, making the waistline of her skirt stick to her skin. Even with the front and back doors of the laundry open, the air was stale without a breeze. The strong odor of dirty linens mingled with the pungency of lye.

She blew at the hair hanging limply in front of her face. The effort only served to plaster the strand to her damp forehead. She paused, lifting the heavy iron from the shirt spread out on the worktable, and rolled her shoulders to ease the ache there.

In the back of the room, Mr. Chung scrubbed at one large tin sink while Becca stood over another steaming tub, plunging garments in and out of the water to rinse them. Sweat dripped like sprinkles of rain from her friend's face, plopping into the water.

Earlier in the day, Kate had protested when Becca insisted on giving her the easy tasks, like hanging the laundry to dry on the long lines outside, or drawing water from the well to refill the tubs, or adding more fuel to the ovens that kept the wash water hot.

But now with the onset of evening, Kate couldn't object, not even if she'd found the energy to do so. The laundry tasks were more exhausting than anything she'd ever done before, even her work in the mill. She'd started there at age twelve as a doffer, replacing the bobbins as fast as she could to keep the spinning frames from stopping for long. After that, she'd tended the power loom as its thread-bearing shuttle rocked dangerously back and forth.

She'd been content enough with the work, until she'd been let go from the factory two years ago when the cotton supply had diminished at the outset of the War Between the States in America. Since then, she'd struggled like all the other unemployed women, relying on charity to keep hunger at bay.

After the hardships of those years, she ought to be grateful for employment in the laundry, no matter how difficult it was. *Stop complaining,* she inwardly chastised herself as she returned the heavy black iron to the shirt and pressed it along the rumpled hem. But her efforts were to no avail, because the iron had grown too cold to take away the creases and smooth the fabric to perfection the way Mr. Chung liked it.

With handsome features, Mr. Chung was younger than she'd expected. He'd warmly welcomed Becca since they were friends from the days when he'd lived and operated a laundry in Victoria. But upon meeting Kate, he'd narrowed his eyes and spoken sharply in Mandarin before walking away, shaking his head in disgust.

Later, Becca had informed Kate that Mr. Chung didn't think she was strong or sturdy enough for the hard labor of the laundry. And all day, Kate had been attempting to prove her new employer was wrong.

In some ways, she was also trying to prove to herself that she hadn't made a mistake in turning down Herbert's proposal. She tried not to think about the fact that if she married him, she wouldn't have to work in the hot laundry. And she wouldn't have to stay in the drafty cabin out back, which was every bit the *shack* Zeke had declared it to be. Though tidy, the hastily constructed building was hardly big enough for one person, much less both her and Becca.

With a sigh, Kate returned the iron to the hot stovetop and reached for the spare one that had been warming. Her fingers accidentally brushed the handle before she remembered to use a rag for lifting it. Heat and pain pricked her skin, already burned in several places. Hissing, she stuck her fingers into her mouth to attempt to cool the newest burns.

"Evening," came a voice from the open front doorway.

She jumped away from the stove and hastily dropped her fingers. Throughout the day, a steady stream of customers had been visiting until Mr. Chung said, "These men coming to see you. Maybe you be good for my business."

The men had been polite but curious, some making small talk with her, others simply staring at her while she worked. Whatever the case, Mr. Chung never allowed them to linger for long before shooing them out.

This time, as she turned to collect a bundle of dirty laundry, she halted in surprise at the sight of Zeke standing in the doorway. He was wearing the typical dusty woolen trousers and flannel shirt of miners, and his boots were caked with mud. He swiped off his hat, revealing his dark hair, flattened with the hat's imprint. His jaw and chin were shadowed with stubble. Even so, he was starkly handsome, so much that her breath caught.

His green eyes swept over her. After the long hours on her feet in the overheated shop, she had no doubt she looked her worst. A part of her wanted to turn away and hide until she had time to freshen herself. Her more practical nature held her in place. Being kind was more important than looking pretty.

"Hello, Zeke." She offered him a smile. "Is today your wash day, too?"

"Too?"

"From the business we've had, it would appear this is wash day for most men in town."

Zeke's dark eyebrows slanted together. "Most men?"

Mr. Chung had paused in his washing and now stood facing Zeke with dripping hands. "They come to see the missee." He nodded in her direction.

Kate wanted to deny Mr. Chung, but after her experiences in Victoria as one of the bride-ship women, she would be naïve to believe otherwise. "Mr. Chung hasn't let anyone stay for long."

"Good." Zeke exchanged a long, hard glance with the young man.

Only then did she notice Zeke wasn't carrying a sack or pile of linens. His arms were empty. Did that mean he'd come to the laundry to see her? What if he hadn't felt the need to have an excuse like the other men?

Her pulse hopped at the prospect. She couldn't deny that her thoughts had strayed frequently to him throughout the day—mostly because she was concerned over his wound, although a part of her still held her girlish infatuation.

"How's your injury?"

He moved his arm gingerly. "It hurts like—" He clamped his mouth closed.

She guessed he'd been about to curse but then thought better of it around her, which was a reminder he still was a wandering soul, a man living for his own pleasures rather than God's.

Of course, she shouldn't rush to judge him. After all, no one was perfect, and she could only pray he'd made his peace with God over the past year.

"Did the doctor examine the wound today?" she asked.

"Aye, he cleaned and bandaged it again."

"And is everything looking alright?"

"As well as can be."

"It's probably due for another cleaning and more salve."

"He gave me the supplies to do it myself. They're back at the store."

"Then I'll help you."

"First, I'll treat you to dinner."

He was asking her to dinner? She'd always dreamed of Zeke asking her to do something together but had never expected it to be a reality. She wanted to jump up and down with a little squeal but forced herself to respond calmly as she started toward him. "Sounds perfect."

"Not right now, missee." Mr. Chung paused in his scrubbing and glared at her. "We finish work first."

Kate halted, an iron still in her hand. "You're right." What had she been thinking? She couldn't just walk out.

She offered Zeke an apologetic smile. "I'll finish, then meet you later." Her gaze slid to the piles of dirty laundry yet on the floor waiting for washing, and her shoulders sagged. At the rate they were going, they'd be working halfway through the night at least.

"How many hours have Kate and Becca been working?" Zeke directed his question to Mr. Chung.

"Does not matter. We keep going until work is done."

"You might be able to work all day and night." Zeke crossed his arms. "But don't expect it of the women."

Mr. Chung cocked his head slightly as if he was mentally translating. Then he glanced sideways at Becca.

She hadn't paused and was still plunging linens up and down in the steaming tub. The sweat continued to drip from her face, and the back of her shirt was plastered to her skin.

"Once the women have worked eight hours," Zeke continued, "let them be done for the day."

Mr. Chung's eyes widened. "Eight?"

"No more than ten."

Becca stopped working to stare first at Zeke, then at Mr. Chung. Her expression contained none of the usual wariness, only curiosity. And something else. Was it admiration?

Kate lifted fingers to her mouth to hold in a gasp. Did

Becca like Mr. Chung? She studied her friend's face with more care. Kate had no doubt Becca had told her the truth about coming to Williamsville for safety. But was it also possible she'd traveled to the mountain town to be with Mr. Chung? Had Becca already developed feelings for the handsome Chinese man when they'd known each other in Victoria?

"They need time to rest, Lee." Zeke gentled his tone. "You have to allow them breaks throughout the workday as well as the evening."

Kate's knees wobbled together, the weariness of the past long hours making her suddenly weak so that she had to fight back a yawn. In spite of her aching muscles, she wouldn't have any trouble falling asleep in the cramped shack tonight.

Mr. Chung was silent a moment longer before nodding. "Women done work for the day. Becca and missee go rest, and I will finish."

"I ain't gonna leave you with all this to do." Becca thrust her arms back into the rinsing tub.

Kate's hopefulness evaporated as quickly as the hot water in the large pots. "I'll stay too," she offered quietly.

"No." All three of the others spoke at the same time.

The quickness and certainty of their answers made Kate smile. "Are you sure?"

"As long as Zeke promise to get you a fine dinner." Becca smiled in return, one that radiated with genuine happiness. Maybe Becca wanted some time alone with Mr. Chung. Kate would be only too happy to comply.

"What do you say, Zeke?" Kate asked.

55

"I promise." Zeke spoke solemnly but with a hint of a twinkle in his eyes.

"Then how can I resist?" She set the iron back on the stove, a new lightness in her steps. It didn't matter that she was still dirty, overheated, and perspiring. She was blessedly done and free to spend time with Zeke. She couldn't think of a better end to the day.

As she approached him, he bowed slightly and held out his elbow, as though he were a wealthy gentleman and she a courtly lady and they were going to dinner with the queen.

Tucking her hand into the crook of his arm, she relished the hard contours beneath his shirtsleeve along with the fact that she was touching Zeke. The gesture was likely only polite on his end, something he'd do for his sister, and she shouldn't read more into it. Nevertheless, she flushed inside at the contact, marveling again that she was doing something she'd only fantasized about.

As they stepped outside, she halted at the vista that greeted them. With the sun beginning to sink behind the high peaks directly to the west, the range was a glow of every shade, tone, and tint of red and yellow possible. She'd unpacked her paints and palette last night, eager to start something new. But in the crowded and dimly lit confines of the shack, she'd stuck to her sketching.

Maybe tonight after returning from dinner, she'd recreate the glory and grandeur spreading out before them, the unyielding mountain peaks touched by the ever-changing beauty of light.

She took in a deep contented breath.

"In all the time I've lived up here, I've never once gotten tired of this view." Zeke stood beside her on the plank sidewalk, ignoring the gawking men passing by on horse and foot. His face was pointed in the same direction as hers, his sights set upon the mountain peaks.

She followed his lead and ignored the onlookers. "I can't wait to paint the scene."

Zeke swiveled so she could feel his gaze upon her. "You paint?"

"I try." She stared straight ahead, fighting a wave of embarrassment at her admission. It wasn't as though she'd hidden her artistic pursuits from her friends and family.

"Do you have any recent paintings with you?"

"I sold everything in Victoria before I left."

"Then you're good enough that people will purchase your paintings?"

"Don't act so surprised." She swatted his arm, glad he'd offered her the one that hadn't been injured. "Believe it or not, some people like my work enough that they're willing to pay for it. Not much, mind you. But every little bit helps."

"I'm not surprised. Well, maybe I am. But even more than that, I'm proud of you."

Pleasure welled up and spread through her body in a way she couldn't explain. When he tugged her along, she couldn't focus on the sunset over the mountain range any longer. All she could think about was the spectacular man walking next to her, how he was easily the most handsome and charming man in town.

She answered more questions about her painting and

sketching and didn't pay attention to where they were going until he drew them to a halt in front of a two-story house on the far end of town. It was constructed of planks rather than hewn logs and had been painted a crisp, fresh white with black shutters, reminding her of the homes in Victoria. Though the structure was simple, it was unarguably the biggest and nicest place she'd yet to see in Williamsville.

"Does the doctor live here?"

Zeke swept his gaze over the shingled roof, gabled windows, and portico over the porch. His mouth curved upward into the beginning of a smile. "I live here."

"You do?"

His smile inched higher, bringing out his dimples. "Aye."

"Why Zeke Hart," she said, letting her amazement spill out with her words. "Now it's my turn to be proud of you."

"Thank you." He reached up and squeezed her hand still tucked in the crook of his arm. His fingers were strong and warm, and his touch did strange things to her insides.

For a short while, she plied him with questions about the house, and she learned he'd opened a sawmill last fall, and the first thing he'd built was his house. The construction was completed by the first snowfall, and he'd been living in it ever since. "Mr. Peabody," he finished, "Wendell's grandfather, lives upstairs and helps me with the upkeep."

"Then you can show me around since you shouldn't have any messes to hide." She tugged him toward the door, giving him no choice but to follow.

"Mr. Peabody has dinner waiting for us."

"He does?" Kate pulled up short, her heartbeat tripping ahead of her. "That's so kind of him."

"I have a feeling you'll love Mr. Peabody."

"I'm sure I will." She couldn't keep from studying Zeke's features and had the urge to skim her fingers along the planes of his cheeks and brow, and around those green eyes—which were intently tracing her face with as much interest as she was his.

Was he interested in her as more than a childhood friend and his playmate's little sister? Surely he was seeing her all grown up as a woman. And surely that spark in his eyes meant he liked what he saw.

At the prospect, she silently admonished herself. She needed to put her mind elsewhere, needed to stop letting her thoughts run away from her. "And how, exactly, did you know I'd be able to join you for dinner?" She pulled him forward again. "Didn't you worry Mr. Chung would refuse to release me from my obligations?"

"Nope. No worries. Lee's a good guy. He might work himself to death, but I figured I could sway him to be easy on you women."

"And what if I'd told you I had plans with someone else?"

"I'd have told you to cancel them." He opened the front door and pushed it wide.

"You're assuming I would have wanted to."

"I think you would have." His voice was light and teasing.

She didn't want him to know he was right. Instead, she

shook her head and tried to look nonchalant. "I see you're still as arrogant as when you were a boy."

He chuckled.

A brightly lit front hallway greeted them, along with an elderly man who rushed from what appeared to be the kitchen at the back of the house. He was short like Wendell but lacked his grandson's thinness and was instead plump and red-cheeked. While the top of his head was bald and polished to a shine, he had a curly black mustache as well as a long, pointed goatee.

"Ah, there you are." He wiped his hands on an apron. "The marmalade glaze on the duck is beginning to congeal."

"Mr. Peabody, this is Miss Millington, the young lady I was telling you about."

"Welcome, mademoiselle." Mr. Peabody lifted her hand, kissing the back while at the same time bowing with a flourish.

"Thank you." Kate was conscious again of her work-worn appearance and wished she'd insisted on changing. "Are you French?"

"Moi?" Mr. Peabody waved a hand brusquely and made a noise at the back of his throat. "I wish, but alas, I'm English through and through."

"I see." She glanced at Zeke. He was watching her reaction to Mr. Peabody, his eyes crinkling at the corners. She had the urge to smile and swat him playfully again, but she bit back her mirth and nodded at Mr. Peabody. "I'm looking forward to your dinner."

"I hope you enjoy it, mademoiselle. Duck à l'orange, red beet salad, and mashed potatoes with caramelized onions."

"It sounds wonderful."

"It is." Mr. Peabody stepped into a nearby doorway. "When Zeke asked me to prepare a nice dinner for his lady friend, I decided he needed all the help he could get if he plans to propose."

Surprise zipped along her nerves, joined with a tingling of hesitation. Surely Zeke wasn't considering asking her to marry him tonight. Was he?

six

Plans to propose?

Zeke hadn't mentioned anything to Mr. Peabody about proposing marriage to Kate, but the idea wasn't bad, was it? It would solve his problems about keeping the other men from pestering her. Once they knew she was his, they'd have no choice but to back off.

He hadn't been able to keep his eyes off her for more than a few seconds since first stepping into the laundry. It hadn't helped that he'd thought about her all day. At his mine, knee-deep in mud and water, even with the urgent concerns of a collapsed beam demanding his attention, she'd occupied him so thoroughly, he hadn't been able to concentrate the way he needed to.

"Your dinner awaits." From within the dining room, Mr. Peabody made a grand gesture toward the interior.

Zeke started to move but Kate didn't budge. Instead, her fingers upon his arm tightened, and something flashed in her eyes—something akin to the panic he'd seen there yesterday when she'd been trying to break her engagement with Herb.

He paused and studied her more carefully. Her lips pressed together. It wasn't exactly a frown, but he suspected it was as close as she got to one.

Did she really think he was planning to propose tonight? For a second, he was tempted to let her lack of enthusiasm toward the suggestion bother him. But he pushed aside the feeling. She'd just ended a relationship yesterday and wasn't ready for a new one. That's all there was to it. Besides, he wasn't ready either. Was he?

"Hey," he said softly. "Don't worry. I'm not gonna propose."

"You're not?" Her gaze snagged his, her long lashes highlighting her beautiful eyes.

"Nope. 'Course not."

"Oh good." She released a breath, her shoulders relaxing.

Even if he'd grown up with Kate, he didn't know her. And while she might be pretty, he wasn't in the habit of falling in love with women at first sight.

"Come now." Mr. Peabody poked his head out of the dining room again. "Sit down and let me serve the meal before it's inedible."

"Ready?" Zeke patted her hand, the movement making his shoulder ache. Though his wound still throbbed, the pain had begun to diminish, except for the few times he'd overexerted his arm while down in the mine.

This time, Kate didn't resist as he led her forward. She paused when reaching the wide doorway, her gaze sweeping over the simple hand-hewn table covered with a white cloth and decorated with a jar of wildflowers and long candles. The tableware was neatly set with linen napkins folded upon the plates into an interesting shape.

She released a little gasp and clasped her hands together. "Why, Mr. Peabody. The flowers are masterfully arranged, and the swans are so intricately folded. The effect is simply stunning. A work of art."

Zeke took a second look at the strangely folded napkins. Those were supposed to be swans? He tilted his head, first one way, then another. "They look like shoehorns, not swans."

Mr. Peabody shot him a glare, and Kate seemed to try to hold back a smile.

His housekeeper returned his gaze to the flower arrangement, stroking his goatee. "You don't think I've clustered too many lupines with the paintbrush?"

"Absolutely not." She moved to examine the flowers more closely. "The brilliant azure of the lupines brings out the bright burgundy of the paintbrushes."

"That's what I thought, too." Mr. Peabody's stoic expression grew animated, and he rambled on about how he'd decided where to place the different flowers. She listened with rapt attention, nodding and commenting, before she shifted her attention to the shoehorn swans and made a fuss over them too.

When she leaned in and buried her face into the flower petals, Mr. Peabody watched her with such adoration that Zeke almost laughed. Kate had managed to win over his stodgy housekeeper in a matter of minutes when it had taken him months. How was that possible?

"With such a beautiful arrangement," she remarked as she straightened, "I feel as though I should be attired in something much fancier."

"Not at all," Mr. Peabody gushed. "You're already beautiful enough."

"You're too kind, Mr. Peabody. Zeke said I'd love you, and he was right."

Mr. Peabody's face flushed a red that was almost the same shade as the centerpiece flowers. He stuttered before mumbling about the food and running from the room.

Once he was gone, Kate traced the edge of a plate, still admiring the folded napkin.

"So that's how you do it," Zeke said, unable to contain his mirth any longer.

She looked up, her expression innocent and her eyes beguiling. "Do what?"

"This." He pointed between them. She was doing it again. This time to him. Drawing him in so that he was completely enamored.

Waiting for him to elaborate, she tilted her head, the loose wisps of her hair turning to gold in the candlelight.

She apparently had no idea the effect she had on men, both young and old. Which was all the more reason he needed to step in and protect her, no matter what Wendell had said.

"Let's sit." He pulled out her chair.

She didn't move. "First, tell me what I'm *doing*."

A strand of hair brushed her neck, drawing his attention to the long graceful stretch. Though something deep inside warned him that he needed to be careful, his words found a way out regardless. "You're able to weave a spell over every man you meet."

Her lips rose in a pretty smile. "Every man?"

"Nearly."

She lowered herself into the chair, and he assisted in pushing her closer, before rounding the table and taking the spot across from her. All the while, he felt her unswerving gaze upon him.

He busied himself with straightening the spoon and knife that were already perfectly positioned, and then twisted the coffee cup so the handle faced the opposite direction.

"Well?" she asked.

"Well, what?" She'd nibbled on the bait he'd dangled, but now he didn't know whether to proceed.

"Have I woven a spell over you yet?" Her lashes fluttered and her smile beckoned him.

If she hadn't yet had him in her palm, she did now. "You're close to it."

She laughed, his answer clearly delighting her so that he wished he could spend a lifetime making her happy.

Before Zeke made a fool of himself by dropping to his knees and proposing on the spot, Mr. Peabody bustled into the room with a small bowl in each hand. He placed the dishes in front of them revealing beets, walnuts, crumbled white cheese, and salad greens.

Zeke picked up his fork and poked at the assortment.

He'd grown accustomed to Mr. Peabody's cuisine and to trying strange creations that were supposedly French. But this time, Mr. Peabody had mistaken him for a goat.

Kate cleared her throat.

He glanced up to see that she'd folded her hands on the table in front of her. "Should we say a prayer before eating?"

The expectation on her face brought his pulse to an abrupt halt. He laid down his utensil and leaned back in his chair. How could he explain his fall from grace to this sweet young woman? Did he even want to attempt it? And yet, he couldn't mislead her into believing he was someone he wasn't.

He reached for his spoon and began flipping it, trying to decide how to proceed. He sensed his admission would disappoint Kate, and disappointing her was the last thing he wanted to do.

"Zoe told me that when you left home, you left your faith behind."

He chanced a glance her way. She was chewing a bit of salad and watching him, kindness in her eyes.

"I admit," she continued, "I was hoping you'd figured everything out and made peace with God . . ."

He sensed she was giving him an opening to discuss the matter, but he didn't want to talk about it now—or anytime. "Listen, Kate—"

"You don't have to tell me anything. Until you're ready."

He hesitated. Part of him wanted to unburden himself with this woman and share how difficult his last days in Manchester had been, when he had felt abandoned by everyone, including God. The days of running away and voyaging to British Columbia had been lonely and frustrating and difficult. The first weeks of trekking up into the Cariboo and searching for gold had been hard too.

But he'd made it through all the challenges on his own. Now he had his wealth, businesses, and power—and he didn't need God. And God didn't need him, not with godly men like Zoe's husband, Pastor Abe.

"I'm sorry, Kate. You're probably hoping to hear that I'm back to being the same person I was before—"

"No, of course not. I don't expect you to be the same person. Not at all." She took another bite of the beet salad.

"But . . ."

She swallowed her mouthful. "You'll never be the *same*. You'll be *better*, once you give control of your life to the Lord."

He lifted his fork and stirred his salad, the cheese crumbling and the beet juice turning the pieces dark. He'd already had this awkward talk with his sister and Abe, one in which they both pleaded with him to stop running away from the Almighty. He didn't need another well-meaning person dredging up old memories.

"I'm doing just fine the way I am. I hope you can understand and accept that."

She paused, another forkful halfway to her mouth. "I accept you. But that doesn't mean I agree with you." As her mouth closed around the fork, he watched her lips and the way they glided over the tines. His gut cinched with a need to test her lips for himself. How long had it been since he'd kissed a woman?

He gave himself a mental shake. Where had thoughts of

kissing come from? If he wanted the other men in town to respect Kate, he was gonna have to set the example and think of her as a friend and nothing more.

That's the only reason he invited her to dinner. For friendship's sake. And he couldn't let himself forget it.

As he forced himself to eat Mr. Peabody's salad, he made a point of moving the conversation to safer topics and discovered she was easy to talk to. For any question he asked her, she directed a question back at him, so that the flow was a pleasant give and take.

She told him more about her first days in Victoria, about the onlookers who'd lined up on the shore to greet the bride ship when it arrived, and how hundreds of men had shouted and cheered as the women stepped onto land after almost a hundred days at sea.

He shared how he'd worked in construction for several months before saving enough so he could purchase the supplies he needed to begin his trek up into the Cariboo mines. He explained what his life had been like in those early days in Williamsville. And he answered her questions about the sawmill and general store.

The topic of his gold mine never came up. It was almost as if she assumed he'd given up mining to pursue his other endeavors—like so many other miners did once they became disillusioned with the search for gold. As before, he hesitated in revealing the truth about his riches.

Throughout the evening, Mr. Peabody interrupted them with each new dish he'd prepared. And Kate never failed to compliment the housekeeper about the flavor or texture or consistency. Her words were sincere and each smile genuine. With the pleasure on Mr. Peabody's face, Zeke had no doubt the man would have married Kate on the spot had he been forty years younger.

There was nothing pretentious about her. And the more time they spent together, the more he wanted to be with her. When she could no longer contain yawns behind her hand, he offered to walk her back to the laundry. She insisted first on accompanying him to his store and helping him clean his wound—even when he claimed he could take care of it himself.

"It's been a pleasure to meet you, mademoiselle," Mr. Peabody said at the front door as he bowed and kissed Kate's hand.

"You're an excellent chef and host," Kate said in return. "You really should consider opening your own eating establishment."

"Now hold on." Zeke tugged Kate's hand away from Mr. Peabody and placed it into the crook of his arm. "Don't encourage Mr. Peabody to leave me. I need him."

"Need?" Kate teased. "It's a crime to keep his talents all to yourself."

Mr. Peabody beamed at Kate, his face again turning red.

"Maybe I'll have to wring a promise out of Mr. Peabody that he won't desert me." Wendell's grandfather was just as invaluable as Wendell himself.

Gold fever had brought the two up into the mountains at the height of the gold rush. But Wendell had lasted only a week before seeking out other employment. And Mr. Peabody hadn't gone much longer before realizing just how difficult the search for gold was. The average man could pan a few nuggets, enough to put a handful of money in his pocket. But only a few were as lucky as Zeke to strike it rich on a claim.

Zeke had hired Wendell first. The young man was a genius with figures and investments. Within a few weeks of employment, Wendell had doubled, even tripled, the profits of everything he touched.

When Wendell had asked about employment for his grandfather, Zeke hadn't been able to say no to his most valuable employee and closest friend. At first, Mr. Peabody had worked in the general store, but his finicky nature had driven away more customers than he assisted. When Zeke had hired him instead at the boardinghouse, Mr. Peabody had nearly caused riots every day with his pickiness.

Finally, after Zeke had started construction on his house, he offered Mr. Peabody the position as his housekeeper. Mr. Peabody had been happy ever since, and now Zeke didn't know how he'd get along without the older man's assistance.

"Promise you won't leave me, Mr. Peabody," Zeke insisted as he led Kate out the front door onto the portico. "You wouldn't want to see me go back to eating beans and hard biscuits, would you?"

Standing in the door, Mr. Peabody stroked his mustache, curling up the ends, glancing from Kate to Zeke and back. "There's one way you can ensure I'll stay."

"Name your price," Zeke teased, "and I'll pay it."

"If you marry Miss Millington, then I'll stay forever." The crimson in Mr. Peabody's face spread to his ears.

Kate's laughter was soft but full of amusement. "You're so sweet, Mr. Peabody. But I can't marry Zeke. I just ended a relationship, and I can't rush into another."

Mr. Peabody waved dismissively. "You'll be ready soon enough. And when you are, you'll marry Zeke."

Kate laughed again and ducked her head.

Zeke's pulse quickened. Was it possible she might eventually consider him?

She glanced up at him shyly and then focused on Mr. Peabody. "As wonderful as Zeke is, we're really more like brother and sister."

Zeke might have started off thinking of Kate as a sister, but those thoughts had now hightailed it. Before he could correct her, Mr. Peabody beat him to it.

"Zeke's ardor is much more than brotherly." Mr. Peabody brushed a hand over Zeke's shirt as though dusting away crumbs. "That should be quite obvious with all the trouble he's gone to in warning the other men not to court you—"

"Mr. Peabody!" Zeke didn't want Kate to know anything about his underhanded dealings. But his housekeeper was about as useful at picking up social cues as a donkey was at picking up commands.

Kate's brows rose. "Warning other men not to court me?"

"It's nothing." Zeke slanted a glare at Mr. Peabody.

The older man straightened Zeke's collar and then patted his chest, all the while ignoring Zeke's pointed look. "Zeke had Wendell spread the word that nobody's to seek out your attention or court you unless they get permission from him first."

"Get permission?"

"It's not what you think—"

"You're requiring that men get permission from you before they can come courting?" Her voice was tinged with accusation.

Zeke's gut churned with the need to make this whole conversation disappear. "I can explain."

"I hope so."

Glancing between them with raised brows, Mr. Peabody tilted his ear toward the kitchen. "What do you know? I hear the water boiling. That means I really should be on my way to wash dishes." He dipped his head in good-bye and promptly closed the front door.

Once they were alone, Zeke glanced down the street to the busy thoroughfare scattered with lantern light, men, and horses. His house was set far enough away from the businesses that he had some privacy, but the strains of music and laughter still wafted their way.

He moved onto the street, hoping she'd follow suit and forget about everything Mr. Peabody had just revealed.

She didn't budge but instead crossed her arms and cocked her head. "Well?"

"Well, we really should be going."

"*Well*, I think you should explain why you're scaring the men of this town away from me."

"Guess it didn't work since half the population stopped by the laundry today."

"Hardly a man spoke to me—" Her eyes widened. "You instructed Mr. Chung to make sure the men didn't stay."

"Technically, no—"

Her hands fell to her hips, and she pursed her lips.

"Fine." He released an exasperated sigh—one aimed more at himself than her. "I had Wendell instruct Mr. Chung to send the men away quickly."

"Zeke, how could you? You know I'm here in the colonies to find a husband."

"But you just told Mr. Peabody you're not rushing."

"That's right. But I need to begin getting to know the men. How else will I be able to pick a husband if I don't have the opportunity to mingle?"

"I'll screen the men for you." His process of *screening* would probably involve smashing his fist into their faces, but he wasn't about to admit that to Kate.

"Thank you for your concern." She gentled her voice. "But I don't need for you to be involved. I've been handling my own courtship since the day I arrived in the colonies. And I'm doing alright figuring this out by myself."

"*Alright?* You chose a real winner with Herbert Frank."

"And what's wrong with Mr. Frank?"

Zeke gingerly lifted his shoulder to bring attention to his injury. "For starters, he tried to kill me."

She sighed, stepped off the porch, and strode rapidly down the street.

He sighed too and then hurried after her. "Kate. Hold on."

Thankfully, she halted. But her back remained rigid and her chin high.

"Listen." He came alongside her. "I just want you to be safe."

She didn't respond.

He touched her arm. Then, before he could stop himself, he grazed a delicate path down to her hand. Amidst the buzz of crickets, he could hear her soft intake of breath.

Slowly, he circled his fingers around her wrist, lingering over the spot where her pulse thudded to a tempo that matched his. Surely, she was feeling some of this attraction.

"I'm an adult now, Zeke."

"Believe me. I'm well aware of that." He caressed her pulse with his thumb.

"And as an adult, I can take care of myself." Her voice was definitely breathless.

"Sometimes even the strongest of us can use a little help."

She was quiet for several heartbeats before she shook her head and started forward, breaking contact with him. "This is something I need to do for myself. Please try to understand."

He walked next to her. The scent of smoke in the air had grown thick as the miners who camped outside of town and along the river added fuel to their campfires.

"Please, Zeke?" She was too sweet and her voice too filled with hope for him to resist.

"Fine. I'll try, but I'm not making any promises."

She surprised him by laughing lightly. "You're so much like Jeremiah, it's scary."

"So, we're back to being brother and sister?"

"I think that's a good place to stay, don't you?"

He sensed she wasn't giving him much of a choice. But she'd learn soon enough that when Zeke Hart wanted something, he chased after it, and he usually got it. This time with Kate would be no different.

seven

eke's caress down her arm and around her wrist had seared her skin, so Kate could think of little else as they finished the last steps toward the general store.

The whole evening with him had been like something out of a fairy tale. Several times throughout dinner, she'd wanted to pinch herself to see if she really was sitting across the table from the handsome Zeke Hart.

Now, she was walking next to him on a warm summer night, a sizzling but delicious tension radiating between them. A thousand stars dotted the dark sky, all of them seeming to smile down on her.

Yet a small warning bell clanged inside, telling her she needed to be careful, that she couldn't lead him on in any way, especially now that she knew with certainty he was still rejecting anything having to do with God.

Perhaps she was unwise to agree to accompany him to his store, where they would be alone while she dressed his wound. After all, he'd need to take off his shirt, and just the thought of seeing his bare chest made her stomach flutter.

Her pace began to drag.

He slowed his steps to match hers.

"Zeke," she started hesitantly. She didn't want to hurt him.

He stiffened, cursed under his breath, then began to run.

"What's wrong?" she called after him. Had he sensed she was pulling away and decided to do so first?

His attention was riveted ahead. To his store. Light from the surrounding businesses revealed that the glass in the front window was shattered. Jagged pieces surrounded a large, gaping hole. The door was busted and hanging from its hinges. And the hooks on the beam above the door were empty, the simple white sign gone.

Her heartbeat picked up its pace, and she dashed after Zeke.

Outside the shop, he halted abruptly.

"What happened?" She stopped alongside him.

He toed a piece of glass, before he stepped over it and took hold of the broken door.

She peered past him into the store and released a gasp at the destruction. Though the interior was dark, faint light spilled inside and revealed shelves tipped over, bags slashed open, jars smashed, and barrels overturned.

Hefting—and likely putting too much strain on his injury—Zeke lifted the door away. Then he ducked inside. He righted a chair only to have it tip back over, revealing that one of the legs was broken.

She stood in the doorway, her nerves tightening in anticipation of the culprit jumping out and attacking Zeke. "Why would anyone do this? Were they searching for something? Or maybe someone robbed you?"

Zeke came to a standstill in the middle of the destruction, feet spread, hands fisted at his sides. The shadows obscured his expression, but she could imagine his features hardening with both anger and frustration.

"I'm sorry, Zeke." Her words were woefully inadequate, but she didn't know what else to say or do.

"This isn't a robbery." His voice was tense.

"How can you tell?"

"Thieves are too worried about getting caught to cause this kind of destruction."

"Then who would have done this and why?"

He picked up a tin canister and placed it back on a shelf. "Someone trying to send me a message."

"What kind of message?"

He shrugged but then winced, the movement of his shoulder paining him. "Maybe *someone* decided he didn't like me paying you attention."

The insinuation in Zeke's tone told her who he was holding responsible. "I don't think Mr. Frank would have done this. He may have gotten upset yesterday, but overall, he's a very nice man."

"Let me remind you that your so-called *nice* man stabbed me. I'm guessing you weren't expecting him to do that either."

Kate recoiled at the prospect that Herbert wrecked Zeke's

shop and quite possibly destroyed his livelihood. All because of her.

She shook her head. No, she couldn't—wouldn't—believe Herbert was capable of such destruction. Unless he wasn't the man she'd once believed him to be.

A groan came from behind the counter.

"Wendell?" Zeke stumbled through the darkness, kicking and bumping into items. "Wendell, is that you?" As he rounded the simply constructed planks that served as both shelves and counter, he dropped to his knees.

At another moan, this one louder, Kate maneuvered through the store until she was standing over Zeke, who was in the process of helping Wendell to sit up. Her hand brushed against the unlit lantern, and the glass globe was still warm.

Whoever ransacked the place had done so recently.

At a shifting shadow near the back entryway, her skin prickled. Was the intruder still here?

With fumbling fingers, she searched for matches and set about lighting the lantern. As the flame flickered to life, it revealed the magnitude of the mess—and no trace of the person who'd created it.

She didn't want to accuse Herbert of the crime. But Zeke was right; she never would have expected her ex-fiancé to attack and nearly kill Zeke, not after how kind he'd been in Victoria.

"Where are you hurt?" Zeke asked his assistant.

"Just a bump on my head." Wendell patted the ground around him. "And perhaps a bruise on my tailbone where I fell."

"Did you see who did this to you?"

Wendell shook his head and continued to skim his fingers over the floor until he connected with his glasses, thankfully unbroken. He lifted them, but his hands shook so badly, the spectacles clattered back to the floor.

Zeke retrieved them and situated the wire rims on Wendell's nose and around his ears. Wendell started to rise, but Zeke placed a hand on his shoulder. "Give yourself a minute, Wendell."

The young man nodded. "Maybe I should give myself two minutes. Maybe even three."

"Take all the time you need."

"Very well. I should probably take four, if not five minutes."

"True," Zeke replied with a calmness Kate didn't feel. "In the meantime, while you're counting the minutes, can you tell me everything you remember?"

"You know I can't possibly count and talk at the same time."

"Then tell me what you know first."

"One second I was calculating the boardinghouse ledgers, and the next second I felt something knock the back of my head. That's the last thing I remember."

"So you didn't see anyone?"

"No. I was completely unconscious. How could I see anyone?"

"Before you were hit?" Zeke's tone was still as patient as a parent speaking to a child.

"Whoever it was must have come in the rear door and

snuck up behind me." Wendell rubbed at the back of his head and then hissed.

Kate's stomach pinched with guilt, the same guilt she'd experienced yesterday when Zeke had been hurt. "I'm sorry."

"This isn't your fault." Zeke sat on his heels and took off his hat. The lantern light turned his hair blue-black.

"But if Mr. Frank did this—?"

"You aren't responsible for his actions."

"Maybe I shouldn't have called off our engagement so soon."

"It wouldn't have mattered if you'd waited a few more hours or a few more days. He would have been upset either way."

She pressed a hand against her forehead, trying to think, trying to figure out how to proceed without causing any more trouble. "I'll apologize to him tomorrow—"

"I was only speculating about Herb," Zeke blurted. "We don't know for sure if he was the one who did this. And even if he did, he's not worth an apology."

Kate nodded, but deep inside, she was ashamed of herself for the way she'd hurt Herbert—and the other men who'd courted her. Not only had she canceled engagements with Herbert Frank and James McCrea, but she'd also been engaged to Ronny Earnest before leaving Manchester. Before Ronny, she'd ended things with Thomas Kettle.

She hadn't meant to get attached only to end the relationships. The breakups had always been difficult, and she'd put them off as long as she could, because she loathed causing the men pain. But the truth was, everywhere she went she left a string of broken hearts.

Her pattern had to stop. With the next man she made a commitment to, she would need to follow through. That meant, she had to be absolutely certain he was right before she made any promises.

But was it possible for a woman *ever* to be absolutely certain about a man?

The next morning, Kate couldn't focus on the ironing. Finally, after scorching three shirts with a too-hot iron, Mr. Chung yelled at her in Mandarin and snapped a damp towel in her direction until she had no choice but to veer toward the exit or feel the sting of the towel. The second she was outside, he slammed the door in her face.

For a minute, she didn't move, could only stare at the hewn planks. Behind her, the clopping of horses and crunching of wagon wheels told her the town was awake even at the early hour. How long before someone noticed her standing outside the front of the laundry?

"Miss Millington?" came a timid call a short distance away.

She closed her eyes and slowly counted to five. After last night's destruction at Zeke's general store, she wasn't ready to face any of the men, not when she was too distraught over the possibility that she was somehow partly to blame for the damage.

If only she could put things right. She'd wanted to stay

and help Zeke clean and organize, but he insisted on walking her back to the laundry on his way to speak to several other town leaders.

After retiring to the shack, she'd spent hours sketching the people and places she'd seen in Williamsville—including Zeke—all the while trying to escape the guilt that had followed her up into the mountain town and wouldn't leave her alone.

"Miss Millington?" the man said again, this time closer. "Katherine?"

At her recognition of the Cornish accent, Kate's eyes flew open. Herbert Frank. Maybe she'd finally get rid of her guilt if she made amends. Zeke had told her that Herbert didn't deserve an apology. But she'd feel more peace if she explained how sorry she was for hurting him. And maybe she'd also keep him from inflicting more destruction.

She pivoted to find Herbert standing on the boardwalk only a few feet away. His eyes were bloodshot, his short hair sticking on end, and his shirt and trousers stained and wrinkled—as if he'd slept in them, or worse.

He was in shambles. Because of her.

"Mr. Frank, you're just the fellow I was hoping to see this morning."

"I am?"

"Aye." She took a deep breath and forced herself to do what she needed to. "I wanted to see you so I could apologize for the hurt I caused you. I'm so sorry, and I do hope you can forgive me."

His downcast expression took on a hopeful glimmer. "I've

been thinking about you every waking and sleeping minute. I'm convinced you're the woman for me. Won't you give me a second chance to prove it to you?"

This wasn't going the way she'd hoped. Maybe she ought to go back inside the laundry without saying anything further. After all, she'd apologized. What more could she do?

"Please, Miss Millington—" His voice broke off, and his eyes filled with tears.

"Mr. Frank," she said gently, her chest twisting. "I know this isn't easy—"

"Let me call on you. Give me the chance to show you again the man I was in Victoria."

How could she possibly say no? If she refused, what would he do next? She didn't want anyone else hurt or anything else damaged on account of her.

Maybe she could allow him, like the other men, to call on her occasionally. That would placate him until he had the chance to see for himself she wasn't the woman he needed.

"I'll prove I'm worthy." His chin wobbled.

"I'm planning to have callers from time to time." She couldn't meet with men at the laundry. But perhaps she could arrange to visit with them at one of the eating establishments, giving them each an equal slot of time. Such an arrangement would allow her to get to know the men slowly and carefully. "If you promise not to cause any more trouble for Mr. Hart, I suppose it'd be alright for you to come calling along with the others."

"Really?"

"I cannot promise anything. But at the very least, maybe we can part ways as friends."

"Thank you, Miss Millington." The exhaustion in Herbert's face fell away, replaced by earnestness. "You won't be sorry."

She hoped he was right and prayed she hadn't made another mistake.

eight

utnam reclined in his chair and shoved the sheet of figures away. "No, Hart. It won't work."

Zeke tore his gaze from the door and focused on the two men squeezed into the tight confines of the office at the back of Putnam's Tavern. Hard as it was, he had to keep his attention on the meeting instead of thinking about what might be transpiring several businesses down at J. D.'s Pub.

"I've had my accountant review the numbers several times." Putnam rubbed a hand across his graying sideburns. "As much as I want to support you, we just don't have the financing to back the project."

Putnam, a Yank, was the more talkative of the mining board members and more strongly opinionated. Sometimes his pride was about as big as his mammoth frame.

Blake, on the other hand, was only half the size of Putnam's shadow. Zeke had expected Blake to be more aggressive, especially since he had fiery red hair, but he was unnaturally quiet most of the time. He was English, like Zeke,

89

and had left his family behind in Wales. While he faithfully sent proceeds from his mine home to his wife and four children, he'd been hesitant to pay for their passage to the colony, always having one excuse or another for why he hadn't yet made a home for them in Williamsville.

Zeke twisted his cigar, which was no longer burning and had turned soggy.

Putnam opened the box on his writing desk, retrieved a fresh cigar, and held it to Zeke.

Zeke shook his head.

Putnam then offered it to Blake who held up a hand and also declined. The Yank lifted one shoulder in a shrug and then lit the butt and took a drag. As he exhaled, the puff of smoke rose into the already-stale air.

Usually, Zeke held the board meetings in his store where they had more space to spread out and the ability to get input from miners who were always lingering. But in the week since his place had been wrecked, the store still wasn't put back together completely.

He could admit he'd dragged out the cleanup. With Kate coming over to the store most evenings offering to help him, 'course he'd taken longer. What man in his right mind wouldn't want an excuse to keep spending time with her? Yet, even after the hours they'd worked together that week talking and laughing and getting to know each other, it hadn't been enough. He'd only wanted more.

He'd assumed she was feeling the same way, until he'd gotten word yesterday that she'd made plans to allow interested men to come courting at J. D.'s Pub.

"Now, if our mines were putting out as much as yours," Putnam continued, "I'd be more willing to invest in the hospital."

"I agree," Blake added, his eyes containing a glimmer of jealousy. "Guess we can't all be as lucky and rich."

Zeke *had* been luckier than everyone else so far. But even if Putnam's and Blake's mines weren't as productive, the two had done well for themselves compared to the many other miners who were fortunate to find just a handful of gold dust.

"Fine," Zeke said. "Guess I'll figure something else out." Neither had cared about the hospital before and still didn't. He'd either go at the project alone or abandon the idea until he could rally more interest.

At the bang of the tavern's front door, his attention snapped to the main room, which had steadily grown busier throughout the evening as miners had ended their workdays.

The end of the workday also meant Kate was sitting in J. D.'s Pub waiting for men to come calling on her. At least Zeke hoped that's all she was doing. Waiting. Alone. He'd done his best to discourage any would-be suitors from going, including Herb who claimed Kate had apologized and offered to see him again.

Zeke had wanted to confront Kate last night when the rumors reached him. But he'd been holed up in the mine until late, and by the time he returned to town, her guardian angel, Becca, answered his knock on the laundry door with a scowl and admonition to visit Kate in the daylight.

Instead of heading out to his mine today, he'd spent the majority of time visiting establishments around town and laying hints that Katherine Millington was off-limits and that no one better show up at J. D.'s Pub to call on her tonight.

Had anyone dared to go? What about Herb?

The guilt that had been nagging him all day reared up, reminding him he shouldn't be abusing his power and influence. And yet, the excuses also reared up, telling him he had every right to protect Kate any way he could.

Zeke set his sights expectantly on the open door. He'd instructed Wendell to watch the pub and keep him updated on the happenings, but he hadn't seen his assistant once. Zeke twirled the damp cigar between his thumb and forefinger, the motion imitating the twisting in his gut. Maybe he'd just have to go see for himself what Kate was doing.

It didn't matter that after the first time she'd come to his house, she asked him to understand her need to go courting by herself without anyone—not even an older brother-like figure—assisting her. Fact was, she didn't need to be spending time with so many eager young men without a chaperone. Or at least someone screening the candidates and telling her who to avoid.

Putnam took his cigar out of his mouth and knocked the ashes onto the floor. "I'm certainly willing to go ahead with the benefit supper if you still want to plan one."

"I'm willing to get behind the benefit supper too," Blake added.

'Course they both were, Zeke thought with a burst of frustration. His idea to hold a benefit supper for injured miners in need of aid wouldn't cost them much—the total of providing the dinner and entertainment—with the proceeds going to those suffering the worst.

Though a hospital would benefit the community, especially in the long term, Zeke had to start slow. It had already been that way with his demands for setting into place mining regulations. He wanted all mine owners to institute safe practices that would protect their employees. He'd done so at his mine, including limiting the length of shifts and providing more initial training so new hires were more aware of the dangers. But not all the other owners had been as willing.

Zeke released a pent-up breath, and before he could direct the conversation into the planning of the benefit event, the front door of the tavern slammed again, and this time whistles and calls accompanied the newcomer.

Only the appearance of a woman could elicit that kind of response. It had to be Kate.

He jumped up from his chair. If she was here, then the men had taken his threats seriously and hadn't called on her. No doubt she'd heard he had something to do with it. She was sure to be upset at him, at least at first. But she was too kindhearted to stay angry for long. At least, that's what he was counting on.

As nonchalantly as possible, he ambled to the office doorway and leaned against the jamb. She was weaving around tables and already halfway across the room. The moment she saw him, her lips pursed tighter and her nostrils flared.

Her anger made her more beautiful than ever, which was a feat considering she was already pretty in a blue gown that highlighted her fair skin and her graceful curves. Her blond hair was in a partial updo with the rest cascading down her back. She'd clearly prepared for callers by dressing up.

"Zeke Hart," she said, her brown eyes flashing. "I need to speak with you."

"I'm all yours." He continued his casual pose, hoping his voice didn't betray his eagerness to see her.

"No one came to call on me."

"Good." That's exactly what he'd hoped would happen.

She halted several feet away. "You told me you wouldn't interfere with my courtship process."

"Said I'd try, but I also told you I wasn't making any promises."

The room had grown so silent he could hear the trickle of beer pouring from the tap in the hogshead into the mug the tavern manager was holding. As if recognizing the silence too, she glanced around. Every eye was upon them.

"Can we speak privately, please?" she said in a low voice, her cheeks flushing.

"'Course." He straightened and waved toward a narrow hallway that led to the kitchen. "After you."

She started down the passageway, her crisp steps punctuating frustration.

Once in the kitchen, she stopped and spun on him, her expression animated. At the sight of an older, stoop-shouldered man at the stove flipping fried chicken and staring at her, she closed her mouth, spun again, and aimed for the rear exit.

She stepped outside only to cover her mouth from the stench that emanated from the garbage heap beside the door.

Having festered in the hot sun all day, the refuse not only stank but it buzzed, alive with black flies. At the sight of hordes of flies, she shrank back.

He took her arm and guided her a short distance away to the bottom of the hill behind the tavern. The area was riddled with stumps and dry, scorched grass. And although the backsides of the other businesses also emptied onto the hill, at least for the time being the area was deserted.

As they reached a safe distance from the trash, she lowered her hand from her mouth and took a deep breath.

"Are you alright?" he asked.

She jerked her arm free from his, but some of the fire was gone from her eyes. "You're impossible."

"You're beautiful."

"What?" Her eyes widened.

"Since you complimented me, I'm complimenting you back."

The sparks disappeared from her eyes, replaced by amusement. "You're too much."

"Thank you. You're too sweet."

This time she laughed, a soft, lilting sound that eased the knot in his gut.

He smiled in response. He'd been right. She couldn't stay angry, and he loved that about her.

She faced him, her smile growing. "There come those dimples. I've been waiting to see them. They're adorable."

"Now hold on," he said playfully. "Adorable is the kind of compliment you give a babe, not a man."

"Forgive me," she responded just as playfully. "They're very handsome. Is that better?"

"Aye. Much."

She surprised him by reaching up and fingering first one dimple, then the other. Her touch was feathery but like fire, searing across his nerve endings and skimming down his body.

He reacted without thinking, lifting his hand to her cheek and drawing a line down to her chin.

At his touch, she stalled, her hand still on his cheek, her eyes fixed with his. The brown held questions but also darkened with a desire that sent more heat charging through him. Their interactions all week while cleaning up the store had been strictly platonic. Zeke had been on his best behavior. Even so, he hadn't been able to dampen his initial attraction. And he didn't think he was wrong in assuming she felt something for him. He couldn't be.

Bolstered by her reaction, he glided his fingers up to her other cheek. Her breath quickened, causing her chest to rise and fall more rapidly.

Her skin was smooth beneath his calloused fingers, and he wanted to feel more of her. He let himself explore her cheek, her earlobe, and then down her neck. Each silken inch only awakened within him a deeper craving for more of her.

The problem was he didn't have a right to satisfy his hunger, not now when she wasn't his. Doing so would be selfish on his part.

His fingers stalled at Kate's collarbone.

Her hand dropped away from his face and rested on his shoulder, her touch as expectant as her eyes.

"I threatened all the other men," he whispered, "because I don't want anyone else courting you."

"You don't?" Her face tilted up. Her lips were slightly parted, and her breath gently ragged.

What would it be like to kiss her? To take those lips captive and give her a taste of pleasure? "The only one I want you courting"—he forced his attention back to her eyes—"is me."

Once the words were out, he knew they were true. From the second he'd set his sights upon her, he'd been enamored. The minute he realized who she was, he'd been even more attracted. And with every passing day she was in Williamsville, he thought about her so often he could hardly focus on anything else.

Her lips curved into a smile that moved up to her eyes, causing his heartbeat to do a strange leap followed by a somersault. Never in his wildest dreams had he believed he'd find a woman like Kate.

He slipped his hands to the small of her back, tempted to draw her closer, but he held himself at a distance for fear of scaring her away. From everything he'd witnessed so far about her, he sensed he needed to move slowly.

Her smile wobbled, then began to dissolve. Before he could figure out how to maintain their tentative connection, she stepped back, breaking his hold.

Her brows furrowed. "I'm sorry, Zeke."

"Sorry for what?" He started to reach for her, but she slipped farther away.

"While growing up, I always adored you."

Her admission should have reassured him, but the sadness filling her eyes unsettled him.

"I thought you were the handsomest boy alive on earth." Her smile turned sad, too. "And I dreamed about this day—the day you'd finally notice me."

Was she upset he hadn't paid attention to her in the past? Was that it? "I'm sorry too, Kate. I was a blind fool not to see how beautiful and kind you were. But I got mixed up in the wrong crowd my last few years in Manchester, and I lost track of a lot of important things."

She shook her head. "I don't blame you. Times were tough, and we all did what we had to do in order to survive."

"I pulled away from Jeremiah and my other good friends. I even pulled away from Zoe."

"If you'd liked me then, you probably would have pulled away from me too."

"Probably. So see, maybe it's a good thing I was a blind fool."

She offered him a smile, but the joy was gone from it.

"Kate." His voice turned haggard with a need for her he couldn't hide. "I notice you now. And I like you. Isn't that enough?"

At his bold admission, she dropped her gaze. For a second, she nibbled at her lip before pressing a hand over her chest as though attempting to stop her heart from beating. "I notice and like you too." Her voice was low and wobbly.

"Then good." Relief stole through his veins. "We want the same thing—"

"No—"

"Aye, we like each other. So why not court and see where this leads?"

"We can't court." Her words were laced with anguish. "As much as I want to, I can't."

"You're willing to start courting other men. Why not me?"

She didn't respond and kept her focus upon a thatch of blue-green wood reeds at her feet.

Suddenly, he was aware of the sun baking the back of his neck and the perspiration trickling down his spine. His wound had begun to throb, and the heat that remained from the August day radiated up from the ground and into the soles of his boots causing him to feel as though he were standing in a fiery pit roasting alive.

He wiped a sleeve across his brow. "Whatever it is, we can work it out, can't we?"

"We can't," she whispered. "I'm sorry."

His mind spun in an attempt to understand her refusal. She was scared. That had to be it. "Listen." He worked to keep his tone calm and rational. "I know after calling things off with Herb you want to go slow. And I promise I won't push you. We'll take all the time we need. I'll show you what a decent fellow I am."

"I already know you're a decent fellow, Zeke. You don't have to prove it."

"Then what? What's holding you back?"

Her shoulders slumped. "It's your lack of faith. I can't be with someone who doesn't share my faith in God."

Faith? God? She didn't want to be with him because he'd decided he didn't need God or religion anymore? "That's ridiculous."

Her gaze shot up.

"You're just making excuses is all."

"No I'm not."

"Aye, because you're scared."

"I am not scared." She lifted her chin as though to prove it. "Even though I've always really liked you, I can't be unequally yoked."

"Unequally yoked," he spat the words that came from the Bible, words their ragged school headmaster had told them meant that Christians weren't supposed to marry those who didn't share the faith. As much as he'd respected Mr. Lightness so long ago, Zeke had learned to think for himself. "Can you seriously tell me you'd have been *equally* yoked with Herb?"

"He isn't perfect, but at least he hasn't turned his back on God."

"So you'd rather have a knife-stabbing, store-wrecking man who claims to follow God than an upright man like me who doesn't pretend to have faith?"

"No, I've realized I don't want to marry Mr. Frank either."

"That's why you told him he could call on you?"

She had the decency to blush. "I only did it because I felt sorry for him. But I have no intention of courting him."

"Because, no doubt, you're waiting for someone perfect

to come along." His words came out harsh and angry, but he couldn't stop them.

She didn't respond except to focus on the dried wood reeds again.

Zeke glared unseeingly up the hill to the high mountain peaks beyond, his insides churning with a frustration he didn't understand.

Seconds ticked by, filled with the sounds of the laughter, greetings, and good-natured teasing of the men inside the tavern.

He rubbed the back of his neck. "The night we had dinner at my house, you told me you accepted me. Were you lying to me?"

She flinched.

His words were blunt, but he didn't want to take them back. He waited, his gaze unwavering.

"I do accept you, Zeke," she said quietly. "But as I told you, there's a difference between accepting someone and agreeing with them."

Was she giving him an ultimatum, telling him he had to change or lose out on having her? He shook his head. He might be infatuated with her, but even he knew a relationship would never work if one person changed to earn the approval of another. Even if he'd wanted to do that, he couldn't fake faith. He might not be a man of God anymore, but he also wouldn't make a mockery of religion by pretending to be something he wasn't.

"Then I guess there's no hope for us." He couldn't keep the hint of question from his words.

"I wish there was—"

"I'm not changing who I am for you."

"And I'm not asking you to."

"Good."

Her expression was stricken, her eyes wide and glassy. "I hope we can at least stay friends."

"Really?" He released a humorless laugh. "Do you think I'm a saint?"

"No, of course not—"

"Don't ask for the impossible, Kate. Fact is, there's no way I can be around you without wanting you."

She looked away, but not before he saw a tear spill over.

Regret punched him low. He was letting his anger get the best of him and wasn't being as kind and sensitive to her as he ought to be. "Listen, if it makes you feel better, then let's pretend we never had this conversation."

She nodded and swiped at her cheek. "Okay."

"I'll walk you to the laundry."

"No. I'll be fine. I don't need you to accompany me."

"I insist."

She didn't protest again as he led her around the tavern onto the sidewalk. In fact, she didn't say anything at all as he walked by her side down the street. He was at a loss for words himself, his heart aching too much to pretend otherwise. When she was safely under Becca's watchful eye and the door closed behind her, he pressed a fist against his chest.

He'd offered himself to Kate, but she didn't want him. Now, the pain in his shoulder wound couldn't begin to compare with the pain in his heart.

nine

The steady dripping of water in the mine tunnel soothed Zeke, reminding him that everything went on as usual in the world even if his personal life hadn't been going as he'd wanted.

He held out his lantern as he sloshed through the ankle-deep water, following Phil, his foreman. The craggy ceiling above forced them to stoop low. The slimy cold walls with calcium deposits pressed in, giving them little room to maneuver.

"The vein could be the biggest one yet." Phil's voice echoed with the same excitement it had since he'd approached Zeke's table at the tavern earlier in the evening. Now, after witnessing the discovery and examining the size, Zeke agreed with Phil. The new vein promised greater wealth than he'd imagined possible. With the incentives Zeke offered his foremen and even his workers, they stood to gain a substantial profit too.

If only Zeke could muster the same enthusiasm as Phil.

He'd hoped the trek up to his mine and the hike into the newest tunnel would distract him from the conversation he'd had earlier with Kate. And he'd hoped the sight of the gold would mollify him and remind him of his goals.

Aye, he'd wanted to find gold and get rich quick. Every man who came to the Cariboo wanted that. And he was no different. But he'd wanted the capital so he could start other business ventures that would sustain him and keep him busy long term.

Now after living in Williamsville for a year and a half, he'd come to see it as a place where he could have a fresh start, maybe even a place to put down roots. He was doing all he could to help build the town and turn it into a permanent community, one that didn't fizzle out once the gold was gone. Today's discovery of more gold would only aid his efforts.

Yet, even after seeing the deposit and trying to distract himself, he still couldn't stop from feeling the sting of Kate's rebuff. It hurt more than he wanted to admit that she could so easily dismiss him for not having God in his life. What difference did it make? Especially since they'd gotten along so well all week. That's all that really mattered.

Let her go, Hart. If she didn't want him, then he didn't want her either. After all, before she came and started stirring up things in him, he'd been just fine without a woman. He'd get along just fine again once he got her out of his system.

"Assay those nuggets first thing in the morning," Zeke directed. "We want to validate the grade. No sense in claiming we have a bonanza until we know for sure."

Doing so would only create a frenzy within the miners,

drawing even more men to the area from other mining camps and towns.

"I'm afraid the word has already spread," Phil said. "After the dust settled and the crew began hauling away the ore, the vein was staring us all right in the face."

As they climbed a ladder and reached the main drift, the air was warmer and clearer, especially the closer they hiked toward the end of the tunnel and the outside world. While the ground was damp, it wasn't as wet as the tunnels they'd created under the water table.

The darkness of the night blended with the shadows of the passageway, so that the swaying lantern provided the only light. The place was deserted, lacking the usual steady tap of bits against rock and the heavy ring of iron drifters boring holes to use in the blasting. The trams stood silently, some filled with useless rock that needed to be removed from the mine and added to the ever-growing dump piles.

With the new vein, he'd have to resume using a night watchman to keep thieves away. Maybe he'd finally have to consider a night shift to excavate the gold faster. He could afford to hire more men and pay them better than Putnam, Blake, or any of the other smaller mines. But giving raises to his men would only cause discontent among the other mine workers and lead to tension with area bosses. He didn't want any problems, not now when he was getting along with the rest of the mine owners.

Phil reached the portal first and stumbled over a rope strung at ankle length across the width of the opening. He tripped and fell to his knees onto the rocky ground, yanking the string in the process.

On one side of the entrance, just outside, Zeke caught sight of a sparking flare, like the striking of a match.

He paused, held the lantern up, and attempted to make sense of what he was seeing. When they entered the mine, they hadn't encountered any obstructions across the opening. Who had placed the rope there, and why?

A flashing and fizzling flowed along a line, and the smoky scent of gunpowder rose into the air.

Phil began to rise, grousing under his breath and peeling back the slit at the knee of his trousers to reveal a gouge in his flesh.

Zeke stepped over the rope and watched the spark pick up speed.

"I told them not to dump the ore so close to the portal." Phil pressed a hand against his trousers at the kneecap, blood turning the wool dark.

If Zeke didn't know better, he'd almost believe someone was in the middle of a blasting project. The flare of an ignition, the long line intended to give plenty of get-away time, and the odor of sulfur and charcoal.

He studied the setup again, this time noting the flare was burning faster and heading toward a small barrel. The container wasn't full of gunpowder, was it?

As the spark touched the barrel, Zeke's pulse took a giant leap. In the same instant, he dove toward Phil. "Watch out!" His body slammed into Phil's.

They'd been sabotaged. Someone had purposefully set a

trap, hoping to destroy them and make it look like an accident.

An explosion rocked the air, sending fire and earth skyward. The force blasted into Zeke. Though he attempted to keep his hold on Phil and shield him from the debris, the power of the gunpowder propelled Phil out of his grasp.

Heat scorched Zeke's flesh, and he cried out. The next thing he knew, his body crashed into a pile of rocks. His head slammed against the stones. Pain erupted against his skull. And the world went black.

Kate brushed the charcoal pencil with short, choppy strokes in the areas where dark met light. Her loose markings formed the outline of the mountainous landscape that rose over Williamsville. The heavier strokes in the foreground were bringing to life the businesses and several men lounging in front of the general store. As much as she tried not to, her fingers had a will of their own and sketched Zeke's ruggedly handsome features into the face of one of the men.

She'd hoped the process of drawing something would get him out of her mind. When that hadn't worked, she hoped by bringing him to life on the page she could accept he wouldn't be in her life. She had three pages of sketches with him in each one, and she was still no closer to forgetting about him than when she'd started.

With a sigh, she let her pencil grow idle and leaned against the rough log wall of the shack, the lantern light sputtering at this late hour. Becca was already asleep in her hammock, her hand dangling over the edge, skin cracked and raw but glistening with grease.

Earlier, when Becca had stumbled inside, exhausted and in need of a little doctoring, Kate had pillaged through Mr. Chung's supplies and had also borrowed items from their neighbor so she could make a honey-butter salve for Becca's chapped hands.

Now the sweet scent of the salve mingled with the lye that permeated Becca's damp garments. Wasn't that how life was—a mixture of pleasant and harsh?

Here she was in Williamsville, connecting with Zeke Hart, the man she'd always adored. He'd noticed her as a woman. Said he liked her. Wanted to court her. Thought she was beautiful.

She closed her eyes, unable to stop the smile from curving her lips. He'd not only spoken words of desire, but each of his slow strokes on her cheek and neck had told of his desire just as loudly and boldly, so much so that she'd almost thrown away all caution and wrapped her arms around him in return. Even now, she could feel the graze of his fingers down her neck, and the heat from before returned to her belly and swirled there.

"Oh Lord, help," she whispered.

Her pencil clattered to the plank floor. Quickly she opened her eyes and grabbed it before it dropped through one of the floor slats. She'd already lost a paintbrush that way and hadn't been able to fish it out of the narrow crack.

Lifting her pencil and angling it toward the paper, she studied her sketch, her attention invariably drawn to the center of the page, to Zeke, to his face and the way he'd looked when he tilted his head and asked her: *"Aye, we like each other. So why not court and see where this leads?"*

She'd wanted so desperately to tell him yes. But how could she, when they didn't share the same values? Her parents hadn't been united in their faith, and their marriage had unraveled because the threads holding them together hadn't been strong enough without a common commitment to the Lord.

When Kate had been just a girl of ten, her father left their family on a quest for adventure.

The morning he'd stood in the doorway ready to leave, Kate rushed to him, threw her arms around his waist, and buried her face in his chest.

"Ah, my Katie, my dearest," he crooned, laying one of his broad hands upon her head and smoothing back her hair. "Don't ye be a-cryin' now, d'ye hear me?"

From the bed in the corner underneath the coverlet, her mum's sobs were brokenhearted, laced with the disappointment of a woman who'd begged God for years for her husband's salvation, to end up having him reject not only God, but her.

"I almost forgot." He set down his bag and dug into his coat pocket. "I've got something for ye."

"I don't need anything." *Except for you to stay.* But she'd been too young and in too much awe of her father to speak her mind.

He tugged out a ribbon, long and silky, and a bright rosy pink. "Thought of my sweet lass the instant I saw this."

"It's very pretty." She reached out and stroked it, her throat tightening.

"Not as pretty as ye are." He smiled his handsome grin before he twirled his finger at her. "Turn around."

She obeyed as she always did.

He combed her hair gently, almost reverently. Then he looped the ribbon underneath and wound it to the top of her head. His big fingers fumbled as he tied it into place. "There." He stepped back and took her in. "Every time I think about ye, I'll remember ye just like this, that I will."

She wanted to say something—anything—but she couldn't get her voice to work.

"My Katie." The excitement in his eyes dimmed.

She had to convince him not to go. Maybe he didn't love Mum enough to stay as Mum had accused him, but maybe he'd stay for her. "I love you, Papa," she whispered, unable to keep her lips from trembling. "Please don't leave me."

He hesitated, and his shoulders sagged as they had so often of late. "I love ye too, my Katie, my dearest."

Her hope widened. But then he picked up his bag and slung it over his shoulder. "I just wish I could have been everything ye and yer mum needed me to be. And I'm sorry I'm not." He touched her ribbon, gave her a last sad smile, then turned and left.

Kate hadn't been able to move. Instead, she stared at the open doorway and waited for him to walk back through, pick her up, and toss her into the air like he'd done when she was a wee lass.

Instead, only Jeremiah came through the door. His furrowed brows and brooding eyes told her he'd heard every word of the good-bye. He walked straight to her, took her hand and squeezed it tight, but didn't say a word.

There hadn't been any words to make her feel better, not then and not now.

She slipped her hand into her pocket and grazed the fraying ribbon.

No matter how sweet and handsome Zeke was, she couldn't fall prey to the same mistake her mum had made by courting and marrying a man who didn't follow God or His ways. She'd made the right decision earlier in turning down Zeke's offer. It was for the best, and she'd get over him, especially once she started meeting other men.

She stuffed the ribbon back down to the bottom of her pocket. She didn't know why she hung on to the silly old thing after all these years. She needed to throw it away. It wasn't worth keeping.

A tentative knock on the door startled her. She scrambled to her feet and stared at the door. It was late, well after midnight. And she should have been asleep hours ago, the same as Becca.

Who could be knocking on her door at this time of night? And why?

Zeke's warnings about the men clamored at the back of her mind. Sometimes she was too trusting and needed to use more caution. Was this one of those times?

"Miss Millington," came an unfamiliar voice. "I realize it is quite late—or I should say early—1:46 a.m. to be exact."

Was her visitor Wendell, Zeke's assistant? If so, what was he doing out at this hour?

"It's now 1:47."

Yes, her unexpected guest was Wendell. And the urgency in his tone pricked her. She flung open the door only to catch him in the process of knocking again, this time at the air.

"Miss Millington." His hand stalled in mid motion. His shirt was half untucked, bowtie askew, and hair mussed. Worse, the lantern he held revealed his pale face and grave expression.

The hair on her arms stood on end. "What brings you out at this hour of the night?"

"My grandfather sent me."

She waited for him to explain further.

He stared back as if waiting for her to say something first.

"And what does Mr. Peabody need?"

"He doesn't need anything."

"Then why did he send you?"

"I told him the matter could wait until morning, but he insisted."

"What matter?" She tried to keep the exasperation from her voice.

"Zeke—"

"Aye?"

"He's been hurt. There was an explosion up at the mine."

She'd heard enough about the mines to know explosions could be dangerous, even deadly. "Is he still there?" She stepped outside and closed the door.

"No, he's at home. The doctor's still with him trying to save him."

Trying to save him? Dread coursed through her. He wasn't dying, was he? What if he was already dead?

She pressed a hand against her mouth to stifle a cry. Then, without waiting for Wendell, she darted forward. Even though she'd only been to Zeke's home once, she knew exactly where it was. As the largest home, it stood out, and her feet carried her swiftly toward it well ahead of Wendell, her head and heart pounding with the need to see Zeke and to do anything she could to help.

The taverns along Main Street were still brightly lit, doors open, boisterous talking and laughter ringing in the night air. Thankfully, however, the street was deserted except for a drunken man relieving himself to the side of one of the businesses.

As she stepped onto the portico at the front of Zeke's house, the dread inside her had taken on a life of its own, so that she could hardly breathe. She didn't have time to knock before the door opened wide.

"Mademoiselle." Mr. Peabody wore a long nightcap over his bald head and was attired in a flowing nightdress that fell to his ankles. His ruddy face had lost all color, making his dark mustache and goatee more prominent. "Thank you for coming."

"How is Zeke?"

He shook his head, and tears welled in his eyes. "Not good. Not good at all."

Her pulse, which was already pattering too fast, picked

up pace. She sidled past Mr. Peabody into the hallway where several miners with somber faces waited. At the sight of her, they stared at the floor.

"Where is he?"

Mr. Peabody nodded at an open doorway. "His bedroom is the room across from the kitchen."

She started down the hallway, desperation pushing her. She had to be with him, couldn't let him die, couldn't bear the thought that he'd only just come into her life again and now she might lose him.

"Wait, mademoiselle." Mr. Peabody hurried after her. "I should prepare you first."

"Will he live?" Heedless of the other men watching, she stopped in her tracks and grabbed the housekeeper's arm. "Please tell me he'll live."

He shook his head and wiped at his eyes. "I'm sorry. He's dying."

ten

*K*ate's heartbeat thundered against her rib cage, and fear rose up to choke her. "No." She lurched forward. "No, I won't let him die."

"Wait." The urgency in Mr. Peabody's voice trailed close behind her.

Zeke couldn't die. Not yet. Not without making peace with God. She had to talk to him, try to make him understand reason.

She burst into the bedroom and stopped short. A gasp escaped even as her fingers rose to try to catch it. There, upon his bed, Zeke was laid out facedown, completely unclothed, his bare backside visible.

For several long seconds she could only stare, fascinated, never having seen such a sight before. Then embarrassment hit her. He was naked, and she shouldn't look. Doing so was completely indecent, even at a time like this. She quickly looked away, even as the doctor paused in surprise, and Mr.

Peabody bustled past, muttering his disapproval and grabbing the sheet dangling off the end of the bed.

But it was too late. The image of Zeke's backside was seared into Kate's mind, and no amount of covering or clothing would be able to make it disappear. A firm and muscular body. One that was much too attractive. Even with the multiple abrasions and bandages.

"Why is Miss Millington in the room?" The doctor scowled as he resumed wrapping a cloth around Zeke's head.

"She's Zeke's fiancée." Mr. Peabody jerked the cover up. "In other words, she's the woman he's intending to marry."

Kate started to protest, but as she lifted her eyes and caught sight of Zeke's body again, words failed her.

"I'm quite aware of what the word *fiancée* means." The doctor snipped the bandage with a small pair of steel scissors. "But I don't care if she's the queen of England. She shouldn't be in here."

"She's here to say good-bye." Mr. Peabody finished tugging the sheet up to Zeke's shoulders.

The doctor glared at the housekeeper. "Mr. Hart is not dying."

"He's not?" she asked at the same time as Mr. Peabody, hope and relief springing to life inside her.

"He has a concussion, broken leg, and some painful burns. But he'll live."

"You told me to start making preparations," Mr. Peabody said.

"Preparations for his *care*, not for his death," the doctor retorted irritably. "He won't be getting out of this bed for quite some time and will need assistance all hours of the day and night."

Mr. Peabody grabbed onto the bedpost, his body sagging and his knees buckling. Kate was at his side in an instant, propping him up.

"You're sure he's not dying?" Mr. Peabody's eyes once again watered.

"I'm positive." The doctor packed his items into the leather satchel on the bedside table. "But he won't be able to do anything by himself, not until his body has the chance to heal. That is why I suggested you begin to make preparations, to see that he has the assistance he'll need at all times."

"I live here and can take care of him." Mr. Peabody pulled himself up. Even so, Kate kept a firm hold on his arm, needing his steadiness perhaps more than he needed hers.

"That may well be, but I suggest you hire another care-giver who can assist during those times you're indisposed. When he awakens from his concussion, he'll be in a great deal of pain."

"My grandson, Wendell, will fill in when I'm not able to be here."

"No." Wendell stood in the doorway, wiping his glasses and still breathing hard from the run through town. "I can't be tied down. Zeke would want me to continue to manage his accounts as well as to investigate the explosion."

"I'll help," Kate offered.

The doctor shook his head. "I recommend only married women or widows serve as nurses."

The picture of Zeke's bare backside flashed through her

mind, and she flushed just thinking about seeing him like that again. The doctor was right. It wouldn't be proper for a single young woman like her. Nevertheless, she wanted to help Zeke. It was the least she could do for him as an old family friend.

"Mr. Peabody can take care of Zeke's personal needs," Kate persisted, "and I'll be here to assist in other ways."

"Exactly," Mr. Peabody said.

"Mr. Chung can't abide having me working in the laundry and is putting up with me for Becca's sake. He'd rejoice to have me gone."

"Then it's settled." Mr. Peabody beamed. "Besides, do we know of any married women or widows anywhere in the area who would be able to put their lives on hold to come here?"

The doctor listed several women, but Mr. Peabody had an excuse for each one. Finally, the doctor threw his hands up. "Don't blame me if Miss Millington's reputation is tarnished as a result of this arrangement."

"Have no fear, Doctor." Mr. Peabody smiled for the first time since Kate's arrival. "If I see even the slightest questionable behavior, I'll send word to the preacher and have these two married before you can blink an eye."

"Perhaps we ought to see them married right away."

"No," Kate said hurriedly, and perhaps a bit too forcefully. She offered a smile—one she hoped hid the sudden assault against her nerves. She couldn't let the doctor go on believing she was Zeke's fiancée, especially when there was no hope of a future together. "There's no reason to rush into anything, as I'm not intending to marry Zeke—"

The doctor's brows furrowed into an expression of protest.

"That is, I'm not intending to marry him *soon*." *Not at all.* But she couldn't force those words out.

The doctor studied her face before he turned to Mr. Peabody. "I'll expect you to oversee this arrangement very closely."

"Of course, monsieur. I shall do my best to ensure just the right outcome."

Right outcome? As she took in Mr. Peabody's suddenly eager expression, Kate couldn't keep from wondering if she was making a huge mistake. But, just as quickly as the thought came, she shook it off. Mr. Peabody simply cared about Zeke and wanted the best for him.

Together they'd work to nurture Zeke back to health. And once he was recovered, she'd return to her quest of finding a husband.

The doctor rattled off a long list of instructions as well as supplies for Zeke's burns and lacerations. Then he spoke to the men waiting in the hallway, informing them of Zeke's condition.

Once they'd all taken their leave, Wendell filled Kate in on all that had transpired leading up to the explosion, and she learned that Zeke not only owned several businesses in town, but he also had a prosperous mine.

"Phil said Zeke saved his life," Wendell finished gravely. "If not for Zeke seeing the fuse and pushing them out of the way, the chance they'd both be dead ranges between fifty to eighty percent."

Zeke had taken the brunt of the explosion in protecting his foreman, who had suffered only a mild concussion, a few cracked ribs, and burns on his hands. While Zeke had been heroic to put Phil's well-being ahead of his own, Kate's chest still pinched.

Zeke had almost died.

She brushed a strand of dark hair off his temple. Even in his state of unconsciousness, his features were taut with pain, and she wished she could do something to ease his discomfort.

"You need to catch the culprit, Wendell," Mr. Peabody said from the opposite side of the bed, where he was picking up Zeke's blood-soaked garments from the floor. "First the store. Now, this. The person responsible for the trouble must pay for his crimes."

"I will catch him. You can count on me."

"Good boy."

"Do you think Herbert Frank is behind everything?" Kate asked the question that had formulated while Wendell had been speaking.

Wendell used his forefinger to slide his spectacles up his nose. "I'm graphing a chart of possible suspects, and so far, he's in the lead."

"Maybe I should confront Mr. Frank." If he was behind the trouble, then she was mortified she'd ever considered marrying him.

Wendell shook his head. "For now, I suggest remaining silent on the matter. If the suspect thinks he's getting away with the crimes, he won't work as hard to cover his trail."

Kate brushed another lock of Zeke's hair back. Wendell's advice made sense. In the meantime, she would pray Zeke wouldn't come to any more harm.

Zeke thrashed and moaned in his unconsciousness. The doctor had formed a temporary splint on his tibia to allow for the swelling to go down before making a cast. But Zeke's restlessness only caused more agony.

Kate hadn't wanted to leave Zeke's side, hoping to be there when he awoke. But after the remainder of the night and a full day with no change in his condition, she'd allowed Mr. Peabody to convince her to go home and sleep.

When she stumbled, exhausted, into the laundry at dusk, Becca thumped the iron down and whirled upon Kate. "What's this I hear about you walking in on Mr. Hart while he in the nude?"

Kate stopped short, fresh embarrassment slapping her full in the face.

Mr. Chung, in the process of ironing a pair of trousers, didn't pause, not even to blink, which told Kate, that not only had word spread around town regarding Zeke's near-death experience, but every detail of her time at his house spread as well.

Who was giving out such private information? Had the doctor decided to tell everyone? Or the miners in the hallway? Did they think her experience walking into the bedroom and finding Zeke bare was newsworthy?

"I see." Becca's eyes narrowed upon Kate's face, which apparently revealed every one of her thoughts. "Guess that part about you being engaged to Mr. Hart is true, too?"

"No, of course it's not—"

"It better be real soon, Miss Kate." The concern in Becca's expression softened the chastisement.

Kate rubbed a hand over her eyes. She was trying to maintain a proper relationship with Zeke and didn't want to get involved with a man she couldn't marry. But every turn she made only seemed to push them closer together.

Would it be better to cut herself off completely and not see him again? At that prospect, her muscles tightened in protest. They had agreed to remain friends, hadn't they? Besides, she feared she was partly—if not mostly—to blame for the state he was in. And Mr. Peabody couldn't take care of Zeke by himself and needed her assistance.

"Don't take much to see you fallin' for him. What with all those pictures you been drawing of him."

"Everyone knows about my sketches, too?"

"Just me. You left that book wide open last night after you gone off."

"I guess I need to stop drawing him, don't I?"

"Or you just go on and get married to him. Then I can quit worrying about you every waking moment."

"I'm sorry, Becca. I didn't mean to worry you. You probably wish you'd never met me."

"Don't you go thinking that, Miss Kate. The good Lord put you in my path, and I aim to watch over you best I can, and that includes not lettin' any man take advantage of your sweetness."

The sincerity and love in Becca's eyes melted Kate's resistance. She crossed to the dear woman and threw her arms around her in a hug. "I'm so glad God brought us together."

Becca stood stiffly, having already told Kate several times she didn't like hugs. Nevertheless, Kate wrapped her tight, and a few seconds later Becca's arms slipped around Kate to return the embrace.

"I'll be more careful," Kate whispered. "I promise."

Becca only sighed.

eleven

Flames danced across Zeke's back, twirling and spinning and burning. He wanted to scream at the torture, but the sound stuck in his throat, suffocating him. He had no way out and no one to help him.

Where was he?

He tried to think, tried to figure out how to get away. Had he died? Was he in the afterlife? In a place of torment?

"Hang in there, son," came a kind voice from above him. "You'll make it. I'll do everything I can to make sure of that."

Son? Was his father here?

The flaming torture flared again, and this time a sound slipped out of his mouth.

Gentle fingers shifted him to his side, lifted his head, and pressed something cool to his mouth. Liquid poured in, but his head was raised at an odd angle, and half of it dribbled out.

"There you are," the voice said again.

Zeke pried open his eyes and squinted. The bald head

and fleshy face with the long mustache and goatee didn't belong to his father. His father had never spoken kindly or been there for him. Fact was, his father had always been the one inflicting pain, not saving him from it.

"Mr. Peabody?" Zeke's voice came out a rasp, as though he'd swallowed gravel.

"I'm here."

Zeke tried to stretch out a hand toward the sound of the voice, but he couldn't make his arm work.

Mr. Peabody's fingers wrapped around his hand and squeezed him securely. "I'm here, son. I'm here."

Zeke released a breath. Even though blackness moved in and threatened to swallow him, he no longer felt alone.

Zeke watched the flames pouring out the mill windows and spiraling high into the sky. Black smoke plumed with the faint echo of screams. Had someone been inside when the fire started? He tossed down his ale and bolted upright only to have one of his friends hold him back.

The group of men around him didn't move. They only stared at the fire and continued drinking.

"Someone's inside." Zeke tried to shrug off Chuck. "I heard screams."

His friend's grip tightened. "The place is empty. You're drunk and you're just hearing things."

Zeke replayed the scene from several hours earlier when he'd gone to his supervisor inside the mill and begged to have his job back as a power-loom weaver. But Mr. Shelburne had insisted he had only enough cotton for the handful of workers he'd kept on.

Zeke had walked away angry, accusing his supervisor of playing favorites with his family and friends, leaving the rest of them to starve to death.

Another chilling scream came from the window, louder than the last.

"The place isn't empty." Zeke wrestled against Chuck. They needed to go over and put out the fire—or at least rescue anyone left inside.

"And how would you know?" Chuck asked.

Zeke tore his attention from the flames and only then noticed the accusation in the faces around him. They were all union members. They all acted together. And no one dared to do anything without consulting the other members.

But Zeke had gone by himself when he'd returned to the mill. And he'd done it without asking. Now it seemed they'd found out.

He swallowed the rising fear. "I'm tired of watching my family go hungry."

"We all are." Chuck's grip on his arm tightened. "But you don't see any of us crying about it, do you?"

Zeke hated the man he was becoming, hated that he was lying and stealing and drinking and doing everything Zoe had accused him of earlier in the day. He'd seen the disappointment in her bright-green eyes. Her disgust matched his disgust in himself.

He supposed he'd gone to the mill with the hope that maybe he could rescue himself from the man he'd become.

But he should have known it wouldn't work, that Mr. Shelburne wouldn't hire him back, and that he'd only anger his union friends. "I shouldn't have gone."

They only glared at him and continued to drink.

Shrieks rang out from the mill window, frightened and distressed shrieks.

Chills raced down Zeke's spine. "People are trapped inside."

He jerked in another attempt to free himself, but two other men jumped up and grabbed his arms, twisting them behind his back and immobilizing him.

"What's wrong with all of you?" Zeke shouted.

Chuck stood in front of him, and the gleam in his eyes turned Zeke's blood to ice. "The boss wants to teach everyone a lesson."

The haze that had clouded Zeke's head only moments ago cleared, and suddenly he understood what had happened. The union men had trapped the weavers and started the fire.

"Let me go!" Desperation speared Zeke. Maybe he'd fumed at the lucky ones earlier for still having a job when he had none, but they didn't deserve to suffer and die.

"You won't end up the hero of this accident." Chuck slammed his fist into Zeke's stomach, dropping him to his knees and drawing laughter from the other men. "No, Zeke Hart, you'll be far from a hero when this is all said and done."

Pain had ripped through his shoulder sockets and arms with each frantic movement he made to free himself. But he'd been pinned down and forced to helplessly watch the mill burn until the screams had tapered to silence.

Burn.

Zeke gasped as the flames poured over his back and down his body. He deserved to burn like the trapped mill workers. His burning was just punishment for bringing the tragedy upon them.

If he'd never gone that afternoon and begged for the job. If he'd only been stronger and able to get away from Chuck and the others. If he'd never gotten involved with their crowd in the first place.

His mistakes had cost three mill workers and Mr. Shelburne their lives. He blamed himself for their murders even if he hadn't been the one to light the match. In the days following the fire when he'd been running and hiding from the law, Jeremiah had encouraged him to tell the constables the truth, that the union men had set him up. But Zeke had felt too guilty, had wanted to hand himself over. If not for Jeremiah pushing him to go to the gold fields of Britain's colony in the Pacific Northwest, Zeke would have hanged for his crimes or been killed by the union men.

Would death have been preferable? Sometimes he wondered, especially when the tortured screams of the victims echoed in the corners of his mind, reminding him of everything he'd run from. He'd never be able to make up for the pain he'd caused those poor people and their families.

The burning flames raced over his skin again, and he released a moan.

"A little water, Zeke," came a soft plea nearby, a woman's voice. "Take just a sip."

Cool fingers caressed his cheek down to his chin. "For me. Please?"

He forced his eyes open to find the most beautiful face above his, the face of an angel with the prettiest brown eyes framed by long lashes. Kate.

"You're awake." She smiled down at him, her eyes glistening with sudden tears.

His mind cleared, bringing him back to the present. He'd been injured in an explosion at the mine. His pulse spiked with a burst of fear. "Phil?" he croaked. "How's Phil?"

"He's just fine. His injuries aren't nearly as bad as yours."

Zeke was stomach-down on a bed. His bed. In his room. In his house.

What was Kate doing here? Especially after the way they'd parted? She'd all but told him she didn't want anything to do with him, that he wasn't good enough for her because he wasn't a church-going, God-following man anymore.

"What are you doing here?" His voice came out harsh, but he didn't care.

"I'm helping take care of you—"

"I don't need help."

Her smile only grew wider, making her more beautiful. "Fiddlesticks. The doctor said you can't be left alone and that you need constant supervision."

"Doc doesn't control me." Zeke attempted to push himself up onto his elbows, but pain shot down his torso to his leg. He bit back a cry of agony.

She brushed his hair again, only to make him realize his

head was swathed in bandages and was pounding harder than a pick against stone.

During the explosion, he must have suffered a blow to his head. He squeezed his eyes shut to fight off a wave of dizziness.

"Take another sip." The rim of a mug pressed against his lips.

"I don't want your help." He shifted away, even though it caused more throbbing.

Her fingers against his hair stilled.

"Get Mr. Peabody. He can help me instead."

"He's sleeping now after being up all night caring for you."

"I don't care. I'd rather have him here than you."

Kate pulled back. For a long moment, she was so silent he could hear himself breathing raggedly.

"You're acting like a child, Zeke." Her voice was strained with hurt.

Not only was he behaving like a child, but he was acting like a donkey. He needed to stop talking before he said even more he'd regret later when he wasn't reeling from pain.

The scrape of a chair told him she'd scooted away from the bed, but he didn't hear her footsteps leaving the room. As much as he wanted to see if she was still there, he forced himself to keep his eyes closed.

Moments later, his breathing evened and drowsiness fell over him, lulling him back to a world of oblivion.

The next time Zeke awoke, fresh torment jerked him from his nightmares.

Gentle fingers smoothed salve into a burning spot on his back. A spot very low on his back. And the coolness of the air blowing in his window brushed across his skin. His very bare skin.

Was he naked? In front of Kate?

Embarrassment flooded him. Should he pretend he was asleep and didn't know she was there? She'd be mortified if she knew he was awake while she tended to his wounds.

He lay motionless.

"I know you're awake." The voice wasn't Kate's.

Zeke's eyes flew open, and he strained to see over his shoulder, but the knife wound still pained him. "Mr. Peabody?"

"Of course it's me." The portly man paused and glared at Zeke. "You certainly didn't think I'd subject Kate to such indecencies, did you?"

Zeke lowered his head to hide his disappointment. "She was here last time I woke. So I assumed—"

"She told me you'd rather have my help than hers." Mr. Peabody's tender ministration came to a halt.

"That's right." Zeke tried to keep his voice light.

"Well, here I am."

"Good." The disappointment at her absence crept deeper.

Mr. Peabody moved to a new painful spot on his back and applied the salve, the first touch making Zeke nearly cry out. He waited for Mr. Peabody to elaborate on Kate's whereabouts, but the stubborn man carried on silently.

"What time is it?" The light peeking through the open window told him it was past dawn, but not by much.

"It's six thirty."

"How many days have I been in bed?"

"Two."

Zeke felt as though he'd been lying there for two hundred. Every part of his body ached in one way or another, and he was ready to get up, stretch, and start healing. "You're sure talkative this morning."

Mr. Peabody didn't respond.

Zeke squirmed. He'd obviously made his housekeeper mad. No doubt the older man was tired and ready for a break. And now that Zeke had told Kate to go away, Mr. Peabody wouldn't get any relief. "Listen. I'm sorry."

Mr. Peabody's fingers paused their rubbing. "Sorry for what?"

"For being selfish and demanding of your time."

Mr. Peabody clicked his tongue but didn't speak.

Zeke guessed the housekeeper was waiting for more. "For kicking out perfectly good help and leaving you to do my care alone?"

"And . . . ?"

"And what?"

Mr. Peabody released a sigh that rivaled a winter wind. "And for behaving so abominably toward Kate."

"Abominably?" Zeke released a scoffing laugh, but Mr. Peabody's fingers jabbed him, stopping him short with a flood of pain.

"Fine," Zeke said quickly. "I behaved abominably with Kate. I apologize. You satisfied?"

"No. I won't be satisfied until you apologize to her."

Zeke had already planned to tell her he was sorry for his rude comments. Even if her rejection stung, she didn't deserve his contempt. After all, she hadn't done anything wrong. She had the right to turn down his advances and choose any man she wanted. That's all there was to it.

"It may be a while, but next time I see her, I'll tell her I'm sorry." By then, hopefully, he'd be feeling better and have time to build a few fences around his battered heart.

"Why will it be a while? She'll be here soon."

Zeke stiffened. "She will?"

"Fortunately, she's not scared away by your insolence."

He started to push himself up. "Hurry and help me get dressed. I need to comb my hair and wash my face."

Mr. Peabody chuckled. "I knew you still wanted her."

Propped on his elbows, Zeke reached for the glass on the bedside table, but the water sloshed over. "'Course I want her. The problem is that the feelings aren't mutual."

"Who says?" Mr. Peabody took the shaking glass from Zeke and lifted it to his lips.

"She says," Zeke said, before swallowing several mouthfuls.

"I've seen the way she looks at you, and it's clear she cares about you. Besides, I don't think she would have offered to be your caregiver during your recuperation if she didn't have feelings."

"She offered?"

"When the doctor said you needed someone else besides me, she was eager for the opportunity."

"Eager? Doubt that."

"Rest assured, she likes you." Mr. Peabody patted Zeke's cheek, bringing back the vague memory of the housekeeper calling him son and promising to be there for him. "The problem is that you need to prove yourself worthy of her."

Prove himself? Zeke rested his head against his pillow. "How do I do that?"

"You're a smart young man." Mr. Peabody lifted a sheet over Zeke's body. "You'll figure it out, especially since you'll have her all to yourself for the next few weeks as you heal."

Zeke's chest thudded a new faster tempo. Mr. Peabody was right. If Kate really had offered to be his caregiver, he'd get to spend hours a day with her. He'd have more of her time than any other man. And he wouldn't squander it.

He had to do everything possible to prove he was worthy of her love, so in the end, he could win her—heart, soul, and body.

twelve

Kate's pencil flew over the page, sketching the details of the caribou she'd watched grazing on the hill behind the laundry earlier that morning. Coming back from the necessary at dawn, she'd stopped at the sight of a dozen of the beautiful animals munching silently on the sedges. The sun rays streaming over the eastern range had added an ethereal glow to the morning feast.

She darkened the charcoal that outlined the large velvety antlers before swiftly shading the body and leaving lighter patches around the rump and neck.

She hadn't expected to be able to draw the creatures so soon after arriving at Zeke's house, especially when Mr. Peabody had briefed her in the front hallway and excitedly relayed the news that Zeke was awake and alert and on the mend.

However, when she'd made her way into Zeke's bedroom, he'd been asleep, apparently having taxed himself. She planned to tend to other household duties and relieve Mr.

Peabody of some of his burden, but she'd been unable to resist the temptation to sit down and draw the caribou first.

She'd gotten carried away, and instead of simply drawing the caribou, she'd sketched the entire herd and the hillside.

Pausing, she held her pencil between her teeth while she brushed the charcoal with her fingers, lightening and smudging to blend the lone hemlock tree that stood wild and scraggly, casting its long shadow across the meadow.

As she held the sketch pad at arm's length to study it, she glimpsed Zeke's green eyes upon her, crinkling at the corners with amusement.

Her heart skipped a beat, and she retrieved the pencil from her mouth. "You're awake."

"Aye. And enjoying the view. I'd much rather wake up to your face every morning than to Mr. Peabody's."

His words started a fluttering of warmth in her stomach. "Are you sure?" she asked, not willing to give in to his charm quite yet. "Last time you said you'd rather have Mr. Peabody's help."

"Only because I was an idiot."

She tried not to smile, but her lips curved upward nonetheless.

"I don't know what I was thinking. Doubt I was thinking at all if I wanted Mr. Peabody over you."

This time she laughed. She couldn't help it.

His smile broke free and brought out his dimples. "Do you forgive me for all the awful things I said to you?"

"I already have."

His eyes widened, making their green as lush as a mountain meadow. "You have?"

"Aye. Forgiveness doesn't have to be earned. It's free. Besides, I know you were in a lot of pain and weren't thinking straight."

"I've got no excuse for being rude to you when you're here to help." His sleepy expression was much too handsome, his eyes too beckoning, his lazy grin too enticing.

This was exactly why she'd always been enamored with him, because no matter what he did, she could never dislike him for long. Even so, she couldn't let her attraction surface again, not when there couldn't be anything between them.

"How are you feeling today?"

Zeke shifted, then winced. "Like I took a dive down a rocky cliff."

"You could have died."

"I'm too stubborn to die." His voice contained a note of mirth, even though his smile was gone.

Part of her wanted to shake him so he'd admit his need to make peace with his Maker. But she sensed that even though he'd come close to dying, he still wasn't ready to talk about God, and that to push him to do so would only push him away altogether.

"What are you drawing?" He changed the subject, as if he, too, wanted to avoid the topic of death.

She tipped the sketch pad away from him. "I can't show you until I'm finished."

"You're drawing me, aren't you?"

"No, of course not." Her denial was too quick. And she wished she could keep the flush from rising into her cheeks.

"Hope you're making me very handsome and including my *adorable* dimples."

"No, I'm drawing you more accurately and including a big head."

His laughter tumbled out easily, and the sound of it pleased Kate. She loved bantering with him, something she hadn't been able to do quite as well with any of the other men she'd gotten to know over the past years.

She had no doubt Zeke Hart was a special man. If only he was the man for her.

"Show me." His intense gaze focused upon her and made her wish she'd taken more time with her appearance.

"I told you I can't."

"Is that some kind of rule you artists have?"

Was she an artist? Painting and drawing were activities she did in her free time when she had enough supplies and energy. Even though she'd sold some of her sketches in Victoria, she'd never considered herself an artist.

She tried on the idea and saw herself doing more of what she loved. But just as quickly as the vision came, she let it fade. Life was too busy and had too many demands for her to entertain fancy notions about being an artist.

"If you show me, I promise I won't criticize."

"If I show you before I'm finished, I might lose my muse."

"Maybe I can help your muse. Maybe I can even *be* your muse." He twisted to his side, the tautness in his muscles attesting to the pain he was enduring.

She needed to put her sketch pad away and make him breakfast so that he had nourishment before the doctor arrived to apply a plaster cast. Even so, she skimmed her fingers over the drawing before she flipped it around, so he could see what she'd been working on.

He propped himself up on one elbow, the sheet falling away to reveal his bare chest and arms. Sleek and hard and powerful.

Her mouth went dry, and she made herself look at her creation.

He studied the drawing, his silence lengthening and making her want to snap the cover closed.

"Wow," he finally said. "That's amazing."

"Don't say something just to be nice."

"I'm not." His tone was reverent. "You're more talented than I realized."

Her grip on the pad relaxed. "I still need to finish the baby."

"The calf?"

"Aye, over here. And this must have been the mother." She pointed to a caribou with short antlers that stood close to the baby as though protecting him.

"She looks as if she's scolding her child. And telling him to hurry up and finish his breakfast before the miners come out and disturb the peace with their guns."

Kate angled her head to view the drawing the way Zeke was.

"On the opposite side of the picture," Zeke continued,

"the father is standing guard, watching over his herd and making sure they aren't in danger."

Again, Kate studied the picture, seeing it from a new perspective. "I think you're right."

"'Course I'm right." Zeke's voice took on a playful quality. "And as with most children who think they know everything, the calf's telling his parents to stop worrying, that they're overprotective, and that they imagine danger in every shadow when there really isn't any."

She smiled at Zeke's animation.

"What Cari doesn't realize—?"

"Cari?"

"Would you rather call him Bou?"

She stifled a laugh. "Definitely not Bou. Let's go with Cari."

"Good answer. What Cari doesn't realize is that he's looking for danger in the wrong place."

"He is?"

"Aye. He's facing the town, confident he'll hear the approach of hunters before they can get anywhere close enough to take aim."

She studied the drawing, noting the way the baby caribou was chewing with confidence, his head turned from his mother, as if he was communicating to her everything Zeke was saying.

"While he's watching the town, a silent but deadly predator is slinking down the mountain from the opposite direction."

"What silent but deadly predator?" Kate searched the hillside as if she could see something she'd overlooked.

"The wolf."

"There isn't a wolf."

"Not that you can see yet. And not what our little Cari can see."

She shifted her attention to Zeke, a strange sliver of realization coursing through her. Zeke was a natural storyteller with a big imagination. She should have realized it sooner, especially when they'd worked together cleaning up his store. He'd kept her entertained with silly stories of things that had happened in Williamsville over the past year. Even as children, his tales had always regaled her, Jeremiah, and anyone who'd listen.

For several more minutes, he continued with his tale of Cari ignoring his parents' warnings about the dangers of the world around him, particularly the hidden perils, the threats that crouched closer and closer, waiting to spring up when he least expected them.

With each scene, she mentally sketched the wolf creeping closer, hiding behind a boulder, then within a thatch of tall, thick grass, drawing ever nearer as Cari turned his back on his parents, focusing on the pleasures of the meadow and ignoring the dangers around him.

"In the end," Zeke said, "the wolf snatched poor Cari, dragged him away, and ate him."

"What? No. You're not allowed to kill off Cari."

Zeke smiled much too smugly. "It's my tale. I can finish it the way I want to."

"Well, it's my sketch, and I want a happy ending." He'd pulled her into his story so thoroughly that she'd started to grow attached to the little fellow.

"What if I prefer realism?"

She sat forward on the edge of her chair. "Then find a way to make it both realistic and happy."

"Does such an ending really exist?" His expression lost some of the sparkle.

She suspected their conversation had somehow taken a shift, that Zeke was referring to life and not the story. She pondered his question, wanting to take her time with her answer, needing to give him the truth without it being too preachy.

"God doesn't promise this life will be easy, Zeke. In fact, Scripture warns that we shouldn't be surprised or think it strange when we face fiery trials."

"Fiery?" Zeke released a mirthless laugh.

"We live in a sinful, broken world. Bad things happen to us and to those we love. But through it all, we can't give up hope, because ultimately, someday, we will get our happy ending—if not in this life, then in the next."

Zeke leaned his head back and closed his eyes.

Had she said too much? Even if she had, she couldn't hold back the truth that the way to make it through those fiery trials wasn't by giving up on God but by pressing into Him further.

She closed her sketchbook, tucked it under the chair, and placed her pencil on top. Then she rose and started across the room.

"Kate?" His voice was tired and weak.

She paused.

"I'll come up with a different end to the story."

She wanted to ask him if he'd think of a different end to his story too. But instead, she mustered a smile. "Thank you, Zeke. Cari deserves it."

Zeke did too. She could only pray one day he'd see that.

thirteen

From his spot in bed, Zeke strained to see out into the hallway where Kate was talking to Doc. But no matter how he positioned himself, he couldn't get a view of the two, which sent his frustration climbing to new heights.

For the past week, he hadn't been able to put any pressure against the burns that raged up and down the back of his body. Not only hadn't he been able to don clothing, but he hadn't been able to move off his stomach—at least not without excruciating pain.

Today, for the first time since the explosion, Zeke finally had permission to sit up. With his leg in the cast, the pain there had begun to ebb. If only the agony of his blistered flesh would subside.

At least nothing had worsened, except his ability to tamp down his desire for Kate. The more time he spent with her, the more he craved her. If only she would show some interest in return.

He'd been doing as Mr. Peabody had suggested and made

the most of the hours he was able to spend with her. They'd never wanted for topics of discussion. Sometimes, when she was drawing, he'd pester her long enough that she'd show him her sketches, and then he made up stories to amuse her. Other times, they'd reminisce about childhood escapades, things they loved about life in Manchester, and funny happenings at school.

During the long stretches when he'd been in too much agony to talk, she read to him from a few classics she'd borrowed from a miner who'd once been a schoolteacher. The tales took his mind off his pain.

While he'd grown restless, ready to get back to normal life, he also hadn't wanted the undivided time with Kate to end. He'd been half-afraid today Doc would tell him he could get up and move around without any help. Then he'd no longer have an excuse to have Kate's assistance.

The doctor's laughter wafting in from the hallway was proof of just how easily men caved to her charms. Doc never laughed. Never even smiled. But every time he came, somehow Kate made him like her a little more. And now today, after a week, he was practically falling all over her.

"Kate!" Zeke's tone was testy, but he didn't care.

He'd gritted his teeth during the last few minutes of Doc's exam, hardly able to keep at bay caustic remarks about how Doc was old enough to be Kate's father and had better not think about courting her. But he couldn't hold back any longer. He wanted the doctor to get on out and maybe never return.

"Kate, are you coming?" he called again.

At the sound of the front door closing, Zeke breathed easier, expelling tension.

She stepped back into the room, bringing with her the sunshine in her smile. With her fair hair pulled up into a loose knot, the flyaway strands only softened her face, making her more beautiful. "Well, I guess this is my last day here."

"What?" Panic burst through him.

She began to gather the art supplies she'd left scattered about the room. "The doctor said that since you're sleeping well, Mr. Peabody doesn't need to monitor you at night and can resume your care during the day."

Zeke pushed up, grabbing the blanket to keep himself covered. "Mr. Peabody needs your help so he can keep up with all his other duties."

The scent of freshly baked baguettes drifted into the room, choosing that moment to prove how busy Mr. Peabody was.

She hesitated. "But the doctor—"

"Doc ordered my care in the first place."

She was quiet, as though digesting his reasoning—either that, or thinking of another excuse. "I can't go on living with Becca without earning my keep."

"I'm paying you." He blurted the first thought that came to mind. "Aye, I'm paying you to be my nurse. Didn't you know?"

"I'm not helping you for money."

"You're my employee, just like Mr. Peabody. I'll have Wendell issue your wages today."

Worry glinted in her eyes. "But I *want* to help you."

"I know that, Kate. You're a generous person with a big heart. But I'd have to pay someone else to nurse me. Please let me pay you."

Her lips pressed together in a half frown. "But you don't need me any longer—"

"I'll always need you." The words were out faster than water sliding from a sluice pan.

"I don't want to take advantage of your kindness, Zeke." She resumed tidying and stacking her pencils and paints, thankfully unfazed by his ardency.

"You won't be taking advantage of me."

"But you already employ so many people."

"I can afford to hire you."

"I just don't feel right about accepting a wage from you—"

"Kate, I'm really rich. Rich enough to hire a dozen nurses if that's what I wanna do."

Her mouth stalled around her response. In the silence, Mr. Peabody in the kitchen broke out into song, his voice rising on the strains of an opera aria.

"My gold mine is one of the most profitable in British Columbia. It's made me a millionaire several times over." All along, he'd wanted to impress her with who he was and not his money. But he didn't give one whit about that anymore. If his wealth would help gain her affection, then he planned to use it.

"I could see you were successful." Her voice contained a hint of accusation. "But I didn't realize you'd done so well."

"I didn't tell you because I didn't want to win you that way."

"You should know by now I don't see people for what they have or don't have. That's not important to me."

"Then my ability to buy or give you anything you want doesn't change your feelings for me?"

"Not in the least."

A sliver of disappointment lodged in his chest. So much for thinking his prosperity would sway her. "What if I told you I'd build you a mansion that rivaled the biggest houses in all of England?"

"No. It wouldn't matter. I don't want a house like that."

He paused. What did women want? Clothes? "What if I told you I'd hire a seamstress to create a new wardrobe for you with as many gowns as you want?"

She smoothed a hand over her skirt. "I don't need any more gowns. The ladies in Victoria gave us some nice ones."

"Jewels?"

"No."

He held back a sigh. "What about all the best art supplies?"

"I'm getting by with what I have. But thank you for the offer."

If he couldn't sway her with promises of luxury, then how could he win her? "At least let me offer you wages for being my nurse."

She finally smiled. "I see what you're doing."

"What?"

"You're going to a lot of trouble to get your way."

He arched a brow.

"The first day I was in town, you told me you wanted to help me. And because I wouldn't accept your offer, you went and got yourself hurt so that I had to come here and be with you."

He relaxed against the mattress, his nerves unwinding. "Aye, you figured me out."

"You didn't need to use such drastic measures."

"I suppose I didn't." He always enjoyed jesting with her. "And now if you don't give in, you'll force me to go out and blow myself up again."

She chuckled as she started out of the room again.

He sat forward. "You can't leave me yet."

"I'm not leaving," she said over her shoulder. "I'm just getting you a bowl of the soup Mr. Peabody made."

"Then you'll be my nurse and let me pay you?" He fought the need to jump up, grab her, and hold her back.

"I'll be your nurse," she called as she disappeared into the hallway, "but I won't let you pay me for it."

"Then I'll pay Lee Chung for your rent."

"Maybe."

He leaned his head back and closed his eyes. Weariness pulsed through him, but it was overshadowed by a strange sense of contentment that he'd just won a small battle.

Winning Kate's heart wouldn't be easy. Good thing he wasn't afraid of a challenge.

During the next week, Zeke sat up in bed for longer periods

each day. He also made himself stand with a crutch and walk short distances before weakness and pain forced him back to bed.

"Don't worry." Mr. Peabody tucked Zeke's legs back under the covers. "You're getting stronger. Before you know it, you'll be moving around with no trouble."

Zeke wiped a hand across his brow to dry the perspiration that had formed there after just the few moments of exertion. At daybreak, the summer morning was already warm, and his bedroom was stuffy. Though the window was open, the air was muggy from the rain that had fallen most of the night.

The light cotton shirt Mr. Peabody had helped him don was sticking to the wounds on his back and chafing him, as were the light linen underdrawers.

The front door squeaked opened, and Zeke's pulse sputtered in anticipation of seeing Kate. He wished he didn't want to see her so badly first thing every morning, wished he could put her out of his mind. But from the moment Wendell or Mr. Peabody walked her home to the laundry in the evening, he missed her and thought about her until she returned.

He ran his fingers through his hair to comb some order to it. "I should have shaved," he whispered, rubbing his scruffy jaw.

"She doesn't mind," Mr. Peabody whispered back as he tugged the sheet up. "It's clear she cares about you just as you are."

"She tolerates me."

Mr. Peabody brushed a hand over Zeke's hair, smoothing down a strand. He needed to shoo Mr. Peabody away and tell him to stop fussing. But for some reason, he didn't have the heart to say anything, not when Mr. Peabody meant well by it.

The older man stood back and examined him. "Maybe you need to get busy and just kiss her."

"Kiss her?" The words came out strangled, and Zeke glanced to the bedroom doorway, praying Kate hadn't heard his meddling housekeeper.

Someone coughed loudly in the hallway just outside the door, a distinct throat-clearing that belonged to Wendell. "I don't recommend kissing Miss Millington," he called.

As Wendell stepped into the room instead of Kate, Zeke sagged against his pillows, relieved she wasn't there yet to hear Mr. Peabody's suggestion.

"I'm gonna stick to your grandfather's advice." Zeke winked at Mr. Peabody.

"That's a good boy." Mr. Peabody patted Zeke's cheek.

"I wouldn't listen to him this time, boss." Wendell was impeccably dressed in his usual suit and bow tie, with his blond hair slicked back with pomade. "This time his advice could be deadly."

"Morning to you, too," Zeke said wryly. "Aren't you a bright ray of sunshine?"

Wendell, in the process of formulating another sentence, stopped and peered out the window as though expecting sunlight to break through the gloom. "With the cloud covering at about ninety-nine percent, we have a miniscule chance of sunshine this morning."

If Kate had been there, they would have shared a private

smile over Wendell's quirks. As it was, Zeke tried to keep his mirth to himself.

"What new development do you have in the case?" Mr. Peabody asked. "You may as well spit it out before Miss Millington gets here. We wouldn't want to scare her now, would we?"

"No, and this is quite scary."

Wendell would have been scared of a cricket's shadow, but Zeke refrained from saying so and waited for his assistant to elaborate whenever he was ready.

Wendell had been updating Zeke over the past two weeks on any leads regarding who was responsible for the explosion at the mine. After questioning nearly every man in town, Wendell was no closer to solving the crime than he'd been on the first day of his investigation.

They kept circling back around and pointing the finger at Herb. But Kate's jilted fiancé had hotly denied being anywhere near the mine on the day of the explosion. In fact, Herb appeared to have an alibi; he'd been playing cards at Kelly Saloon all evening and several men had vouched for him.

Wendell dug into the inner pocket of his suit coat and retrieved a folded card, which he held out over the end of the bed.

"What is it?" Zeke reached for the item.

Wendell's glasses slipped down his nose. He jerked the card back and used the same fingers holding the card to slide his spectacles up.

Zeke kept his hand outstretched.

Wendell leaned forward again, holding the card toward Zeke, only for his spectacles to once more slip down, this time, falling off one ear and hanging from the other. Wendell retracted his hand again to fix them and struggled to get them in place.

Mr. Peabody muttered, grabbed the card, and slapped it into Zeke's hand. "You're an intelligent boy, Wendell, but you lack God's good common sense."

While Mr. Peabody lectured Wendell further, Zeke fingered the stiff scrap of paper. Tattered around the edges, it appeared as though it had been torn from the inside of a book. He unfolded it to find scrawling print: *She's not yours. Stop spending time with her or next time you'll die.*

A chill raced through Zeke's veins. Someone was threatening him. Again.

"Where did you find this?" Zeke asked Wendell, interrupting Mr. Peabody's sermon.

Wendell jerked his head up so once again his spectacles came loose. He quickly snatched them off, glancing sideways at his grandfather as if expecting more censure. "It was wedged in the door at the store when I arrived this morning. I knew you'd want to see it right away."

"Was anyone else out? Anyone suspicious-looking? Or anyone who might have seen who stuck it in the door?"

"I'm sorry, boss. I didn't look. I was in too much of a hurry to bring you the death threat."

Mr. Peabody sucked in a wheezing breath. "Death threat?"

Zeke held the note out to his housekeeper but focused on Wendell. "Do you recognize the handwriting?"

"It doesn't look familiar."

Mr. Peabody read the card, his eyes widening with each word. "Your attacker doesn't want you to be with Miss Millington."

"That would account for about ninety-three percent of the town."

"I thought it was ninety-five percent?" In spite of the gravity of the threat, Zeke couldn't keep from teasing his assistant. "Guess that means two percent decided I'm worthy of Kate after all?"

"No. It means a group of men got tired of mining and left town three days ago."

"Whatever the case," Mr. Peabody returned the note to Wendell, "a lot of men don't like you."

"They never have," Zeke replied. Ever since he'd struck pay dirt, he made more enemies than he thought possible. Now that he'd let the men in town know he wanted Kate too, no doubt they thought he was as greedy as a king.

"Take it back to the store," Zeke instructed his assistant, "and start comparing the handwriting to signatures in the ledgers, as well as the mail." In handling the mail that came and went from the town, Wendell, of anyone, would be able to match it to a letter he'd seen at one point or another.

"Yes, boss. But my suspicion is that whoever wrote the threat purposefully disguised his handwriting so the note couldn't be traced."

"Then, what about checking books around town and finding one with a missing front page?"

"What if he tore the page out of someone else's book?"

Zeke shrugged. "Investigate all the possibilities, Wendell. You never know what you might find."

"Very well, boss." Wendell turned to go.

Mr. Peabody stopped him with a touch to his arm. "Wait now. Someone already tried to kill Zeke once and just threatened him again. Don't you think you need to involve the law?"

"I've already sent a letter to Judge Begbie, but I've calculated we'll be waiting at least twenty-three or twenty-four more days before he arrives."

"So, you're telling me we can't do anything?" Mr. Peabody's voice rose a decibel. "That a crazy killer could attack again at any moment, and there's nothing we can do to stop him?"

Wendell's Adam's apple slid up and down. "We don't know who the killer is, Grandfather."

"What about Herbert Frank? After stabbing Zeke, that's enough evidence to lock him away."

Wendell shook his head, but before he could speak again, Mr. Peabody whirled on Zeke, his face masked with worry. "What should we do, Zeke? Hire guards? Build a wall around the house? Stock up on guns and ammunition?"

"This isn't a war. It's just a threat—"

"A death threat!"

"I'll be fine."

"Need I remind you that you were recently almost killed?"

"But I wasn't, so stop worrying."

"Well, someone needs to worry if you're not going to."

"Worry about what?" A voice from the doorway startled them, drawing their attention to Kate. She wore her hair in a long, loose braid with wisps framing her face. Her cheeks were flushed and her eyes dreamy, likely filled with all the images she'd witnessed in the early morning, when all manner of critters came out to forage for food. She'd taken to sketching first thing after arriving, claiming she needed to draw what she'd seen before she forgot.

'Course he never protested. He loved watching her at work, the way her fingers flew over the page, the way she tilted her head to follow the flow of the drawing, the way she nibbled at her bottom lip when she paused to examine her work. More than that, he loved it when she'd hold the picture up and ask him what he thought, as if she truly cared about his impression.

She searched each of their faces, and as usual, the very touch of her gaze sent a sizzle into his blood, making it pump at double the speed.

"Zeke got a death threat," Mr. Peabody said before Zeke could warn him not to mention it.

Kate pressed a hand to her lips, holding in the dismay that easily moved into her eyes and darkened the brown.

Standing near the door, Wendell handed Kate the card.

"Wait." Zeke sat up. "Let's not bother Kate with the details."

But she was already reading the note. Her fingers pressed more firmly against her lips. When she finished, she read it again before she passed it back to Wendell. She was quiet a moment before meeting Zeke's gaze.

"I'm to blame for what's happening to you—"

"Nope. Not at all."

"Next time they plan to kill you."

"There won't be a next time." At least he hoped there wouldn't be. Even so, he wasn't living in fear because of this threat. That's exactly what the person wanted him to do.

"You're right." Kate's expression filled with determination. "There won't be a next time. Because I know just what to do to make sure you won't get hurt again."

fourteen

It was a pleasure meeting you, Mr. Wood." Kate pushed out of her chair and stood in front of the open window, praying for a breath of fresh air to blow inside the house but getting none.

"The pleasure was all mine." Of medium build and fair features, Mr. Wood remained in his chair on the opposite side of the parlor by the fireplace. The heat of the early September evening made a fire unnecessary, but Mr. Peabody had lit one anyway and had continued to enter the room and add fuel to it throughout the evening until it was blazing and crackling, making the room nearly unbearable.

On several occasions, Kate had thanked Mr. Peabody for his kind efforts and informed him they were just fine. Unfortunately, he hadn't taken her hint and had been in and out at least a hundred times—not only to replenish the fire, but to complete other chores he'd insisted needed doing—sweeping, dusting, washing the window, and more.

Each of the men who'd come calling had attempted to

move his chair away from the fireplace and position it closer to the window. But Mr. Peabody had insisted they return to the spot upon the hearth, rebuking them for not keeping an appropriate distance from her, although she suspected they were merely attempting to find relief from the heat.

She used her hand to fan her flushed face, wishing again for a breeze to cool her down. Her gown clung to her body, and loose hairs stuck to the back of her neck. But she wasn't perspiring quite as much as Mr. Wood, who had streams trickling steadily down his forehead and cheeks.

She'd expected Mr. Wood to rise and exit eagerly, as her other callers had done. But he remained in his chair, peering over at her with the same wide smile he'd worn for the entire visit.

At another thump and bang against the far wall followed by shouting, she cringed. Zeke had been short-tempered and moody all afternoon. After his glaring and sulking, she'd been relieved to finish her day with him and begin accepting callers.

He'd made no pretense that he loathed her plan to resume courting the men of Williamsville and had begged her not to go through with the meetings. But ever since the note he'd received two days ago, she'd made up her mind to put an end to the threats once and for all. To do that, she had to show everyone she wasn't engaged to Zeke and that friendship was the only thing happening between them.

Another bang against the wall seemed to shake the house and brought Mr. Wood up out of his chair, his smile finally dimming under the shadows of concern. "Mr. Hart must still be in a great deal of pain."

"He's certainly acting that way tonight, isn't he?" She had a hunch he'd been throwing things at the wall to disturb her, and she had half a mind to march into his room and scold him for his antics.

Mr. Peabody was standing in the hallway, glaring into the parlor at Mr. Wood, his arms crossed, his feet spread. The housekeeper had given each of the men the same glare, one that was frightening enough to send them scurrying from the house.

"As much as I'd like to stay longer." Mr. Wood wiped his sleeve across his forehead. "I can see that Mr. Peabody would like me to leave."

"It is getting late," she concurred, "and I don't want to impose on his hospitality any longer than necessary."

"Next time, may I suggest dinner and a walk?" he asked hopefully, as he stepped into the hallway.

She passed by Mr. Peabody who was shaking his head and mouthing the word *no*. She'd already had to squelch Herbert Frank's hopes to participate in the courtship. Though he denied any part in the most recent threat, Kate had forced herself to stand her ground with him this time. But she had no reason to turn down this request from Mr. Wood. Did she?

"Perhaps," she said with caution. "Although maybe we should spend more time getting to know each other first."

Mr. Wood's smile rose back into place. As he said his good-byes and stepped outside, she watched him stride down the street for a few seconds. Mr. Wood was the finest of the

men who'd called that evening. He was the schoolteach-
er-turned-miner who'd loaned her the books she'd read to
Zeke. Not only was Mr. Wood interesting and well learned,
but he'd talked about the need to build a church and have a
regular minister in town.

"Your thoughts, mademoiselle?" Mr. Peabody asked.

"He's a nice man." She closed the door.

"He's too polite."

She chuckled. "Can anyone be too polite?"

"He's polite to the point of being uppity."

"Fiddlesticks. He's a perfectly fine gentleman."

A crashing came from Zeke's room, followed by an angry
bellow.

Mr. Peabody clicked his tongue while she pressed her lips
together. Zeke was behaving like a child, and she ought to
simply leave without another word to him.

"Don't be too upset with him," Mr. Peabody whispered.
"He's just jealous."

Kate released a frustrated sigh. "You know I'm doing this
to keep him safe from the attacker."

Mr. Peabody gave a solemn nod, his face flushed and
sweating from the heat spreading throughout the house. "I
understand completely. But perhaps you need to reassure
him this is only a ruse and that you're not intending to get
serious with any of the men."

"Mr. Peabody." The truth was she had every intention
of getting serious. She'd already had the conversation with
the meddling housekeeper several times, but apparently she
hadn't explained herself well enough.

"Is anyone planning to help me?" Zeke called. "Or do I have to sit here on the floor all night?"

She rushed forward at the same time as Mr. Peabody. As she reached Zeke's bedroom door, she stopped short at the disaster. Shoes and clothes were strewn about. His pillows and blankets littered the floor. And he was sprawled out in the middle of it all.

Features contorted in pain, he clutched his plastered leg.

"What happened?" She dropped to her knees beside him.

"I tried to get up," he said through gritted teeth. "But my crutch slipped and I fell."

She assessed his leg, looking for anything amiss. "You're not supposed to get out of bed without assistance."

"Should I fetch Doc?" Mr. Peabody asked.

"Nope," Zeke said testily. "Kate's had enough callers for tonight."

"The doctor is not one of my callers."

"He sure acts like it."

"Zeke Hart, that's enough. You're behaving badly." She ran her hand along his cast. "Now, are you hurting anywhere else besides your leg?"

He shook his head. "Just my pride."

Her frustration returned in full force. "If you ask me, your pride needed a good fall."

For several minutes, she worked with Mr. Peabody to lift Zeke until he was standing, and then they helped him hobble to his bed and lowered him to the edge.

"Are you sure you don't want me to fetch the doctor?"

Mr. Peabody smoothed his mustache and goatee back into place.

"Fetch the volunteer fire department." Zeke's tone was laced with mirth. "The plan to overheat the men has overheated the house."

Kate gasped. "The plan to overheat the men?"

Mr. Peabody's face turned from rosy red to a dark crimson. "Time for me to be going along. I need to finish weeding the garden." He bustled from the room, as though the success of the garden depended upon how much weeding he accomplished in the remaining few minutes of daylight.

Once they were alone, Kate crossed her arms.

Zeke stared at the floor.

She tapped her foot. "Well?"

"It was Mr. Peabody's idea."

"Then you're telling me you had nothing to do with overheating the men?"

"That one was his. Mine was throwing things against the wall."

"Zeke Hart! You're too much." As soon as the words were out, she slanted him a glare. "And that's not a compliment."

He grinned as if proud of his conspiring with Mr. Peabody.

"With the death threat, you know I was meeting with the men to help you."

"I don't need your help."

"Fine. Then you have to accept the fact that I'm meeting with the men to find a husband."

His glare came back in full withering heat. "Not in my house."

"I've already planned the meetings. Tomorrow night. With four more men."

"Cancel them," he growled, his brows furrowing above flashing eyes.

She wavered only a moment before lifting her chin. "No."

"It's my house. I refuse to allow it. And that's all there is to it."

At the challenge in his raised voice, she stiffened. "You refuse?"

"Aye. I refuse to let you flaunt yourself in front of a parade of strangers." He was practically shouting.

"I'm not flaunting myself!"

"I heard you tonight with those men, and you were flaunting."

Her anger was growing hotter with each passing comment. She wanted to reach out and shake him and make him see reason, but she squelched the impulse and instead spun to go.

He grabbed her hand and tugged her. The motion set her off balance making her fall against him. Before she could right herself, he tugged her again, and this time her momentum landed her squarely on his lap.

She sat motionless, too stunned to move. His face was only inches from hers, and their ragged breathing filled the space between them. She'd been trying so hard over the past month to ignore her attraction to him. But his green eyes were too close and intense, his hard jaw flexed with determination, and his strong mouth pressed together with stubbornness.

Why did he have to be so handsome?

She started to shove against his chest, but he slipped a hand behind her neck and guided her closer.

She could see where he was leading her, and a part of her warned her to resist. But another part of her had been waiting for this moment her entire life. As silly as it might be, she'd dreamed of the day she'd be this close, and he'd finally kiss her. Now her nerves tingled with the desire to experience this, to sate her curiosity and her need for him.

His attention had shifted to her mouth and his lids dropped halfway, revealing his long dark lashes. He angled in but then hovered just out of reach, the warmth of his breath tantalizing her.

The very moment of waiting was wrought with exquisite pleasure that unraveled inside her. As he leaned in even closer, he still held himself back, as though testing how far he could go before she cut him off. Or perhaps he was giving her a chance to say no.

Her chest rose and fell in anticipation, and she couldn't make herself move away. Instead of jumping up from his lap and behaving as a true lady would, she tilted her head a fraction closer to his.

Apparently, the slight movement was the final invitation Zeke needed. He closed the distance by leaning in, and she met him in the middle with too much eagerness. His mouth covered hers at the same time she opened up to him.

He deepened the kiss so that it was at once passionate

and consuming. Fire, hotter than the flames that had burned upon the parlor hearth, spread through her veins.

She'd kissed men before. Chastely. Sparingly. But no kiss could compare to this one. Nothing could compare with the sensations rippling along her nerves.

Her hands had a mind of their own, lifting to his shoulders, skimming down his arms, and gliding over the muscles she'd admired over the past weeks when he'd gone without a shirt.

At her touch, his hand at the back of her neck grazed her braid to the end. His fingers deftly untied the leather strip and began to unravel her hair. All the while, his mouth had possession of hers, tasting and feasting as if he'd never get enough.

When he freed her hair, he delved his fingers in deeply, tangling and tugging and losing himself there. A low moan at the back of his throat couldn't escape past their kiss, but it reverberated through her.

This passion with Zeke was better—far better—than she'd ever imagined. And she didn't want to stop kissing him. Didn't want to break free of his magnetism. Didn't want to do anything but melt into him.

The loud clearing of a throat penetrated her hazy passion, but Zeke's hand intertwining into her hair kept her locked against him. She didn't have the will or strength to tug away.

"Monsieur." Mr. Peabody spoke from the doorway. "Please forgive me for interrupting."

Kate attempted to pull back, but Zeke pursued her, capturing her mouth again and in the process somehow making her his willing captive.

"Monsieur." Mr. Peabody's voice hinted at mirth. "I regret to inform you that your company has arrived."

Company? Who was Zeke expecting?

She released Zeke and pushed against his chest to free herself.

"No, don't go," he whispered hoarsely even as he tried to hold on to her. "I'll send them away." He grazed his lips across her chin to her jaw and then to the sensitive skin on her neck.

"Zeke," she said breathlessly. Her body responded with the need for him, but her mind urged her to stand up and cool off.

At a cough in the hallway that was deeper and more pronounced than Mr. Peabody's, her eyes shot open. Her gaze landed upon Mr. Peabody in the doorway. His mustache curled up with a smug smile, as though he'd stumbled upon something that pleased him immensely.

Was he happy she and Zeke were kissing? Was this another one of their plans tonight? Maybe he'd left so Zeke would have the opportunity to kiss her.

Indignation began to pool inside. But before she could jump up and question either one, her gaze snagged on the two men standing in the hallway behind Mr. Peabody. Both had removed their hats and were staring with wide eyes at her and Zeke. She'd seen them in meetings with Zeke before and had finally understood that they, like Zeke, owned profitable mines, and together the three had formed a mining board.

"Oh dear!" This time she wrenched upward, giving Zeke no choice but to release her.

"Wait." Even though he was injured, he was fast. He snagged her around the waist and began to drag her back toward his lap.

"You have visitors," she whispered, mortified by the unsteadiness of her breathing.

He shrugged, his half-lidded, long-lashed eyes regarding her with undeniable desire.

"And I need to go." She forced a firmness to her tone she didn't feel and then broke free, this time moving beyond his reach.

He fumbled for his crutch, as though he planned to stand and come after her. "Don't go yet, Kate. We need to talk."

She crossed to the door, sensing every eye upon her. Her cheeks burned with the growing realization that these men had witnessed her sitting on Zeke's lap and passionately kissing him. What must they think of her now?

And what of Zeke? If word spread that she'd been kissing Zeke, his attacker would surely strike again. He'd be in worse danger than before.

"Please, Kate," Zeke called.

Thankfully, Mr. Peabody stepped aside to let her pass. The men in the hallway moved back to give her plenty of room as well. She could feel their curious gazes upon her as she strode to the front door. But she didn't acknowledge them. She doubted she'd be able to look them in the eyes ever again, not after embarrassing herself so thoroughly.

As she exited the house and closed the door firmly behind

her, she didn't care she'd forgotten her sketch pad and pencil, or left behind the tin of beignets Mr. Peabody had set aside for her to take home after she'd raved over the sweet delicacy.

All she could think about was Zeke, his kisses, and how much she wanted to keep kissing him. Even though she could never let it happen again.

fifteen

eke's heart hammered against his chest with the need to chase after Kate. For a reason he couldn't explain, he sensed that he had to pursue her, or he might lose the ground he'd just gained.

With his crutch under his arm taking the weight off his broken leg, he took a wobbly step. But with all the items scattered over the floor, he hesitated, not wanting to trip and fall over something again. His leg still ached from landing on it before.

"Help me, Mr. Peabody," Zeke said, as he fought a wave of dizziness.

Mr. Peabody was at his side in an instant, steadying him. "You're not going anywhere tonight, son."

"I need to go after her and talk to her." He lurched forward another step, inwardly cursing his broken leg for slowing him down.

"Mr. Blake and Mr. Putnam are here for your board meeting." He nodded toward the men who were standing in the hallway, both tugging at their collars and fanning their faces with their hats.

Zeke swiped again at the perspiration running down his face. "Sorry fellows, but I'm in no frame of mind to discuss anything tonight."

"Sure, you go and *talk* to her." Putnam's grin was lecherous. "When you're done, I'd like to *talk* to her too. How about you, Blake?"

At Putnam's elbow in his gut, Blake offered a knowing smile beneath his red beard. "Sure, I like talking."

Anger ripped through Zeke, along with the need to plow headfirst into the men. "She's not that kind of woman. And if I hear you talk about her that way again, I'm gonna make you wish you hadn't."

The laugh lines around Putnam's eyes disappeared. He pulled himself up to his full height, at least a foot taller than Zeke, and he glowered. "You might be able to order around everyone else in this town, but you're no boss of me."

Blake didn't add anything to Putnam's statement, but his eyes glinted with resentment that stabbed Zeke, even a dozen feet away.

Zeke rubbed a hand over the back of his neck to ease the tension. Here he was again, using his authority to threaten people. But this was about Kate. He'd do anything for her, even abuse his power, if necessary. "Kate Millington is a sweet young woman. She's completely innocent—"

"Sitting on your lap on your bed and kissing the way you two were going at it?" Putnam scoffed. "The two of you have a thing going here."

"Aye." Blake nodded, his expression still hard. "The way I see it, neither of you is innocent."

"We don't have a *thing* going. That's the first time I kissed her." Zeke didn't want news of his indiscretion with Kate to spread around town. It would ruin her. Men would say vulgar things about her the same way Putnam and Blake were doing. And it was his fault.

Mr. Peabody patted Zeke's arm. "You know what all this means, don't you? You simply must get married."

"Aye. We're gonna get married. As soon as the traveling preacher comes to town."

"That's right," Mr. Peabody said. "You do the honorable thing and propose to her."

"In the meantime," Zeke leveled what he hoped was his most convincing glare upon his guests, "neither of you better mention—"

Putnam's eyes narrowed, and Blake leaned back as if he expected a blow.

"I'd appreciate it," Zeke forced a calmness he didn't feel to his tone, "if neither of you mention anything about this incident around town."

Blake shrugged, as noncommittal as always.

"Please," Zeke added. "Not for my sake, but for Kate's."

Blake remained silent, but after several long seconds, Putnam grunted. "Fine. But even if she's as innocent as you claim, you need to do the right thing and marry that gal by the week's end. If not, I'll drag you both to the preacher myself."

"Two weeks," Zeke countered, trying to buy himself

more time. "It might take that long before I can get someone here to perform the wedding."

Deep inside, he knew the real trouble wouldn't be getting a preacher to come in two weeks. That would be the easy part. The real trouble would be convincing Kate to marry him.

"Miss Kate, go on and wake up now." The tip of Becca's shoe prodded Kate's ribs. "You in big trouble."

Kate pulled up her cover and burrowed against her pillow. "Please, Becca," she replied, unable to open her groggy eyes. "It's too early."

"Early?" Becca chortled. "Girl, it ain't early. We been working for two hours already while you been sleeping."

Two hours? Kate pushed up from her pallet, blinking at the bright sunlight flooding the shack from the open door.

After being awake most of the night, she'd fallen asleep just before dawn. She'd only planned to slumber for a little while before getting up. But she'd overslept.

All because of that kiss.

"What time is it?"

The scent of lye hung in the air, and Becca stood above her, damp skirt inches from her face. "Time to get married, that what time."

Kate laughed. "Time to get married. Very funny."

"Do I look like I'm being funny?" Becca pressed her lips in a straight line.

Kate sat up farther, disentangling her nightgown from

between her legs and brushing aside long waves of hair, only to have them fall back into her face and remind her of the way Zeke had loosened her braid and freed her hair. She could almost feel his fingers stroking and twisting at the same time he'd deepened his kiss . . .

Warmth fluttered in her belly, the remnants of the heat that had plagued her all night long—heat the kiss had ignited. His kiss had been wonderful, magical, heavenly. The kind of kiss that could make a girl forget everything. Almost.

She lifted fingers to her lips as if that could somehow bring back the feeling and taste of his mouth against hers.

"I was gonna ask you if it true what they're saying. But that goofy smile done give it away."

"Goofy smile?" Kate tried to remove any trace of her smile, but it only widened.

Becca's brow furrowed as she stepped carefully over Kate's art supplies and retreated to the doorway.

"What?" Kate brushed her lips once more. Even if she shouldn't have kissed Zeke and never would again, she couldn't deny she'd enjoyed every second they shared. He'd been tender and yet eager, restrained and yet passionate.

"You love him." Becca's quiet statement was a dash of cold water.

"No." Kate scrambled to her feet, scattering the pages of discarded drawings she'd torn from her sketch pad—all of them of Zeke. "No, of course I don't love him."

Becca cocked her head. "You didn't even have to ask who."

"That's because—" What excuse could she give?

"That's because you been thinking about Zeke Hart every day, all day since you got here."

"He's been on my mind lately because—because I've been taking care of him."

"And you been thinking about him all night and that's why you didn't sleep a wink."

Kate met Becca's warm brown gaze. Even filled with censure, the depths of compassion there reached out to Kate and broke down her last defenses.

"I kissed him."

"From the rumors flying around town, you done more than kiss that man."

"Rumors?" Kate's pulse slowed to a crawl as she began to make sense of what Becca had been trying to tell her all along. With a groan, Kate buried her face into her hands. "I wanted to keep Zeke out of danger by taking the attention away from him, and I probably just made it a hundred times worse."

"You the one in big trouble, Miss Kate."

Kate peeked through her hands at her friend. "How so?"

Becca unhooked Kate's skirt and shirt from the peg on the back of the doorway and handed them to her. "You sure you want to hear? It ain't pretty."

"What choice do I have?" Though the morning was warm, Kate shuddered from a chill and clutched her garments against her chest.

Becca cast her gaze heavenward, muttered under her breath as though praying, then met Kate's gaze directly. "The men be saying you on Zeke's bed right on top of him."

Kate covered her mouth with her hand and captured a muffled scream of horror.

"Then it ain't true? The most you did was kiss him?"

Kate's thoughts returned to the moment in the bedroom when Zeke had tugged her down onto his lap. She shouldn't have stayed. She should have risen right away. At the very least, she could have turned her head away when he'd leaned in to kiss her. He'd given her the chance to say no.

"Then it's true?" Becca's voice rose. "You on his bed—?"

"No!" Kate held out a hand as if that could somehow stop Becca's accusation. "I mean, yes. I was on his bed, but not in the way you think."

"And the part about you being on top of him—?"

"No!" Kate dragged in a breath. "Yes, I was sitting on his lap, but that's it. Nothing else happened."

Becca folded her arms, and her brows arched high.

"Please believe me, Becca." Kate lowered her hand, only to realize it was trembling. Her body was shaking, and her heartbeat was erratic. What had she done? With those kinds of rumors circulating, she'd sullied her reputation and likely ruined her chance at making a match with a God-fearing Christian man.

Becca heaved a sigh, her expression crumpling into one of worry. "Miss Kate, it don't matter if I believe you. The men of this town ain't gonna think of you as a lady no more. They gonna treat you like a loose woman."

Tears sprang to Kate's eyes. "Oh Becca, I've made a mess of things, haven't I?"

"Mm-hmm. You sure did."

Kate hung her head to hide her tears as they escaped down her cheeks.

"Come on now. Don't cry." Becca crossed to Kate and brushed at a strand of tangled hair. "Once you married to Zeke, all those rumors gonna go away. Ain't nobody gonna remember them long."

She nodded at Becca's wisdom, then stiffened. "Once I'm married to Zeke?"

"Yep, told you when I first come in this shack that it's time for you to get married."

Kate wiped the tears off her cheeks. "I can't marry him, Becca."

"Sure you can. You gonna have to now."

He didn't share her faith, but was she making too much of that small difference? Maybe eventually she'd be able to win him over. Surely, with enough time and prayer, she'd help him to realize he didn't have to run away from God any longer.

"You love him," Becca said more confidently than the first time she'd said it. "And he sure do love you."

A tiny bud of hope unfurled. "Do you think so?"

"Mm-hmm." Becca glanced out the open door and retied her apron.

Zeke hadn't told her that he loved her. But he'd been open all along about how much he liked her and wanted to court her. If the kiss was any indication of his feelings, then he must feel as deeply for her as she did for him.

Wouldn't that be enough to hold them together?

A needle of doubt pricked her. What if it wasn't enough

someday? What if they needed something stronger to bind them—like a commitment to God and His plan for marriage? Without a solid belief in doing things God's way, what would prevent Zeke from walking away when life grew tough?

Her fingers slid into her pocket. She stroked the thin, frayed ribbon before crumpling it into a tight wad. Then she pulled her hand out and straightened her shoulders.

She'd make sure Zeke never had any reason to leave. And she'd make him see his need for God. He had a firm foundation in his faith and had grown up believing in the saving Gospel. It was just a matter of time and effort before he decided to return to his faith.

"Go on now." Becca finished tidying her appearance and stepped through the door. "That pesky assistant of Zeke's been here a dozen times over the past two hours, checking to see if you awake so he can bring you over to the house."

"Over to the house?" Did that mean Zeke was eager to see her?

Becca nodded. "Don't you be coming back here unless you get engaged, d'ye hear?"

Kate's throat constricted around her answer, and when the door closed, she sagged against the wall. After breaking things off with Herbert Frank, she'd told herself she wouldn't jump right into another engagement, that she'd choose more carefully the next time.

But what other option did she have? If she didn't marry Zeke, she'd only bring more disaster on both of them.

sixteen

"She's not coming," Zeke called, his leg aching from standing for so long near the parlor window.

"Miss St. Germaine assured Wendell she'd awaken Miss Millington," Mr. Peabody replied from across the hallway in the dining room.

"That's what she said last time Wendell went." Zeke took a long look up the street in the direction of Lee Chung's Laundry, but only the usual mix of wagons, teams, and men crowded the street. Still no sign of Kate.

With a slap of frustration against the window frame, he pivoted and slowly made his way to the nearest chair. The tap of the crutch and the unsteady thump of his footsteps echoed in the stale air of the room, the heat from yesterday lingering even though Mr. Peabody had kept the windows open around the house all night.

Zeke lowered himself into the chair and released a groan. He stretched out his plastered leg and gave his underarm a break from the pressure of the crutch. He wearily studied the room, noting the plain white walls without any pictures, the mantel devoid of decorations, and the wood floor bare of a rug. From the simplicity of the interior, no one would guess the riches he'd accumulated.

He'd expected that building the big house would make him feel accomplished and would prove he'd made more of himself than his father had. His father had worked long hours in the mill and had never had much to show for it. After Mum's miscarriage, he'd started drinking. Then when she'd died, he'd all but given up on life and taken to drowning his sorrows and loneliness in drink. His drunken rages had only become more frequent and more violent.

Zeke had vowed he'd be different. But after moving into the house, he hadn't felt different. Fact was, the big, empty rooms only magnified his loneliness.

He still had every intention of buying more for his home—furniture and all the fine items rich people owned. But the trouble with living so far up in the mountainous region of British Columbia was that the transport of such goods was difficult. Even though the Royal Engineers were building a road up the Fraser Canyon, their work was dangerous and wouldn't be completed for many years.

In the meantime, Williamsville relied upon the pack trains that traversed narrow passes and steep gorges to bring in everything from the outside world they couldn't make or produce themselves. While new businesses were springing up every day, the town couldn't keep up with the demands, especially for food and other staples. He'd always figured feeding the miners was more important than filling his house with fancy things.

But now, with his need to get married to Kate, he didn't have just himself to think about anymore.

He bent forward and propped his elbows on his knees, letting his head drop. 'Course, Wendell had been the one to deliver the bad news first thing that morning—the sordid rumors circulating around town about him and Kate being in bed together.

Ever since Wendell's visit and report, Zeke's nerves had stretched until he felt like a lit fuse about to explode. He'd wanted to find Putnam and Blake and punch his fist into both of their faces and ask them why they'd betrayed him, especially after they'd agreed not to say anything about the indiscretion.

He didn't care one whit for himself. But he'd wanted to protect Kate. Wanted to keep her reputation from being sullied. And he'd failed.

Blowing out a tight breath, he jammed his fingers into his hair. He'd failed to protect her because he'd been a weak man. He should've known better than to kiss her in his bedroom, especially on his bed.

Regardless, he hoped to have the chance to convince her to marry him. But she'd probably heard the rumors from Becca and Lee, who'd no doubt gotten an earful from the men dropping off their laundry. Now she'd hate him and never come near him again.

Maybe that was for the best. After the death threat, he was afraid he was putting her in danger by her association with him. He'd told himself that if the attacker cared enough for Kate, he wouldn't attempt anything around her. But what if he did try to injure Zeke, and Kate got hurt?

"Zeke?" Her voice came from the parlor doorway.

He jerked his head up to find her as fresh as a mountain brook in her blue gown that brought out the creaminess of her skin and the rich brown of her eyes—eyes that weren't filled with the anger he'd expected. Instead, her expression was as carefree as it always was.

Had she so easily cast aside their moment of intimacy from last eve? What if it hadn't meant as much to her as it had to him? Or maybe she hadn't heard the rumors after all. Would he have to be the one to tell her?

Dread settled at the bottom of his stomach.

"You're not walking around by yourself, are you?" She started across the room toward him. She'd worn her hair down except for the front strands, which she'd braided and tied back. The braids only served to remind him of her thick plait from yesterday and the pleasure of unwinding it and burrowing his fingers into the luxuriousness.

Get a hold of yourself, Hart. He couldn't think of touching her hair at a time like this. He had to stay impartial and refrain from causing further trouble.

She stopped in front of him and held out a hand. "You look exhausted. Let me help you back to your room."

He took her hand, relishing the softness and gentleness of her touch. She tugged in an effort to help him rise, but he didn't move. Instead, he surrounded her hand with both of his as though that could somehow anchor him with the words he needed to say.

"Kate."

She grew motionless, her eyes widening. Only then did he glimpse her uncertainty.

"I'm sorry," he whispered.

"You are?" she whispered back, her sights dropping to his lips for an instant. But it was long enough to glimpse her curiosity and even desire. Had she found pleasure in their kisses? Maybe he hadn't been wrong after all. Nevertheless, he'd been reckless, hadn't considered how his actions would hurt her.

"Aye, I shouldn't have done what I did."

Hurt flashed in her eyes, and she tugged to loosen her hand. "You wished you'd never kissed me?"

"Nope." He tightened his hold. "I loved kissing you."

"You did?" The hurt disappeared.

He pulled her a step nearer. "I'm planning to kiss you again."

"You are?" Her voice turned breathless.

"Aye." His tone dropped as he studied her lips. The memory of them against his, so pliable and accepting and inviting, fanned to life the heat that had lain dormant all night. He wanted to drag her onto his lap as he had before, wrap his arms around her, and kiss her all day.

At the clatter of dishes in the dining room, he forced his attention away from her mouth. He had to make himself do the right thing, tell her what had happened, even if it ruined everything.

"Kate," he said hesitantly, "I'm sorry because I didn't protect your reputation better, and now everyone's talking about us being together—together, ah, you know . . ."

A flush moved up into her cheeks. She tugged her hand loose from his and started to step away.

"Wait." He took hold of her waist. "Please, don't go. Let me apologize."

She didn't meet his gaze, but at least she didn't fight to break free.

He took hope from that. "Can you forgive me for putting you in this position?"

She was motionless for a moment before relaxing within his grasp. "I forgive you. But you're not entirely to blame."

"Aye, I am." He lowered his head. "I have a way of bringing trouble to the people I care about."

Before leaving Manchester, he'd brought trouble to his family, the mill workers, and his friends. Earlier in the summer, he'd even put Zoe in danger, though he hadn't meant to. Now he was causing problems for Kate.

Her hands tentatively closed over his shoulders. "Don't be too hard on yourself."

She was standing near enough that his bent head brushed against her. He allowed himself to lean into her, the steadiness of her presence lending him peace as it always seemed to do.

She released him, but he wrapped his arms around her waist and drew her closer, unwilling for the moment to end. For several heartbeats she held herself aloof, and he was afraid he'd overstepped himself again. But then she settled her hands upon his head.

Closing his eyes, he breathed her in, a fresh scent as though she'd rolled in wildflowers.

Tentatively, she smoothed down his hair.

He could rest against her all day.

Her hand brushed his hair again, this time roaming farther back toward his collar. She fiddled with a strand at his neck, her fingers brushing his skin and sending shivers down his backbone.

This was where he wanted to be. Always. He sighed, relieved she'd forgiven him.

She threaded both hands in his hair, moving with a possessiveness that sent a shudder of need through him. When her fingers slid to a halt and held him almost fiercely, something powerful and beautiful surged into his chest. He could only describe it as love. Had he fallen in love with Kate?

Aye, the more time he'd spent with her, the more he'd grown to care about her. He appreciated so many things about her—her selflessness in helping him, her boundless optimism, and her genuine interest in others. Not only did he appreciate who she was, but he loved being in her company, even if he was doing nothing but watching her draw.

Maybe he needed to get down on one knee, declare his love, and propose on the spot.

He gave himself a mental shake. He couldn't. He had to be patient and do things right if he had any hope of convincing her to go through with marrying him. She'd already told him they had no future together. And if she told him no again, he wasn't sure he could survive another rejection.

Kate held her breath and waited. For what, she didn't know except that she'd felt Zeke's body tense, his mood shift, and his need intensify.

Maybe she'd gotten carried away by running her fingers through his hair. In the moment, doing so had seemed right and natural. But so had kissing him last night, and look where that had led.

"Mademoiselle and monsieur?" Mr. Peabody spoke from behind them.

Kate jumped away from Zeke, flames leaping into her face at having once again been caught in an intimate predicament.

"Good morning, Mr. Peabody." She smoothed down her blouse the same way she hoped to smooth over the awkward moment. "I'm sorry I'm late. I overslept, but I'm here now and can take over our patient's care so you can attend to your other duties."

"You'll have no duties this morning." Mr. Peabody glanced at Zeke and smiled almost secretively.

"It's no trouble helping Zeke like I have been—"

"I'm getting better," Zeke interrupted. "And I've gotta learn to get around on my own."

Dismay sifted through her. She wasn't sure what she'd expected to happen this morning, but she certainly hadn't anticipated being told she wasn't needed anymore.

"In light of the rumors," Zeke continued, "Mr. Peabody and I decided you shouldn't be here as my caretaker any longer."

They were right. The doctor had been correct from the start that nursing was inappropriate for a single woman. "Well," she forced some cheer to her voice, "if you don't need me, then I'll go back to the laundry and help there, especially since I'm sure Becca and Mr. Chung have been counting the days until I can return to work."

The truth was, Mr. Chung would be sorely disappointed to see her back, but he'd do anything for Becca, including putting up with Kate. She'd seen the way he watched Becca. And Kate suspected it wouldn't be long before he asked Becca to marry him, at least she hoped so.

"Not quite yet, mademoiselle."

"Nope, not quite yet." Zeke situated his crutch under his arm and used it to push himself to his feet.

Since he'd expressed an interest in doing more for himself, Kate resisted the urge to rush to his aid, though she was tempted to do so.

As he straightened and braced himself with his crutch, she noticed for the first time that he'd taken more care with his appearance than he had since the explosion. He was attired in a crisp, clean shirt and dark-blue vest along with trousers, the material of one leg sliced open and loosely covering his cast. He'd even donned shoes.

Zeke held out his free elbow as if to escort her. "Mr. Peabody has been working nonstop since dawn to prepare a breakfast feast for you."

"*Petit dejeuner*," Mr. Peabody said.

"Breakfast," Zeke countered.

Mr. Peabody's long mustache dipped in displeasure even as Zeke's lips curved up.

Kate couldn't find any humor in the exchange. Instead, her heart tumbled low in her chest. Was this a good-bye breakfast? Perhaps a way of saying thank you?

Whatever the case, she couldn't be ungrateful, not if Mr. Peabody had worked so hard to prepare it. "*Petit dejeuner*. That's so sweet of you, Mr. Peabody. I'm sure I'll enjoy every morsel of your cooking, just like I always do."

"I hope so too. I've made omelette Florentine, brioche, and croissants."

"It sounds very French." She sniffed the air that was filled with the tantalizing aromas she'd come to expect whenever she arrived. "And it smells delicious."

"Now come along." He bustled out of the room. "I'm afraid it's not as fresh as it was two hours ago."

As she took Zeke's arm, she was reminded of their first dinner together—the loveliness of the meal and the camaraderie they'd shared. Was this now the end?

She should feel relieved to be cutting ties with Zeke. After being with him so much, she'd grown to care about him far more than was safe. Maybe now, with some distance, she could extinguish the desire flaring between them and maintain a proper perspective.

She forced a smile. "I guess we shouldn't keep him any longer."

Zeke took a shaky step. "Especially since he's been working all morning on a new pattern for the napkins."

"No more shoehorns posing as swans?"

His grin worked its way up. "No, these are more like soup ladles posing as peacocks."

In spite of the conflicting emotion churning inside, she laughed. Zeke had a way of making heavy moments lighter. When they entered the dining room, she exclaimed over the efforts Mr. Peabody had taken to decorate the table just as beautifully as for the last meal, including the flower arrangement and the artfully folded napkins.

Against her protests, Zeke helped her into her chair. As he lowered himself across from her, his forehead had broken out in perspiration, and his face was pale.

"You're overdoing it," she chastised. "You should be abed."

"I've gotta get stronger."

"You will, if you're patient."

"I'm not a patient man, Kate." His jaw clenched. "You should know that by now."

She didn't dare look at his lips. He'd told her he loved kissing her and that he planned to kiss her again. But they needed to stick to just being friends.

"Well, you really must learn to have more patience," she said, as Mr. Peabody entered the room carrying a coffeepot. "I'm sure Mr. Peabody will agree that patience is one of life's most necessary skills."

Mr. Peabody exchanged another look with Zeke before

pouring the dark brew into her cup. "Today, I pressed the coffee just the way the French do."

Kate had no idea how the French pressed their coffee—and imagined an iron like the one she'd used at the laundry. She lifted her cup, breathed in the rich roasted scent, and then tasted a sip. "It's very intense and flavorful."

Mr. Peabody beamed at her compliment as he rounded the table and poured Zeke's coffee.

Zeke took a gulp before he set his cup aside. "I think I'm ready for the main course, Mr. Peabody."

Mr. Peabody's smile widened. "Very well, monsieur."

Once again, Zeke's face took on a pallor, and he shifted in his chair, wincing as he did so.

"You don't have to do this." She waved at the table and the dishes in front of them. "We can wait until you feel better."

"Nope, I want to do this today. Now." He glanced at the door and cleared his throat.

She picked up her coffee but then paused, waiting for him to say more. But he only reached for his cup and took a quick gulp.

Mr. Peabody reappeared, carrying a plate covered by a lid and grinning like a child with a secret.

Zeke sat up straighter.

She set her coffee down and waited as Mr. Peabody placed the covered plate in front of her. Apparently, he wanted to surprise her with one of his creations. "And what do you have for me first, Mr. Peabody?"

He held the lid in place. "Wait to look until I'm out of the room."

She paused, her arm half raised. "Would you like me to wait until you bring Zeke's plate?"

"No," he said, rushing into the hallway, his voice laced with excitement. "You go ahead."

Tentatively, she touched the lid, then she glanced toward the door. Mr. Peabody poked his head around the door frame, watching her.

Zeke picked up his spoon, twisted it, and replaced it with a clatter against his plate.

She smiled at Mr. Peabody's eagerness and removed the lid, expecting an artfully decorated croissant or some other beautifully arranged item. Instead, a strange lump of rock sat on the plate. She stared at it, trying to make sense of why Mr. Peabody was serving her a rock for breakfast.

She glanced up to find Zeke watching her expectantly, hopefully. And Mr. Peabody was still peeking in and waiting for her reaction.

"I—" She dropped her gaze back to the lump, noting the gold tint showing through the dark gray. "Should I eat it?"

Zeke burst out with a laugh.

She joined him, relieved that the strange tension was gone.

Mr. Peabody moved to stand in the doorway and leveled a stern look at Zeke, who cut off his laugh and attempted to smother his grin.

"Tell her it's gold," Mr. Peabody hissed.

seventeen

old? Kate's attention snapped to the rock. She'd imagined that gold was shiny and pretty and, well, gold-colored. But this was dull, odd-shaped, and mostly gray.

"Aye, it's gold," Zeke said with a note of pride. "Chipped out of the mother lode we recently discovered."

She picked it up, turned it over, and examined it. Thick bands of solid yellowish rock made up the entirety of the lump. "It's nice." *Nice* was an inadequate word to describe it, but she couldn't think of what else to say.

"It's worth thousands of pounds."

"Oh, my." She gingerly set it back on her plate.

"And I'm planning to use it to build a church here in Williamsville."

"A church?" Her pulse slammed to a halt, leaving a strange stillness in its place.

"Aye." Zeke grabbed his spoon and began twisting it again. "And once the church is built, I'll do everything I can to get a full-time minister here." His expression was vulnerable and hopeful all at once.

Her heartbeat stuttered. Did this mean he'd decided to make his peace with God?

As if seeing the question in her eyes—or perhaps the excitement in her expression—he stopped fiddling with his spoon. "This might not be exactly what you want, Kate. But this is the best I can do for now."

"I don't understand."

"I won't be turning my back on the Almighty anymore, but I can't make any promises beyond that." His words, along with the frankness of his gaze, told her this was a continuation of the conversation they'd had outside the tavern when she turned down his offer of courtship.

He was making an effort. She had to give him credit for that, didn't she? That was better than nothing at all. And if he was turning back around, surely it wouldn't take long for him to return to God all the way.

"That's good, Zeke." She tried to infuse optimism into her tone. "You're moving in the right direction."

"And that's good enough for you?"

She smiled. "Of course."

"Good enough to marry me if I ask you?"

Her fingers flew to her lips even as she sucked in a breath. His attention didn't waver from her face.

Even though Becca had admonished her to get engaged to Zeke today, she hadn't expected him to bring it up so soon. But maybe with all the awful rumors, he felt obligated to ask her.

"You don't have to rescue me from the rumors. They'll go away eventually." At least she hoped so.

"Maybe. Maybe not. It doesn't matter. Even if there weren't any rumors, I'd still want to marry you."

Her pulse sped. "You would?"

"Aye." Earnestness lined his face. "You're all I can think about, and all I want."

She tried to laugh. "That's because I'm the only woman here—"

"I'd still want you, even if I had the choice of a million others." He wasn't laughing. He wasn't even smiling.

Her racing thoughts slowed, and she tried to comprehend everything he'd just revealed. He hadn't told her he loved her, but he'd come close. Was it close enough? And what about his faith? Was that close enough, too?

"Please tell me you feel something for me too," Zeke whispered hoarsely.

"I do." She may as well be honest with him about her attraction.

"Then you'll marry me if I ask you?"

Her mind flashed back to Mum on that day her father had walked out the door. Mum's sobs echoed in their tiny apartment, until Kate curled up next to her on the bed and tried to comfort her.

Kate stroked her mum's hair, blond and long and pretty, so much like Kate's. After a little while, Mum turned and buried her face against Kate, her tears dampening Kate's bodice. "Don't do it, Kate," Mum said through wrenching sobs. "Don't ever get married. It's not worth the heartache."

Her mum had never gotten over her broken heart. Every day, she'd peered sadly down the street, waiting for Father to return. And every night, she'd crawled into her bed and cried silent sobs.

Kate slammed the door on her memories, forcing them to remain where they belonged—in her past. She was stronger and smarter than Mum and wouldn't make the same mistakes. She'd reminded herself of that the other times she'd gotten engaged, along with the admonishment not to let her mum's heartache stop her from experiencing love and marriage.

And Zeke—well, he wasn't like her father. Zeke had already sought his adventure and found it here in British Columbia. He had everything he wanted and wouldn't have any reason to leave.

She fingered the lump of gold on her plate. Maybe he hadn't made his peace yet with God, but he was getting closer, and that had to count.

Zeke watched her, waiting. From the doorway, Mr. Peabody waited too, his eyes wide, his hands clasped tightly together.

"Do you want to ask me?" she said, unable to keep the tremble from her voice.

"Aye."

"Okay."

"Okay?" Zeke repeated, not sure he'd heard her correctly. Had Kate just agreed to marry him if he asked her?

In the doorway, Mr. Peabody motioned at him. He jerked his head Kate's direction, mouthing the words, *Ask her.*

Zeke pushed to his feet with his crutch and grabbed the table to hold himself steady. Kate was up in an instant and at his side. "Careful." She slipped an arm around him to keep him from falling.

He wished he could get down on his knee and propose properly. But if he did that, with his luck, he'd end up stuck on the floor. Now, with her by his side holding him up, she was but a breath away, and he liked having her near.

"I've got you," she said gently.

"Aye," he whispered, sliding her around so she stood in front of him. "You've got me—heart, soul, and body."

At his declaration, she drew in a breath, one that emphasized her womanly curves and made him keenly aware of her body. She was exquisite, every beautiful inch, from her head to her toes.

"Will you do me the honor of becoming my wife?"

She caught her lower lip with her teeth and hesitated long enough to reveal insecurity. But just as quickly, she smiled and nodded. "I will."

Surprise and relief weakened him. "You will?"

Her arms tightened about him, lending him her support. "I want to marry you, Zeke," she whispered almost shyly.

Happiness spilled through him. He couldn't contain a grin. By the door, Mr. Peabody released a sigh.

Kate lifted her pretty face up to Zeke's, her smile tender and her eyes shining with wonder.

Desire welled, along with a host of emotions he couldn't

begin to name. He lowered his mouth to hers, needing to kiss her more than he needed to breathe. She responded the way she had the first time—meeting him and pressing into him with passion that made everything else around him fade to nothing.

As their lips meshed and as he tasted her, his hunger for her only increased. He sensed he'd never be satisfied with a few simple kisses and that he needed to be careful. And yet, she was intoxicating and took away his reasoning, until at last a voice broke through.

"We should set the wedding date." Mr. Peabody had remained as Zeke had asked him to do, to ensure that he didn't get carried away again.

Kate was the first to break the kiss, her breathing uneven, her cheeks flushed, her expression both shy and embarrassed. She buried her face into his chest as though to hide.

For several seconds, Zeke clung to her and tried to compose himself.

"The wedding date?" Mr. Peabody prompted.

"The day the minister arrives," Zeke replied.

"So soon?" Kate squirmed to loosen herself.

"The minister can't get here soon enough for me." He wobbled, unsteady on his crutch, enough that she grabbed him again. He held on to her more than he needed to, but he wasn't ready to lose his grasp of her just yet.

"With their circuit riding, it could take weeks, couldn't it?" Her voice was too hopeful.

"I'm gonna send out word that I'll reward the first minister to arrive."

"Good idea." Mr. Peabody clapped.

"Surely there's no need to rush," Kate said in the same breath.

Zeke leaned back enough to read her expression and caught a glimpse of the same uncertainty as earlier. Was she still thinking about his lack of faith? He'd hoped his willingness to build the church would reassure her. He wanted her to know he was trying to get past the hurts and difficulties that had once weighed him down. But he couldn't change everything overnight. This was a start, and she could accept that, couldn't she?

"I see no reason for the two of you to put off your wedding," Mr. Peabody said, coming to Zeke's rescue. "It was clear from the moment Zeke came home talking about you that you captured his heart in a way no other woman ever has."

"You talked about me?" The sunshine returned to her eyes, dispelling the shadows.

"Just a little."

"All the time." Mr. Peabody bestowed an endearing glance upon Kate. "And now I know why. You're exactly what he needs to make him a better man."

"Do I make you a better man?" she asked playfully.

He drew her closer. "Absolutely."

She rested her head against his shoulder. Had he convinced her? Something warned him he was falling short, and that if he didn't hurry up and marry her, he'd lose her. His mind raced to find any other reasons that would convince her.

203

"Our marriage will put an end to the danger and threats." He blurted the first thing that came to mind.

She lifted her face, her eyes filling with concern. "Do you think so?"

"Aye. If we're married, then you're no longer available. Whoever else wants you, will have to concede his loss and move on."

She studied his face as though testing his words.

He shoved aside the nagging voice telling him that playing upon her sympathetic nature wasn't the way to gain her cooperation. All that mattered was being together, and she simply needed a little extra nudging.

"You're right," she said. "If we're married, then your attacker won't have any reason to hurt you."

Except that with as rich as he was, and with as much gold as his mine was producing, he'd likely always have enemies. But he refrained from telling her the truth. After all, she was the real treasure and far more valuable than all the gold he'd found in his mine.

A fist closed about his chest and squeezed, reminding him he wasn't worthy and that he didn't deserve someone as sweet and kind and loving as Kate. But he was too selfish to let her go. He brushed his lips across her forehead and silently vowed to spend his life cherishing her, so she'd never have a reason to regret marrying him.

eighteen

Kate carried her painting as if it were a Rembrandt, carefully dodging men as she made her way down the boardwalk toward the general store.

She'd draped a shawl over the canvas in an attempt to hide it from Becca, and now as she walked, the lacey covering was falling off. It had started dragging on the planks coated in mud from the afternoon thunderstorms that had turned the street into a bog.

Kate tossed a glance over her shoulder toward the laundry and released a short breath. Even at the late hour, Becca was still too busy in the laundry to see Kate's departure. If her dear friend happened to look out the window and notice Kate leaving by herself, she would barge out, hands on her hips, and demand that Kate get back inside.

Kate lengthened her stride. She'd spent the past two days painting the landscape of Williamsville, including the laundry shop. She'd shown the painting to Zeke the previous evening when he'd come calling on her. When she explained it was her way of thanking Becca for their friendship, Zeke suggested she bring it to the store so Wendell could take measurements for a local carpenter to craft a frame.

Zeke wanted Wendell to measure several other sketches and paintings so they could hang them in *their* home, as Zeke now called it. "I want to fill each room with your pictures," he'd said earnestly. Ever since, she'd been mentally planning where to hang various paintings and drawings.

She hefted Becca's gift higher, trying to lift the shawl off the ground. Hopefully, Becca would be thrilled and surprised. It was the least she could do for her dear friend, especially after the past week of rising to Kate's defense against the rumors.

Of course, Zeke had done his best to curb the lewd comments and coarse joking, too. Though he hadn't admitted to his tactics, she'd heard from Becca that he'd threatened to cut off supplies for any man he discovered speaking ill of Kate. Even so, Becca had insisted that Kate remain out of the public eye for the week.

Mr. Chung had shooed Kate out of the laundry every time she attempted to help. Finally, Becca told her to take the week off and use the time to prepare for her wedding. Since Zeke had posted word of a substantial reward for the first reverend to arrive in Williamsville, Kate suspected she had only a few days left.

Every night while lying on her pallet in the shack, she wondered if it would be her final night sleeping on the ground alone, if the next night she'd lie on Zeke's bed next to him. She pictured him pulling her down onto his lap and kissing her again, only this time he wouldn't stop.

Yet every morning when she awoke and realized it might be the day the minister arrived, fear paralyzed her. She would remain unmoving, wondering what she was doing and questioning whether she'd made the right decision in agreeing to marry Zeke.

Her thoughts would waver all day and only calmed when Zeke came to call on her at the laundry, which he'd taken to doing every evening. After the fancy meal at his house the morning he'd proposed marriage, Mr. Peabody had insisted that the next time Kate stepped foot into the house, she'd do so as Zeke's wife.

Until then, Mr. Peabody had warned Zeke not to visit Kate unless they were strictly chaperoned. He also embarrassed Kate by ordering Zeke to keep his hands to himself and not to touch her again, not even to kiss her, until they were married.

Zeke had obeyed Mr. Peabody during his visits, making sure to stay a proper distance away from her while they sat on a blanket in the grassy knoll at the back of the laundry. They'd also had Becca's unwavering eye upon them as she watched through the open rear door of the building.

During the time together, talking and resting in the shade of the evening, Kate's worries had diminished, had almost seemed insignificant. Every time Zeke's beautiful green eyes caught hers or she glimpsed his dimples, her heart would tumble over itself, causing warmth to follow in its trail, convincing her she'd done the right thing in agreeing to marry him.

When dusk fell and she walked him to the street, the air between them would spark. From the way his gaze strayed to her mouth and the heat flaring in his eyes, she'd been able to tell he wanted to kiss her. And she couldn't deny she wanted to kiss him in return.

Long after he left, she dreamed about him and convinced herself that everything would be just fine.

"It will be fine," she whispered, even as her pulse pattered with the disquiet that had lingered from the moment she'd forced herself up that morning.

Her steps halted. The shawl dropped to the boardwalk, but she made no move to retrieve it. She had nothing to worry about today. Now that Zeke was gaining strength and learning how to use the crutch, he'd decided to spend the afternoon up at his mine, overseeing the excavations on the newly discovered vein. He warned her he'd be at the mine late tonight and likely wouldn't be able to visit until after dark.

He was busy, and there was no chance of them getting married tonight even if the minister arrived.

As soon as the relief sifted through her, guilt rushed in on its heels.

"Miss Millington," a voice beside her pulled her from her anxious thoughts. "May I be of assistance?"

A man bent down and picked up her shawl. When he stood, she took a rapid step back. Herbert Frank. Attired in a dusty hat and shirt along with muddy trousers and boots, she guessed he'd just finished working at his mine for the day.

While Wendell had never been able to link any of the attacks on Zeke back to Herbert, Kate hadn't been able to shake the feeling he was responsible.

"Looks like you dropped this." He held out the shawl, now streaked with mud. With slumped shoulders, he waited and watched her.

"Thank you, Mr. Frank." She hefted the painting with one arm and tried to free her other hand but couldn't manage it. "If you wouldn't mind draping it over my arm?"

"I'd be happy to carry it and assist you wherever you're going." He watched her hopefully.

"Thank you for your kind offer, Mr. Frank," she said as gently as she could. "But after all the attempts on Mr. Hart's life, I can't give you any more reason to think there could be anything between us."

"Please believe me when I tell you I had nothing to do with the explosion at Hart's mine." He glanced at some of the passersby who'd stopped to watch their interaction. "Ask any of these men, and they'll tell you the same thing."

"No one else has any motivation."

"I've been trying to figure out who's behind everything, too." Herbert placed the shawl over her arm. "I want to clear my name and prove I'm the same God-fearing man you met in Victoria."

She wanted to believe the best about him. Yet, how could she? "I'm sorry, Mr. Frank. There can never be anything more between us, and you really must put me out of your mind. Please."

The strength of her declaration surprised her. Before he

could talk her out of her resolution, she started forward, her heart quavering but her footsteps loud against the planks. In the ensuing silence, she thought maybe she'd finally convinced Herbert to let her go. But the next instant, he called after her. "The reverend arrived this afternoon."

She stumbled to a stop. The reverend was in town? That meant she'd have to marry Zeke tonight or tomorrow. Her stomach twisted into a knot. She most certainly couldn't get married tonight.

"You won't go through with it. You never marry any of the men you're engaged to."

She spun to face him. "You can't say that—"

"I feel partly sorry for Hart because I know the heartache you're about to cause him."

"Zeke's different," she said but couldn't keep the quaver from her voice.

Herbert laughed, but it was bitter and harsh. "You get close, are almost a bride, but then you are always too afraid to go through with it."

"I'm perfectly fine." But even as she said the words, the truth of Herbert's statement reverberated through her down to her bones. *Almost a bride. Too afraid to go through with it.*

"Miss Millington," said a man from behind. "Is Herb bothering you?"

Kate turned to see the redheaded, red-bearded man from the mining board—one of the men who'd witnessed her passionate kiss with Zeke on his bed. Heat rose into her cheeks. She could only imagine what he must think of her.

"I'm William Blake." He stepped closer, shifting his hardened gaze to Herbert. "Herb, haven't you done enough damage?"

"Stay out of this, Blake," Herbert said. "This isn't any of your business."

"I was just heading up to my mine but couldn't keep from noticing you bothering Miss Millington." Mr. Blake waved a hand to the men loitering nearby. "None of us want to see Hart come to any more harm. He's a good man trying to do a lot for this community."

"I'm well aware of that." Herbert scowled. "I was just offering to help Miss Millington since she was having trouble carrying everything."

"Why don't you go on your way and leave Miss Millington alone." Mr. Blake crossed his arms, and his coat stretched back far enough to reveal a revolver tucked into his belt.

Herbert glared at Mr. Blake before muttering something, spinning, and heading for the open doorway of the nearest pub. When he disappeared inside, Kate expelled a tight breath, but it did nothing to relieve the tension pulling her nerves taut.

Herbert's words had settled inside her and were inflating with each breath she took until she felt as though her chest might explode with the pressure. *You get close, are almost a bride, but then you are always too afraid to go through with it.*

"Are you alright, Miss Millington?"

Her hands shook. "I'm not sure."

"Here, now. Let me carry this for you." Mr. Blake reached for her painting, and Kate relinquished it before she dropped it into the mud.

Was Herbert right? She hadn't gone through with any of her previous engagements. What if she did the same thing with Zeke and broke his heart?

"Miss Millington?" Mr. Blake's voice broke through her mounting panic. "You look pale. Maybe we should find a place for you to sit down and rest."

"No." The word came out forcefully. "I need to see Zeke."

Mr. Blake glanced toward the end of the street. "He's still up at his mine—"

"I need to see him now." She followed Mr. Blake's gaze to the edge of town where the road narrowed into a wagon path through a smattering of pines. Although she'd never gone that direction, she knew the trail followed the river and led out to the hills where dozens of miners had claims.

If she walked out to the mine and talked with Zeke, she'd surely push her fears aside. Being with him and seeing him would remind her everything would work out fine. And she could tell him that even though the minister had arrived, she needed a little more time.

"Mr. Blake, would you please deposit the painting at Hart General Store? I must be on my way." Heedless of the men who'd stopped to watch her, she started down the boardwalk.

"You can't go out to the mines by yourself, Miss Millington." Mr. Blake matched his stride to hers, his footfalls heavy against the planks. "It's too dangerous out there for a lady like yourself."

"I'll be fine. Zeke will be there."

"Do you even know where his mine is?"

She faltered, and Mr. Blake grabbed her elbow to keep

her from tripping. "Will you take me to him?" Surely, her request wasn't too demanding, not if he was already going to his mine.

He was silent against the clattering of horses and wagons and the calls of the men coming and going. His attention was riveted on the foothills beyond town. Finally, he nodded. "I have to gather up a few things, and then I'll meet you outside of town in the gulch that leads to the north. Wait for me there."

"Oh, thank you, Mr. Blake." Relief whispered through her. Once she saw Zeke, her worries would go away. This relationship wasn't like any of the others, no matter what Herbert had said.

After seeing the painting to the store, she headed down the street. Most of the men averted their eyes, as if they were afraid to look at her the wrong way. Zeke's influence in town was clearly felt far and wide. His wealth had made him into a powerful man.

If Herbert was innocent as he claimed, perhaps Zeke had other enemies who resented him for his influence. Anyone she passed by might be his attacker, biding his time to strike again.

With a shake of her head, she dismissed the thought. She'd never been one to assume the worst about people, and she wouldn't start now. Nevertheless, she picked up her pace until Main Street tapered into a trail. Grooved wagon ruts filled with muddy rainwater formed a well-worn path. She followed the road toward the foothills as it gradually wound higher, until the town disappeared and the mountain peaks loomed taller above her.

At a fork in the gulch, she stopped to catch her breath and wait for Mr. Blake. To the south through the tree covering, smaller paths branched off leading to rock debris scattered along the hillside, the remnants of all the mining that had taken place over the past two years.

She lowered herself to a smooth boulder at the center of the fork and breathed in the mountain air laden with the scent of pine and damp earth. Ahead to the north, wispy clouds hovered above the peaks as if snagged there by the barren rocky ledges. Tints of rose and lavender streaked through the clouds. Against the cobalt sky made translucent from the setting sun to the west, the scene was worthy of a canvas.

Under normal circumstances, her fingers would have fidgeted, restless for her brushes. And her imagination wouldn't have been satisfied until she'd captured the landscape. The process of creating would have soothed her anxiety and brought a measure of peace.

But tonight as she waited, thoughts of the newly arrived reverend intruded and cast long shadows. The gloom settled over her, growing ever darker, until finally she glimpsed a man with red hair and a red beard approaching from the trail below. As he drew steadily nearer, doubts crowded in. Should she continue up to Zeke's mine? She certainly wouldn't call off her engagement. That's not why she wanted to see him.

No, she simply wanted to reassure herself she'd made the right choice in agreeing to marry him. All she needed was to look into his confident eyes and bask in the pleasure of his smile.

When Mr. Blake turned the path and started toward her, he tipped his hat in greeting but otherwise was almost somber. He apparently didn't approve of her seeking out Zeke. Perhaps after catching them together on Zeke's bed, Mr. Blake believed she had ulterior motives for visiting Zeke, perhaps plans for an illicit rendezvous.

"Thank you for helping me find Zeke," she said, as they started up the northern fork of the gulch. "I know this may seem unusual, but I need to talk to him. That's all."

"It's no trouble. I'm meeting with the foreman at my mine anyway."

"Then your mine is up this way, too?"

"On the claim right next to Zeke's."

"Oh, good. Well, I'm relieved I'm not inconveniencing you."

Mr. Blake responded with a nod but said nothing more as they climbed upward. With bulging packs slung across each shoulder, he led the way, his long steps even and confident and at home in the hills.

She was tempted to ask him more about himself and his family. From the little Zeke had told her about Mr. Blake, he'd left his wife and children behind in Wales and had been apart from them for at least two—if not three—years. Was he lonely? Did he miss his family? Or like her father, was he relieved to be away living his own life and having his own adventures?

During those first years after her father's absence, she'd

prayed every day that he'd realize how much he missed her and the rest of his family, that he'd come running home and scoop her up and tell her he'd never leave again.

But with the passing of time, she'd accepted he wasn't coming and hadn't loved her or Mum or her brothers enough to sacrifice to stay together. Wherever he was, he hadn't cared enough to write and invite them to be with him.

Zeke was different than her father, she reminded herself with each step farther up the mountain. And her marriage would be different than her parents'.

As the path followed a winding stream, the evidence of gold mining littered the bank—the remains of rockers, flumes, sluice boxes, pans, piles of pebbles, and blackened campfires.

"How much longer?" The evening shadows were deepening, turning the sky overhead into a dusky purple-blue.

"Not far now." Mr. Blake's gaze darted to the crevices and canyons as if he expected wild animals to jump out at them.

The path turned rockier and steeper, and Kate could only guess how hard the trek up into the mountains had been for Zeke with his crutch. He'd likely reached his mine tired and sore after his weeks of inactivity.

Would he be too tired to see her tonight?

She halted abruptly. What was she doing here? Why was she allowing Herbert's accusations to drive her? Maybe she ought to turn around.

"Just up around the bend." Mr. Blake paused and readjusted his sacks.

She glanced back down the gulch. The return climb would be easier. She'd be in town in no time.

But even as she debated, Mr. Blake started hiking again, and she pushed herself to follow. She couldn't stop now, especially after Mr. Blake had gone to the trouble of bringing her this far.

A few minutes later, they reached a level area that contained several buildings and the mouth of a mine. Surrounded by wooden beams, the entrance was marked with a crudely made sign with painted block letters that read *Hart Mine*. Rock debris covered the hill outside the entrance, forming a thick layer. Metal tracks led inside the mine, with wagon-like carts resting along the entrance, some still partially filled with rocks.

Mr. Blake lit one of the lanterns hanging by the opening before he ducked under the beams and started down a dark passageway that seemed to stretch on forever. Kate crept in after him, wishing for her own lantern as the darkness enfolded them. The temperature dropped the farther they walked, the chilled air almost as cold as the January air had been in Victoria when she'd first arrived on the bride ship over six months ago. After the exertion of the hike, however, the coolness soothed her flushed skin.

Ahead of her, Mr. Blake hunched low to prevent his head from bumping against the beams that seemed to be keeping the tunnel from collapsing on itself. After walking two dozen paces, the beams ended, and jagged rocks formed the ceiling. Kate hesitated, before she ducked lower so she wouldn't accidentally hit her head and suffer injury. She'd heard the tales of miners being maimed and severely injured. But she hadn't comprehended the severity of their working conditions.

Now she better understood Zeke's drive to establish a hospital in Williamsville, as well as his proposal to compensate workers injured on the job. He'd indicated that Mr. Blake and Mr. Putnam weren't as supportive of his plans and preferred not to get involved, other than funding a benefit dinner. Zeke complained that while the dinner was something, it wasn't enough. Now, after only a few minutes in the mine, she was inclined to agree with him.

As the tunnel slanted downward, it grew slick and muddy. She slipped on several occasions, catching herself by grabbing on to the rock walls that were damp with trickling water. When the path leveled out again, Mr. Blake's swinging lantern illuminated the thin layer of water covering the path.

"Do you know where to find Zeke?" She tiptoed forward, her voice echoing in the cavern.

"I imagine he's down a level."

Her shoes squished as the cold water seeped through the leather. "Is that far?" Just as she asked, they turned a corner and came upon an opening in the floor. Mr. Blake held up his lantern, showing a ladder descending into the deep hole cut through stone. Next to the ladder was a pulley she guessed was used to haul up stone and gold.

"This is as far as I go," he said.

She peeked over the edge. A glassy layer of ebony shimmered in the light at the bottom. More water. She stifled a shudder. "Zeke's down there?"

Mr. Blake nodded and cocked his head. "Listen and you'll hear the drill."

She stood motionless and strained to hear above her breathing. A steady distant thundering came from the hole. How had Zeke managed to climb down with his broken, plastered leg? Had he perhaps used the pulley?

She reached for the ladder.

"Are you sure you want to go down there?"

"Of course." She stepped onto the first rung, holding her skirts with one hand to keep her feet from tangling. "I've come this far. Why stop now?"

"You'll be in water ankle-deep."

She carefully moved down a step. "My shoes are already wet, so it won't matter now."

Mr. Blake steadied the ladder and held the lantern above her, so she could see her way down. It was longer than she'd realized, at least the length of several men. The narrow walls of the opening closed in around her, and she halted. Should she proceed?

"I'll be fine," she said, more to reassure herself than Mr. Blake.

"Follow the sounds, and you'll find the men."

She paused, clutching the rung, her fingers already stiff from the cold, damp air. "What about a lantern? How will I be able to see?"

"The glow from their flames will guide you."

She wanted to insist that Mr. Blake give her his lantern, but she guessed he needed it to find his way back to the mine entrance. When she lowered her feet into the water, she sucked in a breath from the frigidness. How did the miners work in such conditions all day?

"Go straight ahead," Mr. Blake called. "You'll find them soon enough."

The light down the tunnel drew her forward, as did the echo of voices. She splashed a dozen paces before she realized she hadn't said thank you to Mr. Blake. She turned, but the cavern behind her was black. Mr. Blake was gone and had taken his lantern with him.

The coldness seeping between her toes matched the coldness in her heart. Suddenly, she knew exactly why she'd come to the mine. Because deep inside she knew Herbert Frank was right—she was too afraid to go through with marrying Zeke. She had to break the engagement before she broke his heart. Hopefully, she wasn't too late.

nineteen

"Zeke! I'm sorry but I can't marry you!"

At the sound of Kate's voice echoing in the drift, Zeke straightened and nearly bumped his head on the granite above him. He had to be hearing things. Kate couldn't be here, down in the tunnel, could she?

He squinted in the direction of the shaft that led to the main drift. His foreman, Phil, and several other miners who'd stayed behind grew silent. When they parted, their lanterns highlighted Kate's beautiful face and form. She stood a dozen paces away, her expression etched with the same panicked look he'd seen the day she broke her engagement with Herb.

His pulse spurted with dread. "Kate, what are you doing here?" He started toward her, his crutch sticking in the sediment beneath the water and slowing him down.

"I can't marry you, Zeke," she said again, this time more firmly.

"Don't say that—"

"I'm sorry." She held out her hand to stop him from advancing, her eyes wide and frightened.

He froze. He didn't know what was going on, but it wasn't good. He glanced at his men who immediately dropped their gazes to their tools, all except Phil who caught Zeke's eye and cocked his head in the direction of the shaft.

Zeke nodded in return. "Looks like we're finished here, everyone. Head out and give me a moment."

Silently the men gathered the rest of their tools and belongings and shuffled past Kate. Phil halted several feet away, his gaze compassionate. "I'll wait for you yonder by the ladder."

Zeke swallowed hard, his mouth and throat dry. "Thank you."

As soon as the men disappeared down the tunnel, Zeke advanced another step toward Kate.

"I'm sorry, Zeke." Her eyes welled with tears. "I'm so sorry."

"What happened?"

"I hoped being near you again would help." Her voice rose a pitch and her breathing escalated. "But it only made me realize I don't want to hurt you."

"Now hold on." He drew nearer with caution, as one would to a wounded wild creature. "We'll work through this together."

"The reverend arrived today," she blurted the words as if they were a curse.

He hesitated. What should he say? Every day, he'd been waiting for word of the traveling minister's arrival. With each delay, his anxiety had mounted. Had a part of him known Kate would have second thoughts the longer they put off the wedding?

"Listen, Kate." He forced a calmness to his tone he didn't feel. "I know you've had some hesitations about me. But we're working through the issues, aren't we?" He'd been trying to have an open mind about God, had even asked Wendell to find him a Bible. But this wasn't something he could force, and Kate wouldn't want insincere faith.

She crossed her arms, tucking her fingers under her sleeves, but not before he noticed her shaking. "Mr. Frank stopped me on the street this evening and accused me of never going through with marrying any of the men I'm engaged to."

"That's because none of them have been the right man is all." He moved so he was standing only a hand's width away. "None have been me."

"He told me I wouldn't go through with marrying you either."

"You will."

"He said I get close to being a bride but then am always afraid to go through with it."

"You can't be listening to anything Herb says. He's just jealous."

She lifted her troubled brown eyes. "I think he's right." For several minutes she relayed all that had happened on the street—carrying Becca's picture, Herb stopping her, his accusations, along with her confusion. She shared about Blake coming to her rescue and guiding her up to the mine.

"We'll be fine, Kate," he whispered when she finished, touching a strand that had come loose from her plait.

"I'm afraid."

In the quiet of the tunnel, the plopping of the runoff echoed loudly. "You're just nervous. Aren't all brides?"

She chewed at her bottom lip. "Maybe. Except for Zoe."

"Don't compare yourself with my sister." He stroked Kate's hair. "She's too daring for her own good."

Kate's lips rose in the hint of a smile, one that started to untangle the knot inside him.

"You've got nothing to worry about." He still had a long way to go in easing her worries and convincing her to go through with their wedding, but he was making a start. "I promise I'm different."

"That's what I told Mr. Frank."

Did he dare hold her? Gently he touched her shoulder. When she didn't pull back, he slid his arm around her and drew her closer. She came to him without a moment of hesitation.

He released a tense breath and then settled his chin on top of her head, holding his crutch in one arm and gripping her as tightly as he could with the other. She rested against him for several long minutes before she pulled back and gazed around curiously.

"I've never been down in a mine before. Where is the gold?"

He tried to shove aside his anxiety as he showed her the new vein and explained how they extracted the gold. She was full of questions, and he hoped that meant she'd forgotten all about her encounter with Herb. But even as he told her about how the rock was transported above the surface to the mill, where a machine known as a crusher would grind the ore to separate the gold from the granite, he couldn't shake his fears.

As he leaned past her to point out another smaller vein of gold, with his hunched head and stooped shoulders, his face brushed against hers at the perfect angle for kissing her. The softness of her cheek and the tickle of her hair beckoned him, and his lingering anxiety prodded him. Maybe if he kissed her, he could convince her the best way he knew how that they belonged together. He tilted and leaned in, his mouth hovering just above hers.

Her eyes widened, and she sucked in a breath.

He brushed his lips against hers, letting her feel the heat of his desire before pulling back and touching foreheads, then noses.

Her breathing turned shallow, assuring him her desire was still as strong and alive as his. He'd just needed to remind her of it.

While the cold, watery depths of his mine wasn't the ideal place to share a moment of intimacy, somehow the darkness and privacy of the tunnel seemed to give him the permission he'd denied himself all week. 'Course he'd promised Mr. Peabody and himself he wouldn't touch her again until they were married.

But here, now, in the darkness, alone with the realization the reverend was waiting to marry them tonight and only her fears to hinder them, he pushed aside all reason. He slid his hand to the back of her neck and guided her mouth to his. He teased her again with almost-kisses.

When she released a breathy gasp, he gave in and let his mouth mesh with hers. Desire welled inside his chest. How had he ever lived without Kate? How could he ever go on without her? He needed her, needed her kisses, needed her life more than he needed his own.

"Zeke." She broke away.

He didn't know what she wanted to tell him, but he didn't want to chance any more protest. He cupped her face, letting his crutch fall into the water. And he let himself say the words that had been building, words that scared him. "I love you, Kate."

Her breath hitched, but he didn't give her the chance to respond. He kissed her again, this time going deeper. Maybe knowing of his love would frighten her even more, but now that the words were out, he couldn't take them back, didn't want to take them back.

Instead of pulling away, she lifted her hands to his face. Her fingers splayed across his cheeks, and she pressed closer.

He lost himself in their kissing, in her, and in their passion. At a low rumble in the walls, he paused. Crumbling pebbles and dust sifted onto his head. A second later, the roar and crash of stone came from down the tunnel near the shaft.

He broke away from Kate and tried to make sense of what was happening. He hadn't ordered blasting anywhere in the mine tonight, as he sometimes did to create new drifts or shafts. Even if he had, Phil would have made sure everyone was out before detonating the fuse. He always did in order to give rocks and dust time to settle before the men returned in the morning to clear out the rubble.

Kate lifted her arms above her head to shield herself. He swept her against his chest and sheltered her in the curve of his body. His lantern swayed, and he grabbed it to keep it from falling off the outcropping and into the water.

He huddled above Kate and held her as pebbles rained down. When finally the rumbling ceased, he straightened and held up the lantern, assessing her. "You okay?"

"Just frightened. That's all." She rubbed her arms, glancing around the tunnel with wide eyes. "For a minute I thought the tunnel was collapsing on top of us."

He took a step but almost fell, realizing too late his crutch was in the water. He bit back a frustrated curse. Already seeing his dilemma, Kate was bending and plunging her hand into the water, feeling around. A second later, she produced the crutch.

He handed her the lantern and took the carved stick. At the crumbling of more rocks down by the shaft, fear swelled inside Zeke's chest and nearly cut off his air.

"Phil, you there?" He hobbled forward.

Kate followed closely behind. The going was slow, as it had been when he'd slogged his way down the drift earlier.

At the sound of a moan, he tried to pick up his pace, relieved Phil was alive, hopefully not injured too badly. His mind raced ahead with all the possibilities of what might have happened. A gas leak could have caused an explosion. Or maybe the pressure of the recent rainwater had caused a cave-in up in the main drift.

As the lantern light fell upon the beginning of the tunnel, Zeke's heart plunged hard. Rocks of all shapes and sizes littered the tunnel floor along with a broken ladder and the remains of the windlass. The shaft opening was completely blocked, large boulders and rocks having wedged inside as they fell from the drift above.

Worse, Phil was sprawled out, holding his head, blood oozing between his fingers. If all the rocks had fallen, he would have been crushed and killed. But thankfully, he'd been spared.

With crumbling stones continuing to fall and the possibility of the large ones dropping at any moment, a fresh sense of urgency propelled Zeke. He had to get Phil away from further danger.

"Oh dear." Kate brushed past Zeke and veered toward Phil.

He grabbed her arm. "Stay back, Kate. Let me pull him loose."

Only then did she seem to see the seriousness of their predicament.

Zeke tried to hurry his steps despite the crutch, one eye on the rubble above and the other upon Phil.

"Be careful." Her voice was wobbly.

"Aye, I will." The more he evaluated their situation, the more dread settled over him. From what he could tell, they were trapped in the drift with no way out. But he refused to worry Kate. Not yet.

Instead, for the first time in over three years, his thoughts shifted heavenward. *God help me.* The plea came out before he could think about it.

"Phil?" he called as he reached his foreman.

Phil groaned and moved his head but was only half-conscious.

Zeke surveyed the debris, then he tossed aside his crutch, grabbed Phil under his arms, and hauled him backward. The pain of the pressure on Zeke's broken leg nearly made him crumple. But he gritted his teeth and heaved.

As soon as he was out from underneath the shaft, Kate was at his side and took hold of one of Phil's arms so that together they managed to slide him a safe distance away. Once Phil was propped against the tunnel wall, Kate checked his wounds.

With her attention fixed upon doctoring Phil, Zeke braced himself against the wall and closed his eyes. The throbbing in his leg moved throughout his body, weakening him and causing him to slide down.

He didn't want to get wetter than he already was, especially not his cast. With the temperature in the tunnel hovering around forty degrees, being wet would only add to the misery. He lifted his thoughts heavenward again. *God help me. Not for my sake but so I can help Kate and Phil survive.*

Fact was, Zeke didn't deserve any help from the Almighty. After the misery and death he'd caused the mill workers on the day of the fire, God would be justified in ignoring him and letting him suffer.

I'll suffer and willingly die. But please spare these two, es-

pecially Kate. She's innocent and beautiful and has so much life ahead of her.

"He's got several deep lacerations." Kate's prognosis drew Zeke back to the direness of their predicament. "I'll try to staunch the bleeding until help arrives."

Help arrives? He could only hope his workers hadn't been too far from the mine to hear the explosion. Even if they'd heard the rumble and saw the cloud of dust rising from the entrance, they might not think anything of it, assuming he and Phil had planned a blast after they left. And when the night guards arrived in a little bit, they wouldn't think to check this far back.

The frightening truth was that the three of them might be stuck in the drift all night until the first miners arrived in the morning and discovered the cave-in. Even then, depending on how much debris littered the upper drift, it could take hours of digging and chipping to clear away the rubble before reaching the shaft.

Zeke glanced down the tunnel. The new drift wasn't long. How much time did they have before they used up the oxygen and had nothing left? Even if they had enough breathable air to sustain them, how would Kate survive the cold for hours, especially having wet feet?

He couldn't wait around to find out, had to do something now. But what?

Turning his attention to the entrance, he surveyed the jagged pieces of rock that had already fallen. Maybe he could force the rest of the rocks out of the shaft. By standing close and poking at them, he'd put himself directly into danger. He might get caught in an avalanche of granite and end up like Phil or worse. But if he could work the rocks loose and they dropped from the shaft, he'd be able to clear the way out. At the very least, additional oxygen would flow down into the tunnel.

Zeke crawled forward and grabbed his crutch from where it had wedged between several fallen rocks. Then he pushed himself up, trying to ignore the fire shooting through his leg.

"Can you help me rip my petticoat?" Kate probed Phil's scalp. "The hem is wet but higher is dry and clean."

He was tempted to tell her Phil's injuries were the least of their concerns. But at the earnestness of her expression, he nodded. Helping Phil would occupy her for a while and keep her from figuring out how grim their situation was.

She lifted her skirt to reveal her petticoat. Under other circumstances, he would have marveled at the sight of her ankles and slender calves. But now, all he could think about was how wet and cold her feet already were and how he needed to find a way to dry them and keep her warm.

He helped her rip several strips. Once she was busy bandaging Phil, he limped toward the shaft. The ladder had snapped in two, and half of it was wedged along the side of the tunnel. He hoisted it, and then before he could talk himself out of acting, he shoved the ladder against the rocks stuck in the shaft.

"Zeke! Don't!" Kate called, apparently paying more attention to him than he'd realized.

He thrust the ladder again harder. This time a rumbling was followed by a sprinkling of dust and dirt. In an instant, she was at his side, yanking him back. Already unsteady, he stumbled, his momentum propelling them both away from a new shower of debris.

For endless seconds, they huddled together against the tunnel wall, waiting for the downpour to cease. When only a trickle of dust remained, he started to move, but Kate slapped her hands against his chest, forcing him to remain against the wall. "What do you think you're doing? Trying to get yourself killed?"

"I'm trying to find a way to get us out of here."

"You won't get out if you're buried under the rubble."

"I have to try something."

"Don't you dare try that again, Zeke Hart." Her eyes flashed, making her more beautiful than he'd ever seen her. She was near enough he could feel the warmth of her breath. He had a sudden urge to wrap her in his arms and kiss her until they were both senseless.

What if they only had hours left? Why not spend their last moments in each other's arms?

He shook off the urge, frustration swelling. He broke away from her and staggered toward the other side of the tunnel. "I've made plenty of mistakes in my life." He spun around and faced her. "But I won't cower away this time. I'm gonna do what I have to do in order to save you."

"I won't let you kill yourself in the process." Her voice rang with anger.

From where Phil sat propped up against the wall, he released a low groan, as if agreeing with Kate.

"If I die, maybe I can finally make up for all the lives I cost others." As soon as the words were out, he wished he could take them back. He didn't like to talk about what had happened in Manchester at the mill. He'd worked to keep his memories locked away. And most of the time, they stayed well out of sight.

From the softening of her expression, he could see that she knew what he was referring to. "I know everything that happened that day, Zeke. And you weren't to blame for any of it."

Zoe had already told him the same thing when he'd visited with her earlier in the summer. He hadn't believed Zoe then any more than he believed Kate now. Neither of them would be able to understand that even if he hadn't been the one to light the fire that killed the workers, his careless actions had been the impetus behind the crime. If not for him, all those people would still be alive and with their loved ones.

Kate waded across the tunnel and stood in front of him. "We all make mistakes. For a while, those mistakes might hurt others and us. But we can find healing, if we seek after it."

"Healing?"

"Like your leg. If you'd done nothing after the break, your leg may never have healed—at least properly. But with time and the right care, someday it will be as good as new, or nearly so. The same is true of our inner wounds. If we ignore them, they'll fester. But with time and the right doctoring, eventually they'll heal too."

He studied her face, as sweet and sincere as always. "You've never made mistakes the same way I have."

She ducked her gaze. "I've hurt people too, Zeke."

"Can't imagine how."

"Like Mr. Frank." A note of distress echoed in her voice. "And the other men I was engaged to marry. I hurt them all by making promises and then breaking them."

Like she'd almost done with him and still could do. "Hey." He gentled his tone. "If I have inner wounds that are festering, maybe you do too."

She stuck her hand in her pocket and fidgeted for a moment. "You might be right."

He waited for her to expound, but she withdrew her hand and held a dirty, frayed piece of cloth. On closer examination, he could see it was an old ribbon. "I'm guessing one of your previous suitors gave it to you."

She twisted it between her fingers. "No, my father did."

In the far corners of Zeke's mind, he had a faint image of her father, a tall and handsome man, full of life and energy, always joking and teasing and laughing. One day he'd been there and the next he was gone, changing Jeremiah from a fun-loving friend to a serious young man with the weight of his family's welfare resting on his shoulders.

Had Mr. Millington's leaving affected Kate too? Causing wounds no one could see?

"He tied it in my hair the day he left," she whispered.

"And he told me he was sorry he couldn't be everything my mum and I needed him to be."

"He was a fool for leaving."

Kate continued to stroke the worn ribbon. "Did you know he didn't share my mum's faith?" When she lifted her eyes, his heart ceased beating. He knew then what he'd been trying to deny all along. Kate needed a better man than him—a man who was following the Almighty and His ways with all his heart. Not someone who was trying to appease her with spiritual platitudes and promises of a church.

"Maybe because of the way he left," she continued softly, "I get scared of being left again. Or maybe I don't want to end up like my mum."

"That makes sense." Pain stabbed his chest at the realization he wasn't the godly man she needed. He wanted to be that man. But he also couldn't—wouldn't—fake his faith to have her. He'd never had much of an example with his own father. Maybe his father hadn't left the same way hers had, but he'd been absent in all the ways that mattered. Zeke didn't want to be like that, like either of those men—her father or his. But he'd already run away once. What would stop him from doing it again?

As much as he wanted to marry Kate and make her his, he couldn't put her in a situation where she'd always be wondering if she married someone like her father.

"I guess that's why I only get so far in my relationships," she said. "I hadn't thought of it before, but maybe I have inner wounds that need healing too."

The ache in his core spread to his limbs. As she studied

his face and waited for his response, he was afraid she'd see his resolution. He reached for her, and did the cowardly thing by wrapping her into an embrace so she wouldn't read the truth.

He'd been selfish to convince her to marry him, had only been thinking of himself and what he needed. Now, no matter that it might kill him, he had to let her go so she could find a man who was worthy of her.

But first, he had to find a way to free her from the mine. Or nothing else would matter because they'd all be dead.

twenty

_K_ate shuddered, the damp cold of the tunnel penetrating deep and waking her. Zeke's arms tightened around her, his body bringing her some warmth but not quite enough.

"How's Phil?" She wiggled her toes, which were frigid but dry and wrapped in Zeke's coat after he'd made her take off her wet shoes and stockings.

"He's still unconscious." Zeke's voice rumbled near her ear in the darkness.

Hours ago, they'd positioned several of the biggest rocks together in order to move Phil out of the water and give him something to lean against. While they couldn't do anything about his wet trousers, at least his feet were mostly dry since he'd been wearing his waterproof mining boots.

She'd stopped the blood flow of two deep lacerations on Phil's head and bandaged them as best she could. She'd cleaned a handful of smaller cuts, but the bruising and swelling on the left side of his head was most worrisome.

"Maybe I should light the lantern and check on him again." She tried sitting forward, but Zeke held her in place.

"I will in a few minutes."

Light-headed and weak, she settled back into the curve of his body. Similar to what they'd done with Phil, they'd hauled rocks until they formed a pile, which allowed them a dry place to sit out of the water where his cast could stay as dry as possible under the circumstances. Zeke had leaned against the damp wall and pulled her down in front of him, insisting on keeping her dry and warm.

Though the rocks were uncomfortable beneath her and she'd grown colder with each passing hour, she didn't complain. She was dryer and warmer than Zeke who was sacrificing for her comfort.

Amidst her protests, Zeke had made several more attempts at knocking the debris from the shaft in order to clear it. While small stones and dust had filtered down, the largest of the avalanche remained stuck, jagged pieces wedged too tightly for any one human to move on his own.

Finally, Zeke had given up heaving against the rocks, his shoulders slumped in defeat and his face taut with the pain his exertion had cost him. Though the stab wound was healing and the burns on his back had scabbed over, the doctor had indicated Zeke needed to be in the cast for several more weeks. She had no doubt he was exhausted.

She shivered, and Zeke immediately rubbed her arms,

causing friction that brought some warmth back to her skin. He was so kind.

And he loved her.

She hadn't wanted to think of his declaration when they'd been kissing, had simply given herself over to the passion that so easily flared between them. But now, hours later, she relived his soul-stirring kisses along with his bold words. Though he hadn't spoken of love again, she'd felt his love in every effort he made to protect her.

Was it possible she could put her fears to rest? She'd admonished Zeke to give himself a chance to heal from his past mistakes and hurts. Didn't she need to do the same? Was it time to push her father's rejection behind her and move on?

Zeke rubbed her arms and hands a moment longer and then moved up to her shoulders before he enveloped her, wrapping her against him. She snuggled in, and even though she was stiff and uncomfortable and tired, she knew she was exactly where she wanted to be. In his arms.

The whisper of *I love you* hovered at the tip of her tongue. She wanted to tell him how she felt in return. He was as handsome and charming as he'd always been while growing up, but now even more so. In addition, he was generous with everyone who worked for him, cared about the community, and was a man of integrity among his peers. He was self-disciplined and worked hard, and yet he also had a relaxed and playful side to him. He would be a good provider. She'd never have to worry about being in want ever again.

The truth was, he was everything she could ever dream of

having in a husband. Except for one thing—he didn't share her views on God.

Once again, she told herself it didn't matter. He was searching and would hopefully find the Lord. But as she justified her choice, the steady tap of his heartbeat resounded in her ear, reminding her of the wounds deep inside him.

Was it possible he might use her and their relationship to cover over his past? Maybe loving her eased his aches and made him forget about his mistakes instead of taking them to the only One who could truly heal and restore wholeness.

Weariness tugged at her, towing her back into the world of sleep. She tightened her hold on Zeke, not wanting to let him go. But even as she tried to keep her grip, a sharp sense of God's truth prodded her to release him in order to give him the chance he needed to turn his heart back to the Giver of Life.

Flames blazed into the air, and Zeke fought through them, scorching his flesh. Kate was on the other side, and he had to save her before the fire consumed her.

Kate! Hold on. I'm coming to rescue you!

"Zeke?"

Cold fingers against his own startled him awake. His eyes flew open to blackness instead of burning light. For a moment, he couldn't focus, couldn't get his thoughts to cooperate to tell him where he was and what was happening.

"Zeke?" came the groggy voice again. Kate.

Iciness hit him harder than a Cariboo winter storm. He

was trapped in his mine. Had been for hours. The carbon dioxide levels in the tunnel were increasing, and he hadn't found a way to save Kate.

"I need to check on Phil," she said.

"I'll do it. Then you don't have to get wet."

She was too tired to protest, which wasn't a good sign. Earlier she'd complained of dizziness along with difficulty concentrating, further signs their oxygen levels were diminishing.

He carefully set her aside, and without his body to keep her warm, she started shivering. He fumbled for a match from the small bag of supplies Phil had brought down with him for emergencies. Zeke's fingers were stiff from cold and refused to move as quickly as he wanted. By the time he lit the lantern, his frustration had escalated making him want to curse and yell.

But yell at whom?

Last time he'd been in so desperate a situation he'd cursed and yelled at God, as though somehow the Almighty was to blame for the problems. But God wasn't responsible for the fire that had killed the Manchester mill workers any more than He was for the mine cave-in.

The truth was, they lived in a broken world tainted by sin, sickness, and the very devil himself. With such vice running rampant, horrible things happened. That's all there was to it. No doubt they needed to do their part to stop the atrocities. But sometimes, even after doing everything right, bad things still affected them.

He held the lantern up to assess Kate first. Her hair was

mussed and her face smudged. But she attempted a smile through her quivering lips.

If only she hadn't come down to the mine. If only just he and Phil had been trapped.

Dragging his casted leg, he started toward Phil. Something about Kate's story in coming to the mine didn't add up and had been nagging him. He hadn't been able to figure it out except that last evening's explosion had felt similar in size and magnitude to the previous detonation that had nearly killed him.

What if the cave-in hadn't been an accident? Had his attacker learned he'd be at the mine and planned the explosion, aiming to kill him but making it appear like a mishap? Maybe the person had been waiting for most of the miners to clear out, so he didn't hurt too many innocent men.

Zeke shook his head to clear the fog. "Phil? Wake up, Phil."

He drew alongside the prostrate form. Phil's eyes were wide open. From the blankness of his stare and his motionless form, a fist of grief punched Zeke in his gut. Phil was dead. How would he tell Kate?

Before he could figure out a way, Phil blinked, then shifted his gaze to stare up at Zeke. "Blake."

Relief rushed through Zeke. His foreman was still living and breathing. But apparently the concussion had knocked the wits out of Phil if he was confusing him with redheaded Blake. Either that or his eyesight hadn't come back. "Phil, it's me. Zeke."

Phil stared at him for a few more seconds, then blinked again. "Aye, I know who you are."

"Good. How are you feeling?"

"Like I got hit with two tons of rock."

"That's because you did."

Phil lifted a hand to the side of his face that was swollen and black and blue. He gingerly touched it before fingering the bandage on his head. "Then your woman is safe?"

"Aye. She doctored you up as best she could."

"Try not to move too much," came Kate's weak voice from nearby.

Phil shifted his head and winced. "Don't think I'd be going anywhere even if I could."

"Hang in there." Zeke tried to infuse his voice with confidence for Kate's sake. "I have a feeling we'll be out of here in no time now."

Zeke didn't want to meet Phil's gaze and disappoint him with the truth of their dire predicament. But at his foreman's steady stare, Zeke finally looked him in the eyes.

"How long have we been trapped?" Phil asked grimly.

"Twelve hours, maybe sixteen."

"Then they're still moving rubble from the main drift to get at our shaft?"

"That's what I'm thinking."

"So, it could be hours, maybe even—"

Zeke cut Phil off with a curt nod toward Kate, and they both fell silent.

"I hope Mr. Blake and all the other miners made it out

before the explosion," Kate said. "I'd hate to learn that anyone else was hurt."

"Blake." Phil started to push himself up but grimaced and reclined again.

"What about Blake?" Zeke had been surprised to learn of Blake's role in delivering Kate to the mine. Blake rarely interacted with anyone in town, much less offered to help.

"I saw Blake in the mine," Phil said.

"Aye. He walked Kate out from town."

"No, I saw someone above the shaft just a few minutes before the explosion. I didn't think anything of it, just figured one of the men had come back for something. But now I realize I saw William Blake."

"Maybe Blake left something behind."

"Or maybe he set off the explosion."

"Now hold on." Zeke's mind raced to piece together what had happened. "Why would Blake want to harm me? He's got his own mine and is doing just fine for himself."

"He's a decent fellow," Phil added. "You're right. Most likely he left something behind."

They were quiet for a moment.

"What if Mr. Frank caused the explosion?" Kate interjected, still shivering and hugging her arms to her chest. "Maybe after our confrontation on the street, he was angry with me again and followed us up to the mine."

Zeke hadn't been able to convince himself of Herb's guilt with the last explosion. From everything Zeke knew, Herb was usually easygoing and more reactionary than calculated. And this attack and the last were too well orchestrated.

"There's no way he'd have gotten the supplies together so fast. And besides, one of the men leaving the mine would have seen him coming in and stopped him."

"Aye, that they would have," Phil said. "And they would have come a-runnin' to warn us."

A wave of dizziness assaulted Zeke, and he wavered against his crutch. At the same time, he fought against the desperation that closed in. If they didn't survive, it wouldn't matter if Herb or someone else was guilty. His priority wasn't solving the crime but surviving.

He offered Phil sips of water from the canteen, helped him get more comfortable, then returned to Kate. After extinguishing the lantern, he pulled Kate into his arms.

Darkness settled around him, and exhaustion made his eyelids heavy and his limbs lethargic. Someone wanted him dead. That much he knew. But exactly who and why eluded him.

twenty-one

*G*od help! Keep her alive. Please just keep her alive.

Zeke brushed his fingers across Kate's cheek and then her mouth. The warmth of her breathing told him she wasn't dead yet. But for the past hour or more, his gentle shaking hadn't woken her. Likewise, Phil hadn't answered any questions, and Zeke hadn't been able to muster the energy to lift himself up and go to his foreman.

During the past hours, he lost track of how long they'd been trapped. He didn't know if hours or days passed. He'd used the last of the oil in the lantern, and he was saving the remaining few sips in the canteen for Kate. But the last time he attempted to get her to drink, she didn't respond, and the precious drops dribbled down her chin.

Though he wavered on the brink of unconsciousness himself, he'd clung tenaciously to wakefulness by reciting every Scripture verse Mr. Lightness had required them to memorize during his years at school. Psalm 23 came back to him quicker than others, especially the verse that spoke about death.

"Yea, though I walk through the valley of the shadow of death, I will fear no evil: for thou art with me; thy rod and thy staff they comfort me."

Every time he silently spoke the words, the truth became clearer. God *hadn't* promised to keep them out of the valleys or from experiencing tribulations, possibly even death. But during their walk through the valleys, He *had* promised to be with them and comfort them.

The more Zeke thought about it, the more he realized that during past hardships, he'd become disappointed—even angry—when God hadn't taken him out of them. Perhaps he'd expected the Almighty to lift him high above troubles and make his life smooth. When things had gotten more difficult instead of less, he'd easily given up on God.

At a rumble from somewhere above, Zeke stirred and tried to open his eyes. He could only hope that meant the rescue efforts were nearby. *Please, God. Please. For Kate's sake. Not mine.*

As he begged God, resignation settled within him. Even if the Almighty didn't take him out of this trouble and even if he faced death, Zeke wouldn't pull away from God and blame Him again. Nope, he'd seek out God's plans and wisdom. He had a long way to go on that path, but now that he'd started, he had to keep going.

And if he died today? Before the rescuers could get to him?

A quiet urgency nudged him. He'd been working toward

making his peace with God, and he couldn't put it off any longer. Whether he lived or died, he had to get on his knees and repent before the Almighty.

He sat forward, but the movement sent needles through his leg. For a second, blackness hovered over his consciousness, but he held on until he was breathing again, even though each intake was shallow.

So much for kneeling. That wasn't important anyway. God would hear his confession no matter where he was or what posture he took.

I'm sorry, he silently prayed. *I strayed from You, went my own way, and did my own thing. But I don't want to do that anymore.*

Zoe had returned the pendant Mr. Lightness had given him the day he'd stood in front of the school and made his declaration to follow and love Christ. At the sight of the bronze circle engraved with a crucifix, he'd been tempted to toss it over a cliff. But he'd hung on to it and had instead tossed it into a drawer.

He vowed now if he made it out alive, he'd never push aside his faith again.

Kate shuddered, and he drew her closer. *God help her!* This sweet, beautiful woman meant more to him than anyone or anything. He'd gladly give up his own life if he could know she'd survive and be safe. If only there was some way to transfer the last of his energy and oxygen into her lungs.

But even as he attempted to think of a final effort to save her, his thoughts turned blurry and distant. And a roaring filled his ears.

Bright light stung Kate's closed eyelids. Was she in heaven? Her body seemed to be moving, almost floating in the light.

"Hang in there, my dearest." A gentle voice that sounded strangely like Mr. Peabody's spoke above her. "You'll be alright. I just know it."

Kate struggled to open her eyes but was too tired.

The light came once more, this time brighter. Warmth wrapped around her torso, her limbs, and even her feet so that somehow the cold had disappeared.

"I need more warm blankets," came Mr. Peabody's voice.

She dragged in a deep breath, and the process of simply breathing in and out revived her. She cracked open one eye and blinked against the sunlight streaming over her face.

"She's awake," Mr. Peabody called.

A shadow crossed Kate's face. "Miss Millington?"

Kate tried to pry her other eye open, but the brightness hurt, bringing tears to her eyes. But even without looking, she recognized the voice belonging to the doctor.

"Miss Millington. How are you feeling?"

She tried to formulate a response, but her tongue stuck to the roof of her mouth, swollen and dry.

"Stand back now, d'ye hear?" Another voice, this one feminine but testy, was at her side. "Miss Kate, think you can lift your head to drink?"

"Becca?" Kate managed.

"Mm-hmm. Who else gonna put up with you nonsense?" Tender hands slipped behind her neck, raising her, and a cool cup pressed against her lips. As the liquid spread into her mouth and down her throat, Kate drank greedily and would have kept going if Becca hadn't pulled away. "Little at a time now, Miss Kate."

With another deep breath, Kate pried both eyes open first to see Becca and then to find herself encircled by men of all shapes and sizes. The light was too intense, and she had to quickly close her eyes.

"Miss Millington, does anything pain you?" The doctor's voice was laced with worry.

She wiggled her fingers and toes. They were no longer rigid from the cold. And though her backside and muscles ached, nothing else hurt. She opened her eyes halfway and found them filling with tears again. "The light is too bright. Would you mind moving it away?"

"It's the sunlight," the doctor said. "After almost forty-eight hours of darkness, your eyes will need time to adjust."

Darkness. The mine. Being trapped. The memories rushed back. What had happened to Zeke? A cord of panic slithered around Kate's middle, and she attempted to push herself up. "Zeke and Phil? Are they okay? Where are they?"

Becca's hands upon her shoulders prevented her from jumping up altogether. "Don't you worry none. They got people tending them too."

"Then they're alive?"

"Yep," Becca answered. "Thank the good Lord."

"How did you get us out?" Kate asked.

The physician pressed his fingers against the pulse in her

neck. "Nearly every man in town has been working in shifts around the clock to clear away rubble."

"Really?" She glanced at the men standing nearby, their faces sweaty and dirty and tired. But they were all smiling, and she offered them a smile of gratitude in return. "I don't know how I can possibly thank everyone."

"No need," said one man to her left. "We're just happy you weren't buried under all the rocks."

"It was a massive cave-in," the doctor continued, "and would have taken much longer to clear away if not for the determination of these fine men."

Kate squinted. Through her watery vision, she gathered she was on the hillside outside the mine. "Zeke? How's his leg?"

Becca lifted the cup again and tipped it, so Kate had no choice but to take another drink. "He gonna need a cast on his other leg when I get through with him."

"He saved my life down there," Kate said, choking up. "If not for the way he kept me dry and warm, I would have frozen to death."

"If he hadn't invited you down, you wouldn't be in this here trouble in the first place." Becca's brows were drawn into a fierce scowl.

"He didn't invite me down." Kate tried to lift a hand to brush at the moisture in her eyes, but her hands were still cocooned in blankets.

Before Kate could find the words to defend Zeke further, the crowd around her was parting. "Stand aside," Mr. Peabody called, "and let us through."

The men reluctantly shifted, and she glimpsed Mr. Peabody guiding Zeke toward her, his arm around Zeke's waist propping him up. Zeke's face was smudged and his dark hair askew. His garments were dingy and damp, and his boots coated with mud. His green eyes searched wildly until they landed upon her.

At the sight of her, he broke away from Mr. Peabody and hobbled faster, scanning her blanketed body as though needing to reassure himself she was really there. Mr. Peabody hurried to keep up with him, scolding him worse than a mother hen.

"How is she, Doc?" The panic in Zeke's voice drew on Kate's compassion.

"I'm just fine, Zeke." She pushed up and let the blankets fall away. She would have stood and gone to him, but Becca's firm hold and the shake of her head stopped Kate.

Zeke stood above her. "Are you sure?"

"As soon as I have a bath and a meal, I'll be as good as new." She half-expected him to bring up their wedding and ask when she'd be ready to marry him.

Instead, he motioned toward the doctor. "If Kate doesn't need you, then you should tend to Phil. He's in bad shape."

The doctor retrieved his medical bag and started to weave through the men.

"And I'll have a crew make a stretcher to carry Kate back to my house. You can check on her there."

The doctor gave a curt nod.

"I can probably walk," Kate offered.

"The crew can carry her back to the laundry." Becca glared at Zeke.

"You can both stay at my house until Kate is recovered." Becca started to interrupt him, but he continued before she could say anything more. "I'll take a bed at the boarding-house."

Becca's response stalled, and she eyed Zeke warily.

"I didn't invite Kate down into the mine." His expression was firm, even sad, and trepidation whispered through Kate.

"Everyone know you did," Becca insisted.

Mr. Peabody shoved aside several miners and stood on his toes, peering over the crowd and waving at his grandson. "Wendell, you come over here and tell everyone what you've learned about the cave-in."

A second later, Zeke's assistant was standing beside his grandfather, his thin face red and perspiring, his gaze darting around the mine yard as though expecting someone to set off an explosion at any moment.

Kate grabbed Becca's hand.

"Don't you be worrying none. That Herbert Frank locked up for good this time."

"Then he's to blame again?" Kate asked.

"Several men saw him argue with you before you went up to the mine," Wendell interjected. "So when we learned of another explosion, he was naturally the suspect."

Zeke rubbed the back of his neck. "Do you have proof he followed her?"

Wendell shook his head. "Only Blake's word that he saw Herb following the two of them up to the mine."

"If Mr. Frank was a threat," Kate said, "then why didn't Mr. Blake warn us?"

"That's the same question I asked Blake," Wendell responded. "Especially when he told everyone he'd taken you up to the mine because Zeke wanted time alone with you."

"What?" Kate sat up, even against Becca's clucking and fussing. Once she'd climbed down into the tunnel, Zeke had sent his men away. Maybe he'd figured that was the only place they'd be able to spend any time without Becca's watchful gaze. Even though Kate's cheeks flamed, she met Zeke's gaze directly. "Is that true?"

"Nope! 'Course not!" He spat the denial as if such an accusation were an insult. "I never even considered it."

Mr. Peabody patted Zeke's arm. "I knew Zeke wouldn't do such a thing. After harming Kate's reputation once, he'd never risk hurting her again."

"Fact was, I promised I'd only visit Kate with a chaperone until we were married. And that's what I aimed to do."

From the sincerity of Zeke's tone, remorse swelled within Kate. She shouldn't question his motives. After all, she was the one who'd sought him out at the mine. If not for her, they wouldn't have ended up alone. In fact, if anyone was to blame for them being together in the compromising situation, she was.

Wendell cleared his throat while pushing his glasses up his nose. "When my grandfather insisted that Mr. Blake was lying, I realized it was possible I'd been looking for the suspect for the crimes in the wrong places. That perhaps the true culprit had planted clues in order to keep the attention off himself."

Zeke glanced around at the miners, his eyes narrowed with suspicion. "Then it's possible Herb was a decoy?"

"It's eighty percent possible."

"That means you've got solid evidence to convict the person who's really responsible for everything?" Zeke asked.

"Yes." Wendell's eyes were wide but guileless. "I searched the suspect's belongings and discovered a book with a missing page that matches the sheet used for the death threat. The handwriting on the note—while disguised—is still very much the same as the other handwriting samples I located from this person. In addition, the supplies used in both explosions also match the supplies that remain among the store of explosives at his mine."

"Who is it?" Kate couldn't hold in the question, her grip tightening within Becca's firm hold. "Is it Mr. Blake?"

"As I said," Wendell answered. "I'm eighty percent sure it's him."

Zeke limped closer to Wendell. "Herb's got motivation to eliminate me so he can have Kate. What's Blake's?"

"Your gold." Wendell responded without hesitation. "I looked into his ledgers, and the numbers show a steady decline in the output of his mine. It's possible he would have depleted his gold by the end of autumn."

Wendell rattled off figures that Kate couldn't understand but were clearly bad since the miners began to murmur among themselves.

"He pretended to be wealthy, but in reality, he was barely

excavating enough to pay his workers. My guess is that he believed if he could get rid of you, he'd be the first in line to acquire your mine since it bordered his. He could also make the case that as the first to arrive in Williamsville he deserved the right."

"Blake was the first in Williamsville?" Kate asked.

"The town is named after him," one of the other miners interjected. "William is his given name."

"So he's been trying to kill me," Zeke asked, "but shifting the blame to Herb?"

"That makes sense." Mr. Peabody brushed at the dust on Zeke's shirt. "The attacks didn't start until Kate arrived, probably because Blake realized he could plot Zeke's demise and pin the blame on her rejected fiancé."

Wendell cleared his throat again. "The trouble is that I'm still missing twenty percent of the evidence."

"It's certainly more evidence than we have to keep Herb locked away," someone countered.

Kate's eyes had finally adjusted, and the sun wasn't as bright as she'd first thought. The sky overhead was a swirl of rose and sienna and lavender against the blue of the fading evening. She shuddered at the realization of how long they'd been trapped.

Becca tugged the blanket back around her more securely and started to give instructions to several men standing nearby.

"I think we might actually have that twenty percent." Zeke's declaration cut Becca off.

"No." Wendell shook his head. "I've already done the calculations—"

"My foreman, Phil, can give you what you need. He stayed behind to lift me out with the windlass. Only minutes before the explosion he glanced up the shaft and saw Blake in the main drift."

Wendell nodded, his glasses slipping down his nose as he did so. "If Phil can give a testimony, then we'll have nearly one hundred percent of the verification we need to lock Blake away for good."

"Phil's still unconscious." Zeke peered past the men toward where the doctor was tending the foreman. "Even so, we gotta lock Blake up before he strikes again."

Zeke's pronouncement set the men into motion, and Kate reclined, closing her eyes and letting her body relax. Everything would be just fine now. Hopefully, Phil would recover. And hopefully, Blake was the real culprit. Once he was captured, they could all rest easier knowing they were safe. Life could go on without any more threats hanging above them.

But how exactly would life go on? As she tuned in to Zeke's voice issuing orders, an ache formed in the pit of her stomach. Her resolve from the time in the tunnel came rushing back. She couldn't marry Zeke—not because she was running away in fear, but because he needed to find his happiness in God first before he could truly be happy with her.

She didn't know how or when she'd tell him the news, except that she needed to do it soon.

twenty-two

Zeke stood in the hallway outside his bedroom door and combed his fingers through his hair. His heart thudded an ominous rhythm, one he knew wouldn't go away until he did what he needed to do.

He blew out a breath and then knocked on the door frame.

"Come in," Kate called so sweetly and eagerly that he hesitated. Maybe he could wait a couple more days to speak his piece. After all, they'd only been out of the mine for two days. She'd been abed most of it.

But the doctor had announced yesterday that she was recovered enough to get up for short periods. That meant she'd be walking around and back to normal soon. With the minister still in town, she'd be expecting him to push to get married and would wonder why he was stalling when he'd been so insistent before.

He stepped into the room. She was sitting up in bed. Her

fair hair was plaited, and the braid hung over her shoulder and down her chest. Her face had lost its pallor and was rosy. And her lips curved into an easy smile.

"Have you come today to finally kick me out of your bed?" Her pencil grew idle above the sketchbook spread out before her.

Under other circumstances, he might have joked with her. But the weight of the news he had to deliver was too heavy. In the process of setting her free, he was afraid initially he'd hurt her, especially now that he was aware of how deeply her father's leaving had affected her.

Yet the more time that passed since his desperate hours down in the mine, the more he was convicted he needed to let go of her. He had to take time to grow in his renewed commitment to the Almighty before he'd be ready to lead a wife and family. And while he'd argued with himself that he could grow in his faith even if he went through with marrying Kate, he always came back around to the same issue— he'd never know for sure if he'd chosen to follow God because of Kate or because he'd wanted it for himself.

At his lack of response to her teasing, her smile dimmed. "Is everything alright?"

"Aye. Still no sign of Blake anywhere in the area."

"Nowhere?"

"We've put out the word to the towns all around, but no one has seen him."

Kate shivered and adjusted the thin coverlet higher over her nightgown.

"Don't be worrying. I doubt he'll come back and try to

hurt me. I suspect that when he learned we'd been rescued and we were alive, he knew it was only a matter of time before the clues all led back to him."

"Then do you think he ran away?"

"With the way he cashed in on all his assets and cleaned out his gold, no doubt he hightailed it back to Wales and his family."

Zeke crossed to the bed. Should he call Mr. Peabody into the room to act as a chaperone while he visited with Kate? Becca had stayed with Kate the first day after the accident but then had returned to the laundry to help Lee.

'Course, the situation wasn't the same as it had been when he'd broken his leg. Kate wasn't incapacitated like he'd been and didn't need constant assistance. And besides, Mr. Peabody was having the time of his life pampering Kate. On his way in, Zeke had greeted the housekeeper in the garden where he was picking and arranging a fresh bouquet for her room.

Zeke stopped at the footboard. If he got any closer, he'd have a hard time resisting the urge to pull her into his arms. And if that happened, he wouldn't be able to say what he had to.

"How is Phil?" She closed her sketchbook, as though she didn't want him to see what she'd been drawing. "I hope he's doing better."

"Phil's a tough one. And Doc remains confident he'll pull through." Having been in his wet garments in the cold, damp tunnel for so long, Phil had come down with pneumonia. With his blood loss and concussion, he'd also been unconscious longer and was suffering from memory lapses. Good thing he hadn't forgotten about seeing Blake in the mine just before the accident and had been able to make a statement to that effect.

"I keep praying for him."

Zeke wanted to admit he'd prayed for Phil too. But his throat constricted around the words. He couldn't say it to Kate. Not yet. He hadn't told her about praying while they'd been trapped in the mine. He hadn't told her about repenting. And he hadn't told her he'd been talking to God every day since then.

He needed to know this was his conviction before he made it known to everyone else, especially to Kate.

"Kate . . ."

Her features tightened, as though she sensed he was bringing bad tidings.

"Kate, I need to talk to you—"

"Hello?" a woman called from the hallway. "Zeke? Are you home?"

He couldn't place the voice, couldn't imagine any other women in town except for Becca and Kate being in his home.

A moment later, a beautiful woman with green eyes and long dark hair appeared in the doorway.

"Zoe?" He blinked, afraid he was imagining her there.

Her anxious eyes took him in from his head down to his boots. "We got news you'd been in an accident with broken bones and burns, so we packed up and left the minute we heard. We got into town late last night, and I wanted to see you right away. I've been so worried, but Abe convinced me to wait until this morning."

"It's been a month, and I'm doing fine now."

"Are you sure?" She studied his plastered leg.

"Aye, I'm well on the mend." He guessed she hadn't heard he'd been trapped in the mine and almost died. He wouldn't trouble her with that news yet. Instead, he crossed to her and grabbed her into a hug. "How are you?"

"Getting bigger." She squeezed him tight before she pulled back and slid a hand over her abdomen, revealing a small swell. When he'd last seen Zoe in July, she shared the news of her pregnancy. Already having several adopted children and a newly opened orphanage down the Fraser River in Yale, Zoe would be busy.

Before Zeke could respond, a tall man holding an infant appeared in the doorway. He bounced a chubby-cheeked native child who cooed and clapped. At the sight of Zeke and Kate, her happy noises ceased, and she stuffed her thumb into her mouth and sucked on it.

"Pastor Abe." Zeke crossed the room and held out his hand toward his sister's husband.

"Good to see you all put together, Zeke," Abe said with a handshake. "The news we received wasn't good."

"Except the news that you're getting married." Zoe glanced at the bed. "We heard rumors you were rewarding the minister who could arrive first."

Zeke shifted, uncertain how to answer.

As Zoe studied Kate, her eyes widened. "Kate Millington? Whatever in the world are you doing here in Williamsville? Last time I saw you in Victoria, you had a whole swarm of suitors vying for your hand, and I thought for sure you'd marry one of them."

Kate smiled. "It's a long story."

Zoe rushed to the bed and wrapped Kate into a hug. "Why are you abed? I hope you're not ill."

"That's another long story," Kate replied. "But rest assured, I'm doing well, and the doctor promises I'll be out of bed soon."

"I'm glad to know Zeke's taking care of you. At least now I don't have to strangle him . . ." Zoe's gaze bounced from Kate to Zeke and then back. "Wait a minute. Was that why you needed a minister? Are the two of you . . .?"

"Married?" Kate filled in the pause.

Zoe's attention zeroed in on Zeke, making him suddenly uncomfortable. He knew how this appeared. Kate was in his bed in his house. "It's not what you think."

"No, we're not married," Kate said at the same time, her eyes revealing turmoil. Apparently, she sensed something had changed in him and his plans. He could only pray she'd give him the chance to explain himself and reassure her this had nothing to do with her and everything with him.

"Oh." Zoe's eyes narrowed. "So the minister request wasn't for the two of you?"

"It was," Kate admitted. "But that's an even longer story."

Zoe sat on the edge of the bed. "Sounds like I need to make myself comfortable so I can hear all these stories."

Zeke rubbed his hand over the back of his neck. How

could he even begin to summarize what had happened over the past weeks?

The child began to fuss. Rather than rising and rushing to the infant, Zoe clasped Kate's hands. "Zeke, would you mind taking Abe to the kitchen so he can feed Violet?"

Zeke hesitated, not sure if he wanted to leave Kate and Zoe alone. But at the gratefulness filling Kate's eyes as she squeezed Zoe's hands, he realized Kate needed a woman to talk to and that having Zoe here was probably the best thing for her. No matter the outcome, he needed to let her unburden herself.

If only he didn't dread the outcome.

twenty-three

Kate swiped at the tears that wouldn't stop flowing after she shared all the stories with Zoe. "So, what do you think I should do?"

Zoe's green eyes, so much like Zeke's, regarded her seriously. "Do you want to hear the truth?"

Kate brushed the dampness from her cheeks again. Did she want the truth no matter how difficult? Or did she want Zoe to tell her everything would be alright?

The men's voices wafted from the kitchen, and Kate guessed Zeke had given Pastor Abe the same details she'd just given to Zoe. At some point, Mr. Peabody had entered the kitchen, and from the higher pitch of his tone, she could tell he was talking to Violet, Abe and Zoe's adopted baby. The scent of his morning baking still filled the house, and if his pattern from the previous days held true, he'd soon deliver the delicacy to her with fresh coffee and a vase of flowers.

If she turned down Zeke's offer of marriage, she'd have to

give up living in his house and the delight of Mr. Peabody spoiling her. More than that, she'd disappoint Mr. Peabody, who thrived in her presence.

Worst of all, if she canceled her engagement, she'd lose the man she loved. Aye, she loved Zeke more than she had any other man. Her brush with death had shown her that, and she couldn't imagine her life without him.

Yet how could she join her soul to his when they didn't share the most fundamental and important of beliefs?

"What is the truth, Zoe? Please tell me."

Zoe squeezed her hand, her expression sympathetic. "The truth is that as much as I love my brother, I'm not sure he's stable enough for you. I'm afraid that until he makes peace with his past, he may always keep running. And I don't want you to end up like your mum, left behind by a restless soul."

Kate nodded. Zoe had been there when her father had left and had witnessed the devastation to her mum. During the voyage to British Columbia on the bride ship, they'd had long conversations about their parents' marriages. And they both vowed to do better.

But was that possible? Were they destined to make mistakes too, perhaps even the same ones?

"I love him," Kate whispered, her chest swelling with the pain of loving a man she knew she couldn't have.

Zoe didn't say anything but drew Kate into her arms and held her. Kate gave way to tears and let herself grieve the loss of everything that could have been. In turning down Zeke's proposal, she was giving up so much.

Finally, she pulled back. "Thank you, Zoe. You're a god-send." She attempted a smile.

Zoe smiled tenderly in return. "What will you do next? Will you continue to work in the laundry?"

"No, I can't." Over the past couple of days of lying in bed, she'd had too much time to think. As much as she loved Becca, she couldn't impose on her friend any longer. It wouldn't be long before Mr. Chung asked Becca to be his bride, and when he did, he'd want to move back into the shack.

Even if Kate found another place to live, Mr. Chung didn't want her in the laundry. And what other suitable work was there for a woman like her in Williamsville? She certainly didn't want to resume her courtship plans anytime soon, especially not to anyone besides Zeke.

"I think I'll need to return to Victoria," Kate admitted, her heart wrenching at the prospect of being so far from Zeke.

Zoe brushed a strand of Kate's hair back. "How would you feel about traveling with us to Yale and working in our new orphanage? We'd love the help."

Kate sat up straighter and drew in a final sniffle. "Really?"

"Really. The house is plenty big. You could have a room to yourself."

"That's not necessary—"

"Abe was just saying he's concerned about me having too much work, especially once I'm further along." Zoe placed a hand on her abdomen, her fingers splaying and revealing a beautiful wedding band with a jade jewel at the center.

Amidst the pain radiating through Kate's chest, a ray of hope broke through. Yale wasn't necessarily close to Williamsville, but it wasn't as far away as Victoria. Though she couldn't cling to the hope Zeke might one day be ready for her, she couldn't stop herself from praying for that anyway.

In the meantime, maybe she needed to focus on getting herself ready. Perhaps all along by seeking after relationships, she'd been trying to fill the void caused by her father's leaving. What if she needed to allow God to fill the void first? Maybe only in the healing could one truly find freedom from making the same mistakes as one's parents.

Whatever the case, she had to accept Zoe's offer. "I'll go."

"Good." Zoe leaned in and gave Kate another hug. "I think you're doing the right thing."

If only it didn't hurt so much.

Relaxing against the fence that surrounded Mr. Peabody's garden, Kate cuddled the sleeping child and pressed a kiss against her head. Kate had offered to watch Violet while Abe and Zoe were called away to visit an orphan girl in need of a home.

Kate hadn't realized how much energy the almost one-year-old had. Though Violet wasn't yet walking, she more than made up for it by crawling everywhere. Finally, the child had worn herself out and fallen asleep in Kate's arms.

The September afternoon was warm, but at least outside Kate could feel the mountain breeze better than she could indoors. Mr. Peabody had fussed about her leaving the house and had come to check on her a dozen times over the past hour.

His concern only heightened the dread of having to tell him about the decision she'd made yesterday when talking to Zoe.

"You're a natural with the babe," Zeke spoke softly. He leaned against the side of the house watching her, his crutch idle at his side. The brim of his hat hid his face in shadows, but there was no disguising his dark, good looks, and the sight of him never failed to make her heart patter faster.

Kate kissed Violet again to hide her face and keep Zeke from seeing her attraction. "It's easy to be a natural when a baby is asleep." From the corner of her eyes, she watched Zeke push away from the house and shuffle toward her. Would he ask to sit beside her and spend time with her as he'd done those evenings before they'd been trapped in the mine? Their conversations were among some of her favorite memories.

Heat stung her eyes, and she nuzzled Violet's cheek while she tried to compose herself.

He stopped several feet away, leaning on his crutch and looping his thumbs in his belt. "Listen, Kate. We need to talk."

Something in his tone and posture sent a shiver up her back. She'd sensed he wanted to share bad news the other morning when he'd come into the bedroom, and she'd been glad for Zoe and Abe's timely arrival, which had prevented him from saying anything.

She'd tried not to think of it since, although a tiny current of anxiety had zipped along her nerves whenever Zeke was around. Thankfully, with Zoe and Abe staying at the house, Zeke hadn't had the chance to be alone with her again.

Until now. "Aye, I need to talk to you too," she said, her heart racing with a strange need to get up and run away.

"Please, Kate—"

"I'm moving to Yale."

His head jerked up. "You are?"

"Aye. I'm leaving at the end of the week and going to work at the orphanage with Zoe and Abe."

He examined her face as if trying to make sense of her decision.

"It's for the best. Zoe needs the help, especially after her baby is born."

"Then Zoe is in agreement?"

"She invited me."

Zeke scrubbed his jaw, blew out a breath, and then stared off at the mountain peaks. Silence settled over them except for the high-pitched whistle of a broad-winged hawk swirling above the hill.

Was he upset? Had she hurt him? "I'm sorry, Zeke."

He continued to peer into the distance, his shoulders stiff and his jaw flexing.

She wished she could voice her inner turmoil and tell him this was just as hard for her, that she didn't want to do it, that she loved him. But she couldn't make herself say the words. "We both have things we need to work through."

"I know."

"You do?" She'd expected him to argue or try to convince

her to go through with the marriage, and his simple agreement took her by surprise.

"Aye. I realized it when we were trapped. I'm not the kind of man you need or deserve. And if I don't change, I'd end up hurting you the same way your father did."

So this was it. What he'd wanted to tell her.

"I'm not the kind of man you need or deserve." Her father had said almost the same thing the day he'd walked away.

She focused on Violet's sleeping face to hide the sudden burn at the backs of her eyes. Maybe Zeke believed walking away from her now would keep her from getting hurt later. But it was too late. She'd already fallen in love with him, and this rejection was piercing her fragile heart and shattering it.

"I want to change." Zeke's voice was hoarse with emotion. "But I have to make sure I'm not doing it for you."

She blinked back tears and prayed none of them would leak out. She didn't want him to know how much this parting hurt.

As she fought her inner battle, a long silence stretched between them.

"Say something," Zeke finally said, his tone anguished.

She swallowed past the lump in her throat and forced a smile. "I hope eventually you'll find everything you're looking for."

Standing nearby with slumped shoulders and hands in pockets, misery flitted across his face. "I hope so too."

Before she could formulate words to express any more thoughts, Mr. Peabody bustled out. As with the other times, he fussed over her and insisted she return to bed. Needing to be away from Zeke, she allowed Mr. Peabody to take Violet, help her up, and guide her inside.

Once on her bed, she collapsed and a sob escaped. But she caught it and told herself she wouldn't cry over Zeke. They were both doing the right thing. If only doing the right thing didn't have to be so hard.

twenty-four

*K*ate gave Mr. Peabody another hug, his long mustache tickling her cheek and his sniffles loud in her ear.

"You'll be back," he said as he already had at least a dozen times.

She couldn't make herself contradict him as she knew she should. Instead, she squeezed his stout frame one last time. "Of course I will. I'll miss your beignets and baguettes too much to stay away forever."

He wiped the tears from his cheeks before he offered her a wavering smile. He'd already cried when she gave him the painting of one of his vases of flowers. And if he kept crying, she wasn't sure she'd be able to hold herself together much longer.

"The pack train is leaving," Abe called from where he waited a short distance away down the street with Zoe, who was holding the hand of the four-year-old orphan while carrying Violet in a cradleboard on her back. "We need to be on our way."

Kate took a step away from Mr. Peabody and tried not to look around for Zeke again. Even though the hour was early, she'd expected him to come to the house to see her off. His absence stung.

She'd thought perhaps he'd arrive at home while she was away delivering the newly framed picture to Becca and saying good-bye to her friend. But upon returning, he still hadn't been there.

She picked up the package she'd saved to give to him. The street was already alive with miners, business owners, and the train of mules and men readying to leave Williamsville. But nowhere in the melee did she see Zeke.

The ache in her chest pulsed with fresh disappointment—the same ache that had been there all week since Zeke told her they needed to go their separate ways. In her head, she knew Zeke had made the right decision. But her heart couldn't stop protesting.

"Will you give this to Zeke?" She handed the package to Mr. Peabody.

"Where is that boy?" The housekeeper narrowed his eyes and glared around. "I don't understand why he's letting you run off like this."

"Don't blame him. We both made the decision that we'd be better off parting ways."

"If I were Zeke, I sure wouldn't let a woman like you walk out of my life." Mr. Peabody shuffled Zeke's package, his face and ears turning red.

"You're too kind, Mr. Peabody."

He muttered more about Zeke being a fool for not marrying her when he'd had the chance. Even as Kate started down the street, Mr. Peabody was still complaining about Zeke and brushing more tears from his cheeks.

With a final wave to the dear man, Kate caught up with Abe and Zoe. She took the other hand of the little orphan girl and tried to distract herself by playing and talking with the child. All the while, the ache in her chest kept growing until she wasn't sure she'd be able to force herself to leave. How could she? Not when the man she loved was still here?

At the first crack of the whip that prodded their pack train to get underway, Kate fell into step next to Zoe. She wanted desperately to turn around and search one last time for Zeke. But instead, she kept her shoulders straight and forced herself forward.

Even as she willed herself to keep walking, tears slipped out. Tears for the man she'd loved and lost.

Zeke leaned on his crutch and stood in the shadows of the boardinghouse, watching the pack train begin its journey. He gripped the hewn log, his fingers digging into the crumbling chinking so tightly, he was sure he'd pull the building apart.

He couldn't tear his eyes from Kate's form as she strolled next to Zoe. Abe strode ahead, already in conversation with one of the expressmen. Under normal circumstances, Zeke would have smiled at his brother-in-law's friendliness and the way he was always thinking of the needs of others.

At first, Zeke'd had reservations about the mountain minister, especially when he'd gotten word of the circumstances of Abe and Zoe's marriage of convenience. But in the end, Zeke couldn't have asked for a better husband for his sister. The two had fallen in love and had much more to their marriage than they'd ever expected.

Zeke had thought he and Kate were falling in love. Even now, his heart felt as though it were ripping from his body and that she was taking it with her. His entire body ached with the need to go after her, beg her not to leave, and tell her everything would work out for the best.

"Let her go, Hart," he whispered to himself through a thick throat. "You have to let her go."

All week he'd been praying and hoping he would change quickly enough that he could go to her and tell her of his new faith. But each time he'd contemplated begging her, he reminded himself he was doing this for her because she deserved better.

He held himself back, watching her retreating form, until she disappeared down the hill. He stared at the spot he'd last seen her, wishing for her to reemerge. Secretly, he hoped she'd run back up and tell him she couldn't leave him.

But as time passed with no sign of her, he leaned his head against the log siding, closed his eyes, and breathed out his frustration. "Did I do the right thing, God?"

"There you are."

The voice startled Zeke, and he limped away from the wall. Mr. Peabody stood on the boardwalk, the early morning sun glistening off his bald head. His housekeeper had a harried air about him, as though he'd been searching everywhere for Zeke.

"I'm coming. Just give me a few more minutes."

Rather than moving on as Zeke hoped, Mr. Peabody climbed down and started toward him. Zeke braced himself for the censure the older man was sure to level at him for hiding away in so cowardly a manner.

Mr. Peabody stopped in front of him and held out a parcel wrapped in brown paper.

Zeke didn't move to take it. "I couldn't say good-bye because I was afraid I wouldn't be strong enough to let her go."

"I know." Mr. Peabody's eyes filled with compassion, making Zeke's heart pinch even more.

"Then you're not mad at me?"

"Of course I'm mad. She's the best thing that ever happened to you, even better than finding the mother lode. And you just let her get away."

"Then should I ask her to stay?" Zeke's muscles tensed with the need to run after her.

Mr. Peabody glanced in the direction of the trail that led away from Williamsville. From the firm press of his lips, Zeke could tell he was contemplating the question seriously. Zeke's blood raced. Should he chase after her and beg her to come back and marry him?

His housekeeper shook his head. "As much as I want Miss Millington to stay, I think you'd only scare her away for good if you tried to force marriage right now."

The statement took Zeke by surprise.

"She needs some time away," he continued, "before understanding you're a treasure worth claiming."

"I need to become worthy first."

"That too."

Zeke inwardly sighed, wishing he was already worthy enough. "What if she finds someone else before I'm ready?"

"Guess you'll have to hurry up and grow."

"You know as well as I do, that real growth takes time."

"If you're headed down the right path, then you don't have to be perfect for her." Mr. Peabody thrust the parcel at him again.

The moment Zeke's fingers closed around the brown paper, he felt the outline of a sketch pad beneath.

"A good-bye gift from Miss Millington."

Zeke had loved browsing through the sketch pads she was always leaving lying around his house. Eventually, she found them, sketched a few more pictures, only to lose them again.

He peeled away the brown paper and flipped open the book. The family of caribou greeted him. At the bottom of the drawing, she'd written out part of his fable in her flowing script. He turned the page to find another picture of the caribou in a different setting along with several more lines from his story.

Once he finished the dozen pages, he reverently shifted back to the beginning. "She's written out my story of the caribou and illustrated it."

Mr. Peabody had been present during some of the times when Zeke and Kate had bantered about the caribou family and their escapades, so the housekeeper was well aware of what Kate had given him.

"What'll you do with it? Seems like it might be more useful to the children of the orphanage. I'm sure they'd love your silly story more than I do. But, it would need to be made into a real book first."

A real book? "How?"

"I'm glad you asked."

"Then you know how?"

"I know *who*." Mr. Peabody smiled and rubbed his hands together. "My brother-in-law is a bookseller and publisher who goes by the name Edward Routledge & Company."

"And you think he'd be willing to take a look?"

"I think the entire world would be willing to take a look at this faraway place through the eyes of Miss Millington, don't you?"

Zeke's mind spun with the possibilities that could open for Kate, a new mother lode, if he went about this in the right way. "True enough, Mr. Peabody. Tell me everything you know about publishing a book."

"First, let's go home." Mr. Peabody crossed to the boardwalk. "We'll have some coffee and breakfast and then discuss the plans."

For the first time all week, Zeke managed a real smile. Maybe everything wouldn't work out the way he hoped. But he could do something special for Kate and show her that he wanted the best for her.

twenty-five

Y ALE, B RITISH C OLUMBIA
A PRIL 1864
E IGHT MONTHS LATER

ate finished fastening the tiny buttons on the front
of the baby's gown. "There you are, my little one."
She tugged up both satiny shoes before smoothing down the
layers of white muslin. "You look beautiful."

The infant cooed up at Kate with her bright-green eyes,
flapping her arms and legs. Kate's chest tightened with longing as it always did whenever she looked into those green eyes
so much like Zeke's.

She bent and pressed a kiss against the baby's chubby
cheek, relishing the smoothness of newborn skin and breathing in the scent of powder. If she'd married Zeke last September, maybe she might have been expecting a baby of her own
by now, a baby just like this one, with Zeke's green eyes.

A tap on the bedroom door was followed by Zoe's breathless call. "Are you ready?"

Kate swallowed her melancholy and picked up the infant from the end of the bed. "As ready as can be."

"Abe went ahead to the church with Lyle and Will." Zoe stepped into the room with Violet, who was dressed in a gown much like the babe's.

"You look very pretty, Violet," Kate said.

Violet smiled, her big brown eyes luminous in her dainty face. Every day the infant seemed to get bigger and was walking all around now and had begun talking.

"What do you tell Auntie Kate?" Zoe prompted, even lovelier than ever since giving birth six weeks ago. Her face and hair seemed to glow, her eyes sparked with energy, and her fancy gown showed off her new matronly form.

"'Ank you." Violet twisted her hands in her skirt, swishing the material back and forth.

Over the past months living and working in the orphanage, Zoe had referred to Kate around the children as "Auntie." Of late, the title had grown heavier and only reminded Kate that she hadn't married Zeke and wasn't really family.

She'd wanted to be real family. All winter and spring, she'd been secretly waiting and hoping Zeke would come for her and tell her he'd do anything to be with her—including making his peace with God.

But after months of silence and continued absence, she'd started to accept that their parting had been final. Of course she hadn't expected him to make an appearance until the spring thaw opened the roads and trails up into the Cariboo region. But with the roads having become passable several weeks ago, she had to stop making excuses for his delay. The truth was, if he'd wanted to come, he could have. He'd simply chosen not to.

Although she still battled old insecurities and feelings of rejection, she'd worked over the past months at not letting fear take root again in her heart. Now it was time to move on. She had to let Zeke go once and for all and give her whole heart to Mr. Donaldson.

"Are you doing okay?" Zoe asked.

Kate forced her brightest smile. "I'm just nervous."

"Fred Donaldson is a good man." Zoe's statement was forceful, as though she was trying to convince them both.

"Aye, he is." Kate tried to make her answer just as certain. After no word from Zeke, Kate had finally decided she couldn't put her life on hold for Zeke forever. Especially because she'd already been putting off taking the next step with Fred.

She couldn't make Fred wait any longer. It wasn't fair to him, not after how patient he'd already been. Besides, he was everything she wanted in a husband. He was kind and considerate and godly. He'd arrived in Yale last autumn as the minister of the newly constructed church, and he'd patiently pursued Kate ever since they'd met.

The only problem was that he wasn't Zeke.

Kate rolled the tension from her shoulders and straightened. "We'd better go. Mr. Donaldson will be wondering where we're at."

Zoe hesitated. "You're sure you don't want to wait until summer? Maybe something's just holding Zeke up."

More than once, Kate had considered giving Zeke additional time. But what if she continued to wait and then lost the opportunity to be with Fred? On the other hand, was she being fair to Fred to move forward if she was still thinking so much about Zeke?

"I'm not the kind of man you need or deserve." Zeke's final words rushed back to remind her of why they'd parted ways. She couldn't marry someone like her father, and Zeke hadn't wanted her to. He'd given her the freedom to find someone who would cherish her forever. And now she couldn't hang on to him and use him as an excuse to avoid marriage.

"I need to move on, Zoe. I have to prove to myself that I'm not letting my past control me anymore."

"But you don't have to prove it this way." Zoe reached out for Kate's hand, but pattering footsteps echoed in the hallway, drawing Zoe's attention. She stepped to the door and captured another of the young orphans, sweeping her up into a hug filled with giggles.

With Zoe's distraction, Kate expelled a breath and bent to kiss the baby again. While she'd loved living in the orphanage with Zoe and Abe and the children, she was ready to have a family of her own, especially after watching the love Zoe and Abe shared as well as helping with the birth of their baby.

Fred Donaldson was eager and ready too. And though she didn't reciprocate his ardor, he'd told her it didn't matter, that over time he'd do his best to make her fall in love with him. And she imagined that one day she would. She just had to make herself go through with the commitment.

———∞———

Anticipation thrummed through Zeke's veins as he stood on the front porch of Zoe and Abe's massive home. He lifted his hat and combed his wayward strands.

The last few miles down the Fraser Canyon, he'd hardly been able to restrain himself from riding ahead of the pack train and galloping the final few miles to Yale. But with Mr. Peabody and Wendell traveling with him, he'd opted to stay with the group. After all, what were a few more hours of painful separation compared with the torture of the last months of being away from Kate?

He stared at the closed door and then knocked again, this time louder. Usually Mr. Ping, Zoe's butler, was punctual and answered the door almost before anyone had the chance to knock. What was taking him so long?

Zeke stepped back several paces and glanced in the wide front windows, hoping to glimpse Kate or anyone. But the house was silent.

With all the additions to the orphanage, the place ought to be much noisier and full of commotion. What had happened? Where was everyone?

"Monsieur!" Mr. Peabody called from down the street in the direction of the busy main thoroughfare. Attired in a suit and top hat, Mr. Peabody had kept his appearance immaculate during the long ride out of the mountains from Williamsville. Zeke didn't understand how he managed it, especially since he'd insisted on carrying on as Zeke's personal cook and manservant during the journey.

Zeke rapped against the door again, then tried the handle. Locked. They were gone.

Puzzled, he retreated down the steps. Hopefully, they hadn't traveled away from Yale. With the coming of spring, they could've ventured to Victoria to replenish supplies. It would just be his luck if they had.

"Monsieur!" Mr. Peabody shouted again, this time with a note of angst that drew Zeke's full attention.

Zeke's footsteps pounded against the boardwalk as he made his way toward his housekeeper. The closer he drew, the more evident the fear upon Mr. Peabody's face, which only made Zeke's heart thud harder.

He wasn't too late, was he? Surely he hadn't lost Kate. Last summer, he'd pulled Abe aside and asked his brother-in-law to put out the word around Yale that Kate was spoken for. 'Course Abe hadn't wanted to lie but had agreed to send word to Zeke if any man showed serious interest in Kate.

Even though Zeke had cringed with every letter that had arrived at the general store, Abe hadn't sent anything. Zoe had penned a short letter a month ago, letting him know about the birth of their daughter. But otherwise, he hadn't heard from them.

"Bad news!" Mr. Peabody called, his face red.

Zeke stumbled to a halt, his blood turning as cold as the damp April air. Though the snow had begun to melt, the trails along the Fraser River had been muddy and slick. And Yale was no different. The streets oozed with thick mud and had puddles the size of small lakes.

Down the street, Wendell stood outside Yale's General Store, talking with Mr. Allard, the store's owner. Wendell was traveling to Victoria and overseeing a shipment of supplies Zeke wanted transported back up to Williamsville. He was also going to the Victoria police headquarters to verify that they had William Blake in custody. Apparently, the miner had been spotted along the main wharf trying to barter with a fisherman to take him out to Esquimalt, so he could board a ship bound for England.

Thankfully, Blake had admitted to his crimes, including both explosions, the death threat, and even the destruction of the general store. Now Blake was locked up and would likely be sent to a prison in England.

"Mr. Allard was just telling us that Miss Millington is at the church." Mr. Peabody could hardly speak the words past his gasping.

"At the church? On a Saturday afternoon?" Zeke strained to see above the businesses to the church steeple.

"He said it's a very special day for Kate."

Dread spilled into Zeke's veins. *Special* could only mean one thing. She was getting married.

"Who's the man?"

In the process of dabbing his brow with a handkerchief, Mr. Peabody paused. "The new minister."

The dread made its way into Zeke's heart and clamped around it. Kate was marrying the minister? Today?

Zeke took off, sprinting down the walkway. The new church Abe had helped construct last summer was located on the opposite end of town. But Zeke didn't care. All he could do as he ran was pray he wasn't too late.

twenty-six

od, please, he prayed with each slapping footstep as he raced down the street. Although Yale had once been a booming mining town, the population had steadily decreased as miners had gone in search of gold higher up in the Cariboo. Even though the town wasn't as busy as it had once been, it was still a bustling place since it was the final stop for steamboats coming up the Fraser River from Victoria. Now he dodged pedestrians and maneuvered around men loaded down with supplies.

Please help me get to her in time. Please don't let me be too late.

Ever since Kate had left, he'd almost traveled to get her a dozen times. But when he'd stopped to pray about it, his urgency had been replaced with calm, one that told him he was doing the right thing in being patient and working on himself.

Fact was, during the past two months of waiting for the

spring thaw, no amount of praying had taken the urgency away or given him peace. So, when the package had arrived last week from London, he threw together his belongings and aimed to leave the same day. Mr. Peabody talked reason into him, and they waited until the next morning to travel with a group.

No doubt he'd been a fool to wait. But he'd assumed that with Abe's silence, he had nothing to worry about concerning Kate, that she hadn't been searching for another husband yet.

Clearly, he'd been wrong. Why hadn't Abe written to him and warned him? 'Course Abe was slow to catch on to matters of the heart—or at least he had been with Zoe, but how could he have missed the fact that Kate was getting married?

With a growl of frustration, Zeke plowed forward. The simple one-room church ahead rose against the backdrop of the mountains. The exterior was rustic and unpainted except for two white-framed windows on either side of the arched door. For an instant, he could picture Kate sketching the scene, delight dancing across her face with each quick stroke of her charcoal pencil.

As he bounded up the steps and reached the door, he drew in a steadying breath. Down the street, Mr. Peabody was shouting again along with Mr. Allard and Wendell. But Zeke couldn't bear to waste another second. If he had any chance of winning Kate, he had to act now.

He pressed a hand against his pendant now hanging from a chain beneath his shirt, whispered a prayer, and then threw open the door. "Stop the wedding!"

Silence descended and gazes swung to him.

He searched frantically among the people standing at the front of the church near the altar until he located Kate. Strands of her long fair hair were pinned up fashionably and the other half hung in silky waves over her shoulders and down her back. Her features were more beautiful than he remembered, her lips parted in a gasp. In a fancy blue gown that hugged her womanly frame, she had a new elegance that fit her well.

She cast an anxious glance at the man beside her. From the clerical collar, Zeke guessed he was the new minister and the man Kate was in the process of marrying.

"Hold on, Kate." Zeke started down the aisle toward her. "You can't marry him."

The minister was a young man, perhaps in his mid-twenties with dark hair and dark eyes, good looking in an aristocratic way. Was Kate attracted to him? Maybe even in love? It was possible the man made her happy and that she'd be better off with a minister.

Zeke's footsteps faltered, but only for a second. He had to try to win her. After how hard he'd worked at becoming worthy of her, he couldn't give up. That's all there was to it.

"Kate." He dropped to one knee before her. "I gave my life back to the Lord."

Her beautiful brown eyes rounded. "You did?"

"Aye, I started when we were trapped in the mine." He reached for her hand but realized she was holding a babe dressed in a long white flowing gown. "But I didn't tell you because I wanted to make sure I was renewing my faith for me and not to please you."

Her expression softened with something he could only describe as tenderness. The sight of it gave him hope.

"Over the past year, I've been reading Scripture and studying the writings of church fathers. I've learned a whole lot and tried to grow into the kind of man who will be able to love and cherish you always."

"Oh, Zeke." Tears welled into her eyes, making them glassy.

"Please tell me I'm not too late."

She opened her mouth to speak, but before she could say anything, Mr. Peabody barged into the church followed by Wendell. Both were breathing hard. "She's not getting married today." Mr. Peabody gasped, bending at the waist and bracing himself with his hands on his knees.

"She's not?" Zeke asked from where he still knelt in front of her.

"I misunderstood Mr. Allard," Mr. Peabody said through his labored breaths.

"I thought he said it was a special day for Kate?"

"It is." Mr. Peabody glanced at the babe in Kate's arms. "It's a special day for the baby Kate."

"The baby Kate?" Zeke echoed.

Kate peered down lovingly at the babe and stuck her finger into one of the little fists rising into the air. "After helping to deliver this little lamb, I'm privileged she's now my namesake and that I'm her godmother."

"Oh." Zeke finally noticed Zoe and Abe standing next to the minister.

"Today's her christening," Zoe said, her voice full of censure. For interrupting the christening or for something else, he didn't know.

He gave her one of his dimpled grins, knowing she'd eventually forgive him.

The minister cleared his throat and slanted a dark look at Zeke. "Shall we proceed?"

"First I need to speak with Kate." Zeke pushed himself up to his feet.

"You've waited this many months to come speak to me." Kate lifted her chin, the tenderness in her eyes replaced with fire. "I think you can wait until the service is over."

"I can't wait a second longer to tell you I love you and want to marry you."

She lifted her free hand to her mouth but couldn't contain the gasp.

Zoe exchanged a look with Abe and smiled.

Zeke took courage from his sister's reaction and continued. "We can talk about things here in front of everyone." He paused and waved a hand at the pews of people watching them, no doubt getting the show of their lives. "Or we can step outside and have a little privacy."

As if realizing he'd trapped her, Kate blew out a breath and handed the babe to Zoe. Then she grabbed his arm and dragged him toward a side door.

Kate stomped into the small lean-to that doubled as the minister's office as well as a storage closet. As she slammed the door, Zeke tripped over a broom and dustpan. He straightened, propped the broom back up, and then spun to face her.

Fortunately, the room had a window that afforded some light, so they weren't standing in the dark together. As it was, the closet was tiny and crowded and Zeke's presence was overwhelming, especially as he took a step nearer.

She held out her hand. "Don't come any closer," she whispered, conscious of the people on the other side of the door likely listening and hoping to hear their conversation.

"Fine." He held up his hands in mock surrender. His green eyes twinkled with a playfulness she adored. But now was neither the time nor the place to indulge him.

"So you're not marrying the minister?"

"Not today."

"Are you engaged to him?"

She hesitated.

"Please tell me you aren't," he whispered.

"He was planning to propose today. After the christening."

"Were you planning to accept?"

"Aye."

"Well, now you can't."

"That's not up to you."

"I'm not letting him have you." His voice turned hard, and his jaw flexed.

"If you still cared about me, you should have written to me." The words were out before she could stop them, containing all the hurt and waiting and wondering of the past months.

"I wanted to write," he admitted, his handsome face beckoning her to touch him, to stroke his stubble, to trace his strong jaw. "But I needed to make sure my faith was genuine before I started anything between us. Couldn't stand the thought of hurting you again."

She mulled over his words, and her anger easily evaporated. More than anything she was proud of him for having the determination to do the hard thing. The truth was, she'd needed the months to work on healing her own wounds, and if he'd come back sooner, she wasn't sure she would have been ready.

She could only pray she was ready now.

"The Almighty's been doing His work inside me, Kate."

She couldn't hold back her smile. "Oh, Zeke, I'm so happy for you."

"I was planning to leave the first day the roads were clear enough. But I was waiting on something to arrive." He held out a brown paper package, similar to the one she'd given him on the day she left Williamsville. Was he returning her sketch pad?

She took it, too curious to resist. Fingering the paper, she attempted to guess what was inside. Although approximately the same dimensions as her sketch pad, it was too hard and thin. "What is it?"

His smile came out along with his dimples. "Unwrap it."

She was almost loathe to look away from his handsome face. But she forced herself to untie the brown string and peel the paper back. At the sight of what appeared to be a children's book, she smoothed a hand over it. "What's this?"

"Open it up and see," he said softly.

She flipped to the first page and startled at the sight of her drawing of the caribou filling the spread of both pages. Underneath in neat type were the words of Zeke's story. She turned to the next page and then the next, realization dawning. She glanced again at the cover to find her name there.

"Routledge & Company loved your artwork and the story. They're planning an enormous print run, and this is the very first copy, sent to me with the fastest delivery service I could find."

Kate lifted her fingers to her lips to catch her gasp only to realize she was shaking. Someone was publishing her drawings into a children's book? How was that possible?

"They loved it and want more from you, Kate. Many more books."

"I don't understand."

"After you left me your sketches, I knew they were something special. So I sent the book to Mr. Peabody's brother-in-law, Mr. Routledge, in London. He's been raving about your work ever since."

Kate paged through the book again, and her heart expanded with gratefulness and love and joy. Zeke had done all this for her, even when she'd walked away from him? Even when he'd had nothing to gain from it?

"What do you think?" Worry laced his voice.

She closed the book and handed it back to him. "I won't accept it."

"You won't?" His eyes widened, highlighting his thick

lashes, making him even more handsome. "But I thought you'd be happy."

"I won't be happy," she inched nearer, "unless your name is on the cover with mine. After all, you're the one who wrote the story."

He searched her face, and then a slow grin emerged. "I've got an even better proposal." He placed the book down and closed the distance between them so she could almost feel the heat of his body.

"What could be better?"

When his hands cupped her hips, pleasure slid down her legs, making her weak. When he drew her against him, the pleasure rippled up her torso, twisting and curling so she could only react by circling her arms around his neck.

"What would be better is having our names joined together on the cover." His voice dropped to a whisper. "Kate and Zeke Hart. What do you say to that?"

She lifted on her toes and tightened her hold around his neck, her face almost touching his. "I like it."

His lips brushed against hers in the tease of a kiss. But the touch was enough to make her gasp out her desire. In an instant, his mouth captured hers decisively, as though he was staking a claim on her and didn't intend to let her get away ever again.

She responded with all the longing that had built within her over the months of separation, maybe even the longing from all the years she'd adored him from afar. All she knew was that she was his and his alone. And she always would be.

He swept her away, the kiss taking them to a place where only the two of them existed.

Until a rapping on the door brought her back to reality. She withdrew, even as he tried to kiss her again. "Someone's at the door." She leaned away, but the angle only gave him access to her neck, and he left a trail of soft kisses down to her shoulder blade.

The knocking became louder and more insistent. "Please come out and finish the christening," came Zoe's muted voice. "You can kiss later, after you're married."

"I like that idea," Zeke whispered between kisses against her chin and cheek. "Can we get married today? After the christening?"

At his eagerness, she laughed lightly. "No, let's not steal the day from baby Kate or Zoe and Abe."

"Then when?"

She needed time to explain to Fred Donaldson she was in love with Zeke and always had been. She owed Fred that much. "Tomorrow?"

"Really?" Zeke's grin was broad and his eyes alight with happiness.

"Really." Even as she said the word, a small part in her quavered with a familiar hesitation.

Zeke bent in and captured her lips, this time with a kiss as sweet and tender and moving as the grandest sunset. She couldn't breathe for the beauty of it.

When he broke the kiss a moment later, he didn't release her but held her tightly.

"I love you, Zeke." She hoped the words would take away that quavering and assure her everything would be all right.

Zeke sighed, the sound contented, almost blissful. "I'll always love you, Kate. And I don't ever want us to be apart again."

"Me either."

She buried her face in his chest and prayed for the strength to go through with her wedding.

twenty-seven

Kate twirled a ringlet of hair around her finger, admiring in the mirror all the curls Zoe had helped her arrange. Zoe had also lent her a fashionable fuchsia gown that had once belonged to the previous mistress of the house. The gown had already been tailored to fit Zoe and now flowed around Kate, making her feel like a princess. She swished the skirt, and it swayed back and forth like a bell.

Laughter wafted up from the lower level. Happy laughter. Excited laughter.

Everyone was assembled in the parlor for the wedding. The guests consisted of the orphans, servants, and friends she'd made during her stay in Yale. And Abe was performing the ceremony. Apparently Zoe had recently prompted Abe to send a letter to Zeke alerting him to Fred Donaldson's interest. But with the unreliable nature of the mail, Zeke hadn't received it before leaving.

Of course, Mr. Peabody had been busy in Zoe's kitchen all morning preparing a feast, and the tantalizing aromas from his baking filled the air.

Once she and Zeke were married, they planned to stay a couple more days in Yale before returning to Williamsville where they could finally start their new life together.

Even with all the plans working out just the way she'd wanted, her stomach pinched, and she pressed her fist against it to make the pain go away. The problem was that it wouldn't leave. In fact, since agreeing to marry Zeke yesterday, the ache had only cramped tighter so that at times she couldn't breathe.

At a soft tap on the door, she smoothed her hands over the skirt.

"Are you ready, Kate?" Zoe asked.

"I'll be ready in a few minutes."

"That's what you said the last three times I've knocked." Zoe's voice contained a hint of worry.

"I just need a little more time. That's all."

Zoe's silence stretched out, filled by the baby's tiny grunting noises. "Zeke's a changed man, Kate. He won't be perfect. No one is. But together, you'll work through any problems God's way."

"You're right." Why was taking this next step still so hard for her? She'd used the months living in Yale to learn to forgive her father and place her fears in God's hands. She'd even burned the old ribbon one night, releasing the grip her father's rejection had on her.

"Please, come down and marry him, Kate."

Kate leaned against the mirror and closed her eyes. "I will. I'm not quite done here."

Again, Zoe was quiet. After a few more minutes, her footsteps receded.

Kate tried whispering a prayer for courage and strength, but her thoughts stuck in her head and didn't go anywhere but in crazy circles. She paced across the room to the bed and then back to the mirror.

Another knock sounded, this one more distinct. Before she could say anything, the door opened to reveal Zeke. As he walked in and closed the door behind him, she took a rapid step back.

He stood absolutely still, as though he might spook her with the slightest movement.

She was being silly to be so frightened. "I'm almost ready." She tried to relax her shoulders. Maybe if she focused on how handsome and dashing he looked in his dark suit, she could forget about the fear holding her captive.

"I know something that might help," he said softly.

Her mind spun back to the day in the mine when she'd run to him, panicked about marrying him. He'd said almost the same thing before kissing her and making her forget her worries. Was that what he had in mind again?

"I'd like to pray with you."

The words took her by surprise.

He stretched out a hand but didn't step any closer. "Will you let me?"

She looked at his hand, then up at his sincere eyes before she accepted his offer.

"Let's kneel here together." He lowered himself and gently assisted her down. When he bowed his head, she followed his example. And when he began praying about them, their marriage, and the future, she could sense God's presence between them and His blessing upon their union. By the time he spoke an amen, tears of gratitude pricked her eyes.

"Thank you," she said as he helped her back to her feet. "That was exactly what I needed—what we needed to start our marriage."

"I agree." He still watched her as if he might yet scare her away.

She reached for his hand and squeezed it. He couldn't be everything *she* needed, but he'd shown her that together, they'd rely upon God to be everything *they* needed. "I'm alright now."

He dug in his pocket and pulled out something. "I was planning to give you this later, but I think now's the perfect time."

"What?"

He opened his hand to reveal a ribbon. Long and silky and unblemished, it was almost the same shade of pink as her gown. "Once upon a time, a man gave you a ribbon, left you, and broke your heart. Today, you deserve a new ribbon, the most beautiful one I could find."

Tears welled in Kate's eyes. "Oh, Zeke."

His expression was serious as he lifted her hair, wrapped the ribbon around it, and brought it to the top where he tied a bow. When he finished, he met her gaze. "With God's help, I promise to stay with you and cherish your heart forever."

Gratefulness swelled with such force that she captured Zeke's cheeks and guided his head down to hers. As her lips touched his, she let her kiss tell him how much she loved him and how she would stay with him and cherish his heart forever too.

When she tugged away a moment later, she wrapped her hands around his. "I'm ready."

"Are you sure?" He bent and stole another tender kiss.

"Very sure." She threw open the door and pulled him into the hallway and toward the stairs.

As they descended side by side, she lifted a prayer heavenward. Their voyages hadn't been easy, but God had been directing them all along and had brought them to this point. They might still encounter rough seas ahead, but she was learning His presence was enough to calm her fears and guide her safely through the storms.

At the bottom of the steps, Zeke paused and raised a brow, as if to ask whether she was okay.

She tucked her hand into the crook of his arm and smiled up at him. "I love you, Zeke, and I'm ready to be a bride. Your bride. Forever."

Jody Hedlund is the bestselling author of over twenty historical novels for both adults and teens and is the winner of numerous awards including the Christy, Carol, and Christian Book Awards. Jody lives in Michigan with her husband, five busy teens, and five spoiled cats. Visit her at jodyhedlund.com.

Sign Up for Jody's Newsletter!

Keep up to date with Jody's news on book releases and events by signing up for her email list at jodyhedlund.com.

Follow Jody!

/AuthorJodyHedlund

/JodyHedlund

/JodyHedlund

/jodyhedlund/

/author/show/3358829.Jody_Hedlund

/authors/jody-hedlund